JODI THOMAS

50

The Little Teashop on Main

D0034603

"*The Little Teashop on Main* is tender, heartfelt and wonderful.... I loved every word."
—RaeAnne Thayne, *New York Times* bestselling author

ISBN-13: 978-1-335-01799-4

EAN

Praise for Jodi Thomas

"Compelling and beautifully written."

—Debbie Macomber,
#1 *New York Times* bestselling author, on *Ransom Canyon*

"You can count on Jodi Thomas to give you a satisfying and memorable read."

—Catherine Anderson,
New York Times bestselling author

"Deeply poignant moments and artfully rendered characters create a rich story that transports readers to an idyllic place."

—*Publishers Weekly* on *Mistletoe Miracles*

"Highly recommended."

—*Library Journal*, starred review of *Sunrise Crossing*

"[*Sunrise Crossing*] will warm any reader's heart."

—*Publishers Weekly*, A Best Book of 2016

"This is a novel that settles in the reader's heart from the beginning to its satisfying end."

—*RT Book Reviews* on *Mornings on Main*, 4½ Stars,
Top Pick!

"Thomas is a wonderful storyteller."

—*RT Book Reviews* on *Rustler's Moon*

"A fast pace and a truly delightful twist at the end."

—*RT Book Reviews* on *Sunrise Crossing*

"A pure joy to read."

—*RT Book Reviews* on the Ransom Canyon series

Also available from Jodi Thomas and HQN

Mornings on Main

Ransom Canyon Series

JODI THOMAS

The Little Teashop on Main

HQN

ISBN-13: 978-1-335-01799-4

The Little Teashop on Main

Copyright © 2019 by Jodi Koumalats

Recycling programs
for this product may
not exist in your area.

This is a work of fiction. Names, characters, places and incidents
are either the product of the author's imagination or are used fictitiously.
Any resemblance to actual persons, living or dead, businesses,
companies, events or locales is entirely coincidental.

This edition published by arrangement with Harlequin Books S.A.

For questions and comments about the quality of this book,
please contact us at CustomerService@Harlequin.com.

HQN
22 Adelaide St. West, 40th Floor
Toronto, Ontario M5H 4E3, Canada
www.Harlequin.com

Printed in U.S.A.

The
Little Teashop
on Main

The
Little Teashop
on Main

foreword

november 2018

Jack Hutchinson

A RARE FOG rolls across Cemetery Road, promising rain, as it whispers of a cold winter to come. I step through a broken gate, refusing to look at the graves. Wild buffalo grass, already stiff and colorless, waves me in. I scan first left, then right, searching, knowing what I will find.

People say a man can never completely know a woman. Men are not wired the same way as they are. But I knew three such creatures. Have all my life.

As I move through the neglected garden of stones, I make out two of those women, dressed in black.

I freeze, not wanting to get too close. This isn't my world. It belongs to them alone. They've never bid me into their circle, and I know I can only observe now.

One spreads a blanket on the ground beside a grave. Another begins to set out cups and a tiny pot. Forever Tea, I think. I've never been invited to join in, but I know the ritual well.

Three women pledged together in friendship. Two of them now saying goodbye to one they've loved closer than a sister.

Maybe I should tell their story. Maybe I'm the only one who can. After all, I'm the one who loved all three. Always have. Probably will through eternity.

But I don't fool myself. They don't belong to me.

If anything, I guess, I belong to them.

Part I: 1988–2001

one

Zoe
Princess Tea Party

ZOE O'FLAHERTY DANCED on the tile floor of the sunroom as if it were a grand stage. Her sun-streaked red hair floated like a cape as it brushed against multicolored geraniums in full late summer bloom.

In her five-year-old mind, today was a perfect day, even if it was raining outside. The best day in her life. Better than Christmas or even Halloween.

Today, Zoe was having her first real tea party. Mommy—or Alex, as grown-ups called her—had decorated with paper stars hanging from the ceiling fan, and she'd bought a Cinderella tea set. They'd made heart-shaped peanut butter sandwiches and tiny cupcakes with a cherry on top of each one. Chocolate kisses sprinkled across the short table with three child-sized plastic chairs. A small box sat on each plate filled with diamond rings as big as suckers and plastic necklaces.

"Now, Zoe, settle down," Mommy said for the magillianth time. "You've got to welcome both girls when they arrive. You're the hostess today. I'll be in the kitchen with the mothers."

"I know. I know." She twirled. When she was a dancer someday, she'd never stop twirling.

The doorbell rang. Zoe squealed and darted to the door, her pink princess dress flying around her so lightly she could almost believe it was made of cotton candy.

"Hi," she said, as a princess dressed in purple floated one step inside the house.

The mother behind her pushed the thin little girl forward. "You must be Zoe. I'm Mrs. Waters and this is my daughter Emily. She's going to be in your kindergarten class. And I, for one, thank your mother for putting this party together so it won't be too frightening for you girls next week. Emily will have two friends she knows in that petrifying environment."

Zoe leaned down when Emily didn't look up. This new princess had long brown braids and fear in her chocolate eyes.

Princess Emily sniffled, hugging herself as if she were cold.

Zoe had never thought about being afraid to go to kindergarten. Or that there would be someone who didn't want to come to a tea party, but this purple princess did not look happy. "I've never had a tea party with anything but dolls. Have you?"

Brown braids slapped against Emily's wet cheeks as she shook her head.

"I like your dress," Zoe whispered. The new princess still didn't look up, but her mother stretched her neck and looked around their room as if she were inspecting the small home.

"Interesting house," Mrs. Waters said, her face wrinkling as if she smelled something unpleasant.

Emily finally raised her head and smiled a tiny bit. "I like your dress, too, Zoe."

Mommy came out of the kitchen and took Mrs. Waters away. Zoe was glad. She was probably nice, but if she'd brought a basket of apples like the queen in *Snow White*, Zoe wouldn't have eaten one.

She took Emily's hand and pulled her to the play table that was set for tea. "Do you like peanut butter sandwiches?"

"Yes, but I don't like my crown. It's too big." Emily leaned sideways and it fell off. "My mommy says I'll never find a prince if I don't keep my crown on."

"Mine's too small." Zoe shook her red curls and the crown bounced atop her head. "And I don't want to find a prince. My mommy says I don't have to find one if I don't want to. She told me sometimes you have to kiss a frog to get one."

Both girls giggled and switched crowns as Zoe's mommy answered the doorbell.

The princesses turned to watch the third little girl

come into view. She was taller than them, had a wrinkled dress and no crown. A man in a dark uniform stood behind her, frowning. He was dressed like an airman and made no move to enter the sunroom, but his hand rested on his daughter's shoulder as if he were on guard.

"My wife told me I had to bring Shannon here for an hour today. Sorry I'm late. It took a while to find the dress."

Zoe stared at the man. Her mommy wasn't married, so she was rarely around men, but this one looked like he might growl at any moment, and she didn't want him at her tea party.

Mommy smiled a sad kind of smile. "You're welcome to come have coffee in the kitchen while the girls have their party, Sergeant Morell."

The man raised an eyebrow. "No thanks. How about I come get my daughter in one hour?"

"That sounds fine." Mommy smiled at Shannon and led her to the decorated table. She introduced each princess and told them to have a great time.

Only when Mommy left, Shannon started crying, and the tea Zoe had looked forward to didn't seem much like a party. One of her special guests was crying, and the other's cheeks were still wet with tears. Zoe decided she was the worstest hostess ever.

"Are you sick?" Zoe asked, guessing if the new princess was sick, the party would probably be over.

Shannon shook her head. "My mommy left my daddy and me this morning."

Emily whispered, "Is she coming back home? Maybe she just went to the store?"

"No. She packed her big suitcase, then slammed her keys on the table like they were too hot to hold in her hand. She didn't even help me find my crown. She said she couldn't look at me. It hurt too much."

Zoe remembered what her mommy told her about being a hostess. She pulled off her crown and gave it to Shannon. "I have another one made of flowers. I'll wear it and be the flower princess."

By the time she got back from digging in her closet to find the ring circled with plastic daisies, Shannon and Emily were giggling. They'd put cherries inside the sandwiches and couldn't wait to have Zoe taste them.

A stem stuck out between the slices of bread, but Zoe played along, acting surprised. Then she poured the lemonade tea, and they all tried it with a Hershey's Kiss dropped into each plastic cup.

As the hour passed, the girls tried on each other's dresses, traded crowns several times and ate all the goodies. They hugged goodbye, all begging to have a tea party every rainy Saturday.

Shannon's father smiled as he knelt to lift up his daughter in one arm. "Come along, princess. I think you've got icing in your hair." His big hand moved over her yellow curls, only smearing the blob of icing more.

She hugged him. "I was afraid you might not come back, Daddy. I thought you would pack your bag and leave me too. But Zoe said you were really a knight who lost his armor and you'd be back."

The sergeant looked down at Zoe. "She's right. I will never leave you. A knight is always there to protect his princess." He nodded once at Zoe. "And, of course, her friends."

"We are friends," all three girls shouted. "Forever friends."

He winked at Zoe. "Next rainy Saturday, I'll have the tea party set up at our house, but you ladies will have to plan the food."

All three five-year-olds giggled as they waved goodbye.

two

fall 2001

Shannon

SHANNON MORELL BROUGHT out her last suitcase as her dad loaded the car she'd got as a graduation present. Her long honey-blond curls had been cut and styled into a short bob since her last high school photos. The summer camp she'd attended in Colorado had honed her tall, lean body into an athletic balance.

"You sure you don't want me to go with you, baby? Five hundred miles is a long drive."

"Dad, you've got to quit calling me that."

Chief Master Sergeant Morell shrugged. "I don't see why. You'll always be my baby. Four years from now you'll probably outrank me, but you'll still be my little girl."

"Come on, Dad, I'm leaving for college, not dying.

All right. We'll make a pact. When I'm here in Laurel Springs, you can call me whatever you like, but when we're at the Air Force Academy, you call me Shannon." At five-eleven, she stood eye to eye with her father, but he'd always be a big man in her mind. He'd stayed. He'd raised her. He'd cared.

Her dad was over forty and tough as leather, but she knew the thought of his little girl being hundreds of miles away wore on him.

"Remember when you went to Iraq twice and I had to stay with Grandma? You promised you'd come back, and, even though I cried, I knew you'd keep your word." She patted his cheek. "Well, I'm only going to Colorado Springs, but I promise I'll be back."

"You got that fancy new cell phone, your extra car keys, your Glock?"

"Yes."

He worried his bottom lip. "You got that roll of quarters in the tray between the seats? Curl your fist around that and you can knock a guy cold with one punch."

She thought of listing all the classes in self-defense he'd made her take over the years, but it still probably wouldn't be enough to calm his worries. "I'll be ready if trouble comes, Dad. I promise." At her height, she wasn't likely to be targeted for mugging.

He followed her over to the driver's door, asking questions. Did she have enough cash? Did she have her AAA card? Did she have a map in case the GPS didn't work?

Hugging him one last time, Shannon answered, "If

I get any more ready, they'll just graduate me when I drive on campus."

Her dad straightened into the airman he'd been all her life. "You drive careful."

She nodded. Dad never said he loved her; he didn't have to. "Don't start clocking my drive yet. I'm stopping over at Zoe's for tea with the girls."

"I know. Farewell Tea. You girls have been having those teas every time you've left for camps or vacations since you were five."

Shannon shrugged. "They're not as much fun as the Hello Teas, but it's tradition."

He looked so sad, like all his happiness was draining out of him.

"Dad, look on the bright side. I'm finally out of the house. You can start dating." He was still a handsome man. "Have a wild fling. Zoe's mother is still single and you like her chicken spaghetti. That seems as good as any reason to ask her out."

"Alex O'Flaherty and I are water and oil, baby. Always have been." He frowned. "How about you and me make another pact? Neither of us dates until you're out of college."

"Not a chance, Dad." She laughed. "And I'm not telling a guy my dad's in the air force and carries a gun. You've got to give me the time and space to go wild."

"I told Jack Hutchinson's mother to tell him to keep an eye on you and make sure you don't do just that. His mom told me all he did was study last year. Didn't even date that she knew about. I guess that makes him safe enough to talk to."

"Dad, I barely talked to Jack for the eleven years we were in school together here in Laurel Springs. Why would I talk to him now?"

"Good. Don't talk to any guy."

She kissed his cheek. "I can't promise that, Dad. It might be fun to talk to someone now and then who doesn't know everyone I know."

"All right. Date and talk, always in public places. That sounds fine." He opened her car door. "I almost forgot. I put a box of Junior Mints and two kinds of Girl Scout cookies in a bag behind your seat. Give them to Zoe when you get to the party. She said she'd need them for the tea."

"You've spoiled her since we were five."

He shrugged. "She thinks I'm a knight. What can I say?"

"And she always gives you a list of what she wants you to send to the party."

"She texted me this time. I liked it better when she sent notes written in crayon with every other word misspelled. It was like I had to decipher a code before I could buy snacks."

Shannon felt the chill of an early winter. "Take care of Zoe, Pop. Of the three of us fairies, she's the one who'll go wild."

"Isn't she headed for New York soon? And you're right about her. With a mother who didn't set down near enough rules, if you ask me, there's no telling about Zoe. After graduation I asked her what she planned to be, and she answered, 'A Wood Nymph.' What in the hell is that?"

Shannon kissed his cheek. "She was kidding, Dad. She just had fun this summer. There's lots of time for her to think about goals. She's broken up with three guys this year, so her heart is pretty beat up, but she'll get over it when she hits the Big Apple. Take the time to visit with her if she comes home before I do. And stop by and talk to Alex. She'll be lost without Zoe."

"Kind of like me without you. But I got a plan. I'm going to work myself to death."

"What else is new?"

"What about shy little Emily? Should I watch over her too?" Shannon knew he'd changed the subject before she could start lecturing him.

"No, her mother's been glued to her side since the doctor cut the cord. Mrs. Waters says Emily can stay home and get a college degree online, but Em really wants to go to some little church school in New England. Last I heard, they were fighting it out. Silent old Howard Waters might side with Em just to have some peace in the house."

Shannon kissed her dad one last time and jumped in the car. "Maybe you should watch over both my friends while I'm gone. I guess I've always thought that was my job."

"I will, and Zoe's mom too. I swear, that woman should have grown up in the sixties. She would have made a perfect flower child. If she didn't own the bakery, I'd never speak to her, but those scones of hers are impossible to resist."

"Don't pick on her, Dad."

"I'd never dream of it. Rule of survival. Never piss off a woman who can cook." He laughed. "She's invited me to drop by the bakery for breakfast any time I'm missing you. I'll probably be fat as a bear by the time you come home for Christmas."

She knew he was keeping it light, making it easy on her, so Shannon played along. "You two will probably run out of anything to talk about long before you get tired of her pastries."

"Oh, we only talk about you girls. That and the weather are our only safe topics. Anything else would probably be a land mine."

"Love you, Dad."

"I know, baby. Now, you'd better get on the road."

He stood at attention beside the driveway until she turned the corner and he disappeared from her rearview mirror. Her mother might have vanished years ago with only occasional phone calls and flyby visits, but her dad was solid as a rock. Maybe that was why she wanted to go into the air force. To make him proud. To follow in his footsteps.

Five minutes later, Shannon ran up the steps of the tiny apartment above the bakery on Main. Three years ago, Zoe's mother had sold her house and moved. She'd said she was downsizing, but Shannon guessed it was to help pay for tuition at the art school Zoe had always dreamed of attending.

Today, they'd have tea on the balcony of the apartment.

Today, they'd say goodbye to each other for a whole semester.

"We're waiting!" Zoe yelled from the balcony.

Shannon felt a lump in her throat. She was the first to leave, the one they'd have to say goodbye to. Emily looked like she'd been crying. Zoe was, as always, dancing around, impatient for the next chapter of their lives to begin.

"We're going to make promises today," Zoe said as Shannon took her seat. "Forever promises that none of us will ever break."

"Forever," Emily said. "I'll go first." She lifted her teacup. "We'll always be best friends."

All three sipped their tea.

"We'll always be there for each other, no matter the miles between us," Shannon added.

Zoe giggled. "And if one of us ever kills anyone, the other two have to promise to bury the body."

They laughed as Zoe straightened and lifted her cup. "Seriously, nothing will ever break our bond. Not boyfriends, lovers or husbands."

As their cups clinked, Shannon whispered, "I don't plan to marry, not for a long time, so that's no problem."

Zoe shrugged. "I plan to have a hundred lovers. Famous actresses do, you know. What about you, Em?"

"I doubt Mom will let me date before I'm forty, so where will I find a lover?"

Zoe lifted her cup one last time. "To Forever Tea. To us."

three

Fuller

A SHADOW MOVED along the sleeping streets of Laurel Springs. He silently crossed through the warehouse district that had been abandoned in the thirties and now loomed, dark and dusty. The barns and workshops seemed to huddle together between threads of winding roads, and had only rodents as tenants.

Here, unlike Main Street or the rows of homes on the other side of the creek, nothing was brightly painted or trimmed. Trash whirled in the alleys and corroded window fans clicked without rhythm through the night. Progress seemed to have faded away here in the shadows.

Along the last row of this area of town a long mile of chain-link fence barred the Wilders' land from the world. Weeds as tall as a tractor's tire wound their way through the holes in the chain, and near the gate, old tires had been stacked to block any passerby's view of what was inside.

The rusty old garage didn't have a sign, but it had a row of bays blocked by locked overhead doors. Everyone knew if the bay doors were raised, the business was open. On a rotting piece of wood near the gate, someone had carved *Wilder's Fort* in letters a foot high.

People said Old Man Wilder could fix anything with an engine. He'd learned his skill while stationed in army bases all over Europe during WWII. He'd stayed in the army another twenty years, claiming he wasn't coming home until he had enough money saved to buy land. When he finally showed up, he bought the abandoned garage in the worthless part of town, built a fence and continued working on cars, tractors and motorcycles. Folks claimed he lived in the garage until he'd married and built a house out behind the junkyard on his property.

The only home at Wilder's Fort. Only one that would probably ever be there.

Before the old man died, he'd left everything at Wilder's Fort—the garage, land and the shack of a house—to his grandson, Fuller Wilder. He'd taught the kid everything about cars, but nothing about life or getting along with people. He'd even bragged that his grandson had driven every teacher he'd had mad.

Said he was feral as the coyotes that roamed the property looking for rats in the junkyard.

Customers complained that something was wrong with the boy; he was too quiet. Didn't have a friendly bone in his body, they'd say. No one ever saw him around town. He seemed to be little more than a shadow who lived only behind the chain-link fence.

Once Fuller dropped out of school, people started to hint that he wasn't right in the head, but no one had any proof, just a feeling when they came to the garage. He never talked more than necessary, but he was a good mechanic who charged fair prices.

They didn't know Fuller Wilder's secret. No one did.

Almost every night he'd crossed the creek and walked their streets. He was no more than a ghost to the community. He never bothered anyone, but he watched people, studied them like a kid studies an ant bed.

He moved alone, shifting from one part of town to another in the shadows of the trees. He found peace in the silence. He let a tiny spark of a dream whisper across his thoughts as he walked. Maybe someday, somehow, he'd belong.

Fuller knew it was impossible. Wilders stayed at the fort; they worked at the garage. He was one of those invisible people.

If anyone did sense him near, they never investigated. They never guessed that Fuller Wilder had a reason. A mission no one would ever know.

He cared about only one person in Laurel Springs:

Emily Waters. And he needed to know she was safe now and then. It helped him sleep even though he'd never said her name aloud.

four

Zoe

New York was still in the clutches of late summer, even though the calendar said it was fall. Women wore sleeveless dresses. Perfect weather for sitting on the stoop outside, but Zoe couldn't sit still long enough to eat her sandwich. She had to explore. She drank the city in like melted peach ice cream.

For her, adventure, love and happiness were just around the corner, and she couldn't wait to find them. In the dark night, she'd miss home and her mother, but now, in the light, all she wanted to do was live.

When the pay phone sounded upstairs, she broke into a run. If she could only afford a mobile phone and not have to use the one hallway phone everyone used, Zoe might be able to have a private conversation now and then.

But phones cost money, and she was living on a tight budget. Until she was a star, of course.

"Hello," she yelled into the old receiver.

A familiar laughter came through first. "How you doing in New York, slugger?"

She grinned. "Jack, aren't you supposed to be at the Air Force Academy?"

"I'm here, working hard. Man, Zoe, you're really out of it. Remember Alexander Graham Bell. He invented this thing you're holding. How about putting in a few bucks and calling me sometime like you said you would the day you left town."

"I remember." Jack always made her laugh. "I know I promised. I've just been busy. I'm in my element, taking in New York. It loves me, you know. The whole town loves me, or they will soon. I love my acting classes. I'll be a star in no time."

Jack's low voice sounded like home. "Of course they'll love you. The whole town you left loved you. Got a boyfriend yet? I know you—without a guy on your arm you'll think you look underaccessorized."

She giggled. "Well, come over and we'll run the streets together. We'll tell everyone we meet that we're lovers, not just friends."

"Can't, slugger. School, remember? Plus, you told me to keep watch over Shannon. How could I do that if I fly off to see my best friend in New York?"

Zoe lost her smile as she allowed a bit of honesty in. "Your best friend is a little lonely up here. Folks aren't like they are at home. People don't say hello when I pass. They don't want to visit on the bus. I miss talking to you and Shannon and Emily."

"You'll make new friends, Zoe."

"I know. Someday I'll walk down the street and everyone will know me. I'll be famous."

"I have no doubt, but until then, keep that left hook up. You might run into someone who needs a lesson. I've seen you in action, remember."

"He was in the third grade," Zoe reminded Jack. "You were in the second grade and about the skinniest kid I'd ever seen. He was beating on you just because he could and I couldn't stand for it."

Now Jack laughed. "Yeah, but you were in the first grade. That third grader took off when you started pounding on him. I might have been on the ground, but I saw the fear in his eyes. You saved me, slugger."

She lowered her voice. "I wish you were here, Jack."

"You'll be fine, Zoe. You know you can always go home if the pace of the city gets too much for you. Give it a few weeks. A few months."

"I know, but I'm going to live in double time for a while. I'll see it all before I come home. I'm going to dance in the streets and wave at the world from the roof."

"And I'm going to hear all about it, Zoe. I'll call you often. While I'm out West marching and studying, I'll be thinking of you having all the fun."

He said he had to go, but even after the phone went dead, she held it to her ear as if somehow she could feel home coming through the wire.

When she made it back to the stoop, someone had stolen her dinner.

Zoe raised her fist and yelled what she'd do if she caught them. No one passing even bothered to look at her, but she didn't care.

She was in New York and she could hear the heartbeat of the world from here.

five

Shannon

SHANNON TOOK LONG strides as she splashed through puddles of rain on her walk from the dorm to the mess hall the cadets called Mitch's. She'd been on the Air Force Academy campus—eight miles north of Colorado Springs—for three months, and every day, every hour, her home in Laurel Springs seemed farther away.

In her mind, she was walking Main. Passing A Stitch in Time, where Mrs. Larady had her quilt shop, and Hidden Treasures, which was packed full of gems no one seemed to want. And the bookstore, run by a white-haired man who smelled of pipe tobacco and Old Spice. She even missed the creek that ran through town, a wild spot woven into the buildings that she'd been afraid of when she was small.

Somehow, walking through her hometown in her mind always grounded her. This month the leaves would be turning in her Texas town. Big oaks and wide willows along Willow Road would offer a gentle rain of color as the season changed. The hundred-year-old houses, each in a different style, always seemed to shine in fall. The road everyone called School Street where three buildings, elementary through high school, stood in a row.

Shannon missed her silent room in the house her father had bought when she was born. Her grandmother's place was three doors down. She missed her friends back in Laurel Springs.

She even missed her dad's never-ending questions. If she took a stand on anything from politics to movies, he'd make her defend it. He might not agree with many of her ideas, but he listened.

No question was off-limits for Dad. Except once, when he'd asked if she'd got her period yet. They'd both blushed so badly they'd agreed never to talk of it again. All sex education for her was left to the internet and friends who were as clueless as she was.

Last summer she and her two best friends laughed about being the three oldest virgins in town. A few in their senior class were pregnant or planning June weddings. But Emily, Zoe and Shannon all wanted to explore the world before they settled down to breed, as Zoe put it.

They'd planned their escape as carefully as prison lifers with shovels. Zoe would go to New York and become famous. Emily would pick a private church school as far away from her mother as possible and finally be able to breathe. Shannon would attend the academy and learn to fly. Then she'd live all over the world, and her two friends would plan trips to see her.

High school dreams, Shannon thought now. The academy, though she loved it, was ten times harder than she'd thought it would be. She woke, slipped on sweats and ran four miles, then showered and started her classes with drills and more exercise sliced in between. She ended the day never done with her list.

She remembered how summer had flown by while she and her friends planned and packed and talked. Then, as the air began to cool, they drank tea in Zoe's mother's tiny apartment. The Farewell Tea. The sad tea. All three agreed they'd follow their dreams and come together for their ritual. Their Farewell Teas, like the Hello Teas, would last a lifetime. They would break out of an ordinary life and fly.

"Someday," Zoe had promised, "the town will put up a billboard saying that the three of us once lived here. Extraordinary women. Best friends."

Right now, Shannon would settle for one cup of tea and talking. She missed them. She missed her town. She missed her dad.

Funny how you don't think the little things are important until they disappear. Her friends seemed a million miles away now. Emailing wasn't the same as talking. Shannon couldn't help but wonder if Emily and Zoe were both happy or just pretending to be, like she was.

Out of nowhere, boots splashed into her line of vision, washing away her melancholy thoughts.

Glancing up, she saw Jack Hutchinson, wearing a tarp of a raincoat. He looked like his own personal traveling mini circus tent. "Get out of my way." She started around him. "I don't want to see you today, or tomorrow, or ever. All you are is scratched-off spots on my calendar, Jack."

He twirled, making the poncho fly out from his stick of a body. "Come on, Shan, get over it. I didn't stand you up. I was just late for our date."

She marched on with him falling into step. "Twenty-three hours late, birdbrain, and this was the third time. No wonder you're having trouble with math. You can't even tell time." When he didn't argue, she added, "And studying isn't a date. I don't date, remember?"

"Then I couldn't stand you up, could I? Right?"

"Shut up. Isn't it bad enough that I had to grow up with you always around? Now you have to follow me to the academy."

"I wasn't following you to school. I came here first. Maybe you…"

"I don't want to hear it. To you everything seems more important than studying. I don't want to be your conscience, trying to make you pass your classes, or your priest when you make up some excuse. Just tell me what you want from me or go away."

"All right. What do I want from you, Shannon Morell?" His sandy-colored eyebrows pressed together to give the appearance that he was thinking. "One, I could offer you a wild freshman affair, for starters. Two, I'd take a million bucks if you have it lying around. And, since you're asking, I wouldn't mind seeing you naked, for the third wish. I've thought about that since the seventh grade."

She doubled her fist before she realized he was kidding. "If I were you, I'd bet on the million bucks appearing because there is no way in hell the other two will."

He had the nerve to look disappointed. This too-tall, too-thin, too-bothersome guy, who she swore had followed her all her life, was also impossible to stay mad at. He reminded her of a stray puppy no one loved, but that she'd probably feel sorry for when someone finally ran over him.

"I just wanted to know if you need a ride home over the Thanksgiving break. I'm driving back, and if you come along, you could study or sleep in the back seat. I won't even talk to you until you hit me in the back of the head and demand a potty stop."

"I'd planned to stay here and work on my term papers. When are you leaving?" She'd been so busy she hadn't thought about Thanksgiving. Two days driving, two days home didn't seem a good use of time. Plus, her dad had flown in and picked up her car a week after she got to school. Some rule about freshmen not having cars.

Jack broke into her thoughts. "Early Wednesday morning. If we leave by eight, we'll be home before it gets dark."

Shannon considered forgiving him for the study dates. A trip home would be great, even if her dad was tied up in Washington. She could stay at the house alone and spend hours catching up with Emily and Zoe. Knowing her grandmother, she'd cook enough food to last a week and leave it in the fridge if she knew Shannon was coming.

If she went home, Shannon would have to plan when to tell her grandmother. Early enough for her to cook but not time enough for Grandma to talk Shannon into going with her to see her sisters in Dallas. Shannon had been trapped into that trip last Thanksgiving. One holiday with those three women, all in their eighties, all arguing, was enough. The three sisters had never got along. When they weren't disagreeing over something, they were telling stories of their fights over a lifetime.

"You want a ride or not?" Jack asked.

"I'll go." She smiled at him. The drive would be worth it to see her friends.

Zoe had emailed yesterday that she planned to be home for a week over Thanksgiving. Her mother always invited Shannon and her father over for the big meal she loved to cook, saying two more would be no trouble. If Dad made it home, even for one day, they'd have a grand meal in the little kitchen over the bakery.

Then she and Zoe would kidnap Emily for a long talk. Emily's house had never been welcoming, even though the girls used to have a playdate there now and then. Emily's mother always orchestrated their playtime, and Shannon had a feeling she usually stood just outside the door to listen in on their talks.

Jack held open the door to the mess hall. "My folks

said Emily is back for good from that church school back East. She didn't last the first semester."

"What?" It always freaked her out a bit when Jack seemed to crawl into her mind. But they were from the same small town, knew the same people, and Jack's parents did live across the street from Emily's parents.

"Mom writes me weekly letters, like I'm off to the war and not at school. In her log of the town happenings, she said that Emily Waters came home a week ago, but she hasn't stepped out of her house. She and her mother didn't even come with the family to church on Sunday."

"Strange. Em's mother thinks having your butt in the Waterses' pew at the First Baptist Church is the eleventh commandment."

"I agree." Jack pulled his slicker off and tried to get his badly barbered hair to stand up, or lie down, or whatever it was supposed to do. "Something's wrong, Shannon, and you've got to go home and find out what it is so you can tell me. Then I can stop worrying about poor little Emily. I was born to worry about that girl. I was in high school before I realized her full name didn't have Poor Little attached to it."

"Shut up," she snapped again, even though she knew he was right. Emily's whole family always smothered her. Strangers frightened Em with just a frown, but Shannon still didn't like anyone talking about Emily.

"I guess she couldn't take that big school so far away." He shrugged.

"Sh."

"I know. I heard you the first two times. I swear,

being around you is like being in Echo Canyon. Are you riding home with me or not?"

She tried giving him a look that would kill, but it didn't work. "I'll go. Pick me up Wednesday."

"Will do."

She nodded a silent goodbye and turned left. He turned right. In the three months they'd been on campus, they hadn't eaten a meal together. She guessed he felt the same way she did. They were here to learn, to grow, to make new friends, not hang around people they'd known back home.

Three days later, a light snow was falling when Shannon climbed into the back of Jack's old Ford. She'd put a change of clothes into her backpack along with books. All her old clothes would be waiting in her room when she got home and, for once, the only things on her to-do list were eat, sleep and talk.

"Ready?" Jack grinned.

"Ready. I've decided since Dad's not home, I'll spend all my free time studying." She was lying, but maybe Jack would get the hint and do the same.

"Me too." He was almost convincing.

She didn't call him out on his lie. Jack never studied. He seemed smart enough to get by and that was fine for him. Shannon didn't even want to talk to him. She just wanted to unwind for a while and watch the beautiful views as they headed south out of Colorado. The edge of the Rocky Mountains melted into rugged land that would soon shift into plains.

Within ten minutes, Jack broke the silence. "You know why there's an Oklahoma Panhandle?"

"No idea."

"'Cause Colorado refused to touch Texas."

"You just made that up."

"No, my grandfather told me. He said his grandpa, they called him Pepa, was half Apache. Born in Oklahoma when it was still a territory, so he should know."

Shannon leaned up between the seats. "You're a wealth of misinformation, Jack. If we ever did study together it would probably lower my scores."

"We've got time to test the theory. The way you're rushing, though, you'll probably beat me to graduation."

She leaned back. "Right. You'll probably still be a doolie when I'm a zoomie."

"I'll do my best to keep up with you." He tossed her a candy bar. "If I don't take summer classes we'll probably graduate together. Engineering is a five-year program."

"A challenge. You're on. I'd better get to work. You keep driving."

An hour later, while he listened to some football game, she used her backpack as a pillow and drifted to sleep.

The day floated by with the changing landscapes.

They stopped for gas and more snacks. She drove a few hours while he slept folded into the passenger seat. Now and then, he'd shift and lean over to put his head on her shoulder. She'd push him off toward his window, and he'd wake up enough to complain.

They argued over switching channels and debated which teacher was the toughest in high school.

When they finally pulled into Laurel Springs, Shannon swore she could feel her heart slow. She was home.

Jack stopped at his father's office to say hello. The Hutchinsons had been builders in Laurel Springs since wagons rolled down Main. Some had been masons, a few architects, but most, like his brothers, Ben and Harry, were contractors. Folks said that Hutchinson took three years to build his home on Travis Street, even hauled trees in before he broke ground, so that by the time the house was finished, the trees were big enough to offer shade. As families moved into town, they wanted him to build a unique house for them on Travis Street. Big or small, Hutchinson built it.

Shannon dug around in the back seat, looking for her tennis shoes. By the time she got them on, Jack was back.

"We got to go." He started the car as he slammed the door closed. "Something has happened to Emily."

"What?"

She got one glance in his eyes before he shot out of the lot, headed toward his house. "What's going on?"

He gripped the wheel so hard she wasn't sure he was listening. Then his words came, slowly. "I didn't take time to get the details. Mom called Dad to say she was going to ride in an ambulance with Emily's mom. They're rushing Em to the hospital. Dad told us to hurry if we want to get there in time."

"No," Shannon said. "This will be the third time she's been in the hospital in three years. Not again."

Jack pressed the accelerator and the quiet streets

became a blur. "We'll drive past her house. Maybe we'll catch up to them?"

When they got to Jack's house, the door was wide open. So was Emily's door across the street. They ran for the Waterses' place.

"Em!" Shannon screamed. "Em!" she shouted again as if her friend might appear and explain that it was all a mix-up.

But no one answered as they entered the Waterses' house.

The TV was on. Vegetables sat half-chopped on the counter. Jack whispered as they moved down the hallway, "No blood. That's a good sign."

Shannon wanted to hit him. A dozen reasons Emily would have been rushed to the hospital came to mind and none of them involved blood on the floor.

She grabbed the phone on the kitchen wall and dialed the bakery. Zoe or her mother might know what was going on. After all, Zoe was already in town.

"Calm down, Shannon," Alex O'Flaherty said in her always-Zen tone. "Zoe called me five minutes ago and said Emily was stable now but still having trouble breathing."

"What happened? Is Emily hurt?"

"There will be time to talk. I'm locking up the bakery and headed out now. I'll meet you at the hospital. I have to go."

Shannon hung up the phone, staring at it as if it could somehow hurt her if she glanced away. "We need to be at the hospital."

"I agree."

Jack drove back down Main Street. Late sunlight blinked across the windows of shops already closed for the evening. Only a few people passed. One waved at Jack, but Jack was concentrating on his driving.

Neither talked. They knew nothing and guessing what was wrong would only cause more panic. They were home. A place so peaceful nothing bad ever happened. Emily was fine. She had to be.

Finally, he broke the silence. "I should have asked more questions. How could Emily have gotten hurt? Or maybe she's sick? Or maybe she tried to…"

"Don't even think it," Shannon whispered. "For as long as I've known Emily, she's felt trapped. If she came home, she must have lost all hope of breaking free. But Em wouldn't…" Shannon couldn't even think about Emily hurting herself, but the possibility seemed to hang between them.

"I don't want anything to change here, Jack. I want to go away and always know that here everything will be the same. This town. My friends."

"It doesn't work like that, Shan."

She hit his shoulder. "Don't tell me that. I don't want to hear it."

He didn't react. He didn't even look at her as he pulled into the hospital parking lot.

When he clicked off the engine, he turned to her, his eyes full of tears he wouldn't let fall. "I can't promise you things won't change, Shan. I can't. But I can promise I'll stand with you now in what you face and later down the road. Whether it's good or bad. Whether you're right or wrong. I'll stand by your side."

She nodded and took his hand as they ran for the emergency doors. For the first time in her life, she saw Jack Hutchinson in a different light.

Like it or not. Ready or not. Her world was already changing.

six

Emily

SHADOWS DANCED ACROSS the walls of Emily Waters's hospital room. Almost real, almost part of her ever-shifting dreams. Emily told herself she wasn't afraid of night's echoes. Sometimes, in her darkest dreams, the shifting shapes were all that kept her company.

They were whispering tonight, telling her this was all her fault. Making her hurt deep inside. Making her wonder what was wrong with her.

There were also whispers from strangers circling around her bed. They tried to be gentle. Tried to help. But how could she tell them where it hurt, when there was no gaping wound, no cuts, not even a bruise.

She was back home in Laurel Springs. Maybe it

would be all right now. Her mother would take care of her.

Her mind drifted through the past few months. The college up North had echoing hallways, and the winter light never seemed as bright as it did in Texas. The whole world seemed hollow there. She'd known after the first week it wasn't for her, but she'd stayed, hoping. She'd made it almost to the break before she left.

"Breathe, Emily," said one of the strangers. "Just keep breathing and you're going to be fine."

Emily closed her eyes and simply drifted. She wanted to tell the stranger poking a needle into the back of her hand that sometimes it wasn't worth it to keep breathing.

But she couldn't think of a real reason to stop, and someone had told her once that a person has to have a reason to die.

She slipped into sleep. Maybe she'd think of the reason tomorrow. Tonight, she was just too tired.

seven

Zoe

ZOE O'FLAHERTY PULLED her feet up onto the waiting room's plastic chair, hugged her knees and curled into a ball. "Disappear," she whispered. "Just vanish and all this will go away." She liked the parties and bright lights and laughter of the Big Apple. She did not like this hospital waiting room. It smelled of dying and loss and heartache.

The walls, the floor, even the chairs were stark white, and the room seemed cold and hollow. Sadness and pain lingered. The only sound was the swishing of automatic doors that the wind set off every few minutes. The double doors would open long enough to let a ghost in, or an invisible spirit out, then swish back into place.

She closed her eyes, not wanting to see the empty waiting room. Her mother had talked Anna Waters, Emily's mother, into walking down to the break room for coffee, but Zoe couldn't leave her post. Not even for a moment. Her friend was just beyond the emergency room doors, and somehow she, Zoe, had to stand guard. Emily's spirit wouldn't slip out without Zoe knowing. She'd keep death's shadow from getting past. She'd pull Emily back to happy times.

A custodian in the corridor behind her was sweeping his broom from side to side. The rhythm of the thuds against the wall almost sounded like heartbeats.

In her mind, Zoe began to dance to the beat. A slow, lonely ballet of worry.

Her mother told her once that if she closed her eyes she could go anywhere she liked. All she wanted to do right now was stand beside Emily. Whatever her friend faced beyond those emergency doors, they'd face it together.

All three could survive if they were together. They'd sit down to a Welcome Home Tea on the balcony above the bakery. Shannon would join them, of course. They'd laugh and tell of their adventures since they'd parted at summer's end.

"Everything will be just as it's always been," Zoe whispered aloud.

A few hours ago she'd been boarding the plane, excited to be heading home for Thanksgiving. Thinking of all the stories she'd tell when they were back together again. But trouble had hit in her hometown while Zoe was in the air.

Part of her wanted to run back to her new life in New York. There, she was among strangers. No one's problems could touch her. Here, in her hometown, she knew almost everyone. She cared.

Zoe didn't know if she could stand to see Emily in the hospital for the third time in three years. Each time, she'd looked thinner. Each time, she'd faded just a bit.

She wished she could run back to the bright lights. She'd lock herself in her little room in the Village and not think of home and what was happening beyond the emergency room doors tonight to her dear friend Em.

Zoe decided she'd only come back to Laurel Spring for the happy times. Weddings. Graduations. Birthdays. And Christmas, of course. Her mom always made Christmas the most superdelicious day of the year.

But reality kept echoing through her brain. Life didn't play out in acts of happiness. Emily, her forever friend, had complained of headaches for years. She blamed them on an accident she'd had when she was fifteen. She'd been out walking on a cool March night, when someone, driving way too fast, had hit her. Maybe the driver hadn't seen her. Moonless night. Back road.

But Emily had suffered a broken arm, a few deep cuts along her neck and headaches. After the accident, the world frightened Em.

Her mother pushed medicines on Em like some parents push vitamins. Over-the-counter. Anything a doctor would suggest. Health store cures. "Even late-night commercial claims are worth trying," Anna Waters would say to Emily. She didn't want her daughter to suffer, to ache, to be anything less than perfect.

A year after the accident, Emily had taken too many of the "cures." The overdose had frightened everyone. An accident. Overmedicating.

Zoe fought down her anger as she waited for news. Emily wouldn't have overdosed, not again, not this time. Mrs. Waters was wrong even to whisper it as a possibility. Emily wouldn't. She had dreams and goals. She wanted to be a missionary and work with children. She told Zoe when they were in grade school that someday she planned to have a dozen kids. Maybe those weren't her mother's dreams for her, but Emily had them just the same.

Somehow, this was Anna's fault, Zoe decided, as she shifted in the hard chair. Anna Waters loved her daughter, but she held on too tight. She wanted Emily to be and do everything she hadn't had time, or been brave enough, to do.

Footsteps ran toward Zoe as wind blew through the open doors again. A moment later, Zoe was hugging Shannon, both girls crying and talking at the same time.

"She's going to be all right, Shan. I'm sure the doctor got to her in time. She's going to be all right. I know it." If Zoe repeated it often enough, it just might come true.

Shannon, as always, wanted details, and Zoe had few.

"An accidental overdose on pills from a prescription two years old." Zoe echoed the words Mrs. Waters had said.

"It happened before." Shannon said what they both knew. "How could she be so careless again? She almost died last time."

"I don't think it was as bad as last time," Zoe whispered. "Mom said they're only keeping her for a few days. Running some tests. That's all I know."

Shannon looked disappointed. Zoe knew, for Shannon, the world always had to make sense, and a second overdose couldn't be right.

"It was just an accident, Shan. Just an accident."

Shannon didn't look like she believed her.

Jack Hutchinson silently stepped from behind Shannon and hugged Zoe. One of those total, feel-good kind of hugs. He asked more questions, but Zoe didn't have any answers. All the while they talked, he held her against him.

When Shannon turned to say hello to Mrs. Waters, Zoe hugged Jack harder. "I'm glad you're here," she whispered.

"Me too," he answered.

"You always give the best hugs, Jack," she mumbled against his shoulder. "I swear, you're getting taller. When we were in grade school, I remember we were the same."

"Hugs are what friends are for." He kissed the top of her head. "And I'm not getting taller. You're shrinking. Is your light shining bright in New York?"

She dried her cheek on his shirt. "Not yet. It's kind of blinking off and on. The school is great, but there's a lot of talent out there. Some days it's like I'm one of a thousand applying for every part."

"You'll make it, slugger."

Zoe had dated Jack her junior year. He'd been a senior and she badgered him into taking her to the prom. Both knew what they had was a friendship, not first love. He was focused on going to college, and the last thing she wanted was to be tied down. Jack was a rock to her, but she knew he thought of her as a butterfly that flew past him now and then.

She stood on her toes and kissed him on the lips, just as she had a few years ago on prom night. "You taste like root beer."

"Yeah, I started drinking it about the time Shannon started driving. We just drove in and heard Emily was rushed here."

Zoe pulled away from him as Jack's mother walked up with two cups of coffee. Since she was dressed in scrubs, Zoe knew Jack's mom was working late tonight. His mom handed Mrs. Waters one cup as she smiled at her youngest boy in that way that only mothers of sons do.

Zoe's mother followed with two more cups, handing Zoe both of them. Zoe's mother—Alex to everyone—thought she was the den mother to all of her daughter's friends. Her wild red hair fit with her name.

"I have to get back to the bakery," Alex announced. "I'll leave you three here. Call me with any news. I'm only ten minutes away if you need me. Emily is going to pull through this. She's stronger than she looks."

Zoe wasn't sure if her mom was telling the truth,

or simply wishing. Alexandra O'Flaherty had taught her daughter well. Always wish for the best. "Hoping hard this time, Mom."

Alex folded her daughter in her arms, then turned to first Shannon and finally Jack. She didn't have to say a word. She was there to offer comfort, not guesses or advice. No matter the mess Alex O'Flaherty walked into, she added a bit of peace to the mix.

After patting each one, she left, with only a silent nod to Anna Waters.

Mrs. Waters did not seem to notice. She sat three chairs down from the little crowd and drank her coffee with shaking hands. Jack's mom sat beside her, offering a few moments of company before she had to get back to work.

Zoe felt sorry for Emily's mother, who was older than most mothers of her daughter's friends. Mrs. Waters's hair was salt-and-pepper gray. Her face looked like it had never seen moisturizer, much less makeup. She had a way of being short with people, even when she wasn't angry.

Emily had told them once that she was a change-of-life baby. The three girls had no idea what that was. They thought all babies were change-of-life.

Zoe watched as Shannon suddenly punched Jack in the back. "I saw you kissing my friend. Don't do that again," she ordered, sounding half joking and half serious.

"Why?" he shot back as he dodged a kick. "Zoe and I are friends. Men and women can be friends, Shan, but you wouldn't know anything about that."

He sounded angry, but Zoe saw the sparkle in his eyes. Picking fights with Shannon seemed to be a new hobby he'd developed.

Before she could answer, a doctor stepped up to Mrs. Waters, and they all huddled close to listen, as if they were family too.

Anna Waters seemed too busy mutilating a tissue to notice them.

"She's weak, but resting now." The doctor's voice sounded tired, as if he'd said the same words too many times. "I don't want to downplay this, Mrs. Waters. Another hour or two and it might have been too late. She's way too thin and her blood pressure is far too low. She told me she couldn't remember the last meal she'd eaten. We're seeing all the signs of clinical depression here."

Anna Waters wiped tears off her cheek with the palm of her hand. "I told her not to take more than four pills. But she said her head hurt. If she'd just listened to me. I've tried everything to get that child to eat, and since she's been home from school all she wants to do is sleep."

She's not a child, Zoe almost shouted, but she just stared at the strange lady. Mrs. Waters heard only her own voice.

"My other two kids never had depression."

Jack's mom moved to hold Emily's mother as if they were friends. "It's all right, Anna. We got her here in time. It wasn't your fault. You can't blame yourself. It was just an accident."

Mrs. Waters kept nodding like a bobblehead doll,

and Jack's mom kept repeating the same thing over and over.

"I'll call Howard after I see her. He'll want to know the facts, even if he can't come home until tomorrow." Mrs. Waters blew her nose and continued, "He'll be expecting Thanksgiving tomorrow no matter what, and I have no idea when I'll have the time to cook." She straightened and added, "I had a feeling this was going to be a lousy Thanksgiving and now I don't care what we eat. I just want my baby to be all right."

The doctor opened the examining room door and waited for them to step in.

They huddled together as they moved through the doors and down the hallway to Emily's room.

No one spoke as they crowded around the bed. Emily was curled up in a fetal position, her long brown hair spread across the white sheets. She looked like she was simply sleeping.

Finally, the doctor set the agenda: "We'll move her upstairs as soon as the room's ready. Should keep her for a few days. Watch her vitals. Check her meds. Encourage her to eat. She's resting now, but she'll probably feel like visitors tomorrow." He raised an eyebrow as if daring any one of them to argue with him.

When no one asked him any questions, the doctor nodded a good-night and vanished down the hallway.

"I'm staying with her—" Zoe glanced at Mrs. Waters "—while you call your husband."

"Me too," Shannon added.

"Not tonight, ladies," announced a nurse at the doorway. "Go home and get some rest. She'll probably sleep all night, and tomorrow is soon enough to visit." When Zoe frowned, the nurse added, "Doctor's orders, miss. We'll watch over her tonight."

Anna Waters took Jack's arm. Tears were dripping off her chin, but she didn't wipe them away.

"I'll take you home to rest, Anna," Jack's mother said as they passed the nurse's station. "My shift was over hours ago. I'll be right across the street if you need me."

Anna Waters moved away with Jack's mom.

They turned toward the door as Mrs. Waters said, "I don't know how to make her better. That's a mother's job."

Jack put one arm around both Zoe and Shannon and walked them out.

At the parking lot Shannon grabbed her backpack from his car and told him she was going home with Zoe.

Zoe realized Shan had read her mind. She didn't want to be alone and the little apartment above the bakery had always been Shan's second home. Shannon might be able to handle anything that came along, but Zoe always felt a little out of place when she wasn't part of a party. The quiet times, the sad times, always left her doubting which way to turn.

The apartment would be perfect tonight. When she meditated in her acting classes and was told to go to her happy place, it was always her mom's apartment over the bakery. Funny how she wanted to do everything in life, see it all, but in times like this the small space overlooking the little town was just right.

"Don't worry, Shan. She'll need our help more tomorrow than tonight." Jack didn't move to join them. He probably knew he wouldn't be invited. "Besides, they'll have machines hooked up to Emily. If she even misses one heartbeat, the nurses will be running her direction. I've watched that happen in all the movies."

"I know," Shannon snapped as she stormed toward Zoe's Volkswagen.

Zoe patted his arm. "She's just upset at the world tonight, not you, Jack."

"I know. I'll see you tomorrow. And, Zoe, call me if anything happens."

She nodded and ran to catch up with Shannon while he stood watching. They were all upset, feeling helpless.

eight

Jack

JACK WATCHED ZOE drive out of the parking lot like she was a NASCAR racer. She was always in a hurry, always dancing through life at full speed. Zoe O'Flaherty had been the star of every school play, the soloist in every church pageant, the queen of every ball. But she didn't see herself out front of the crowd. She might shine, but never enough in her own mind.

She was Shannon and Emily's best friend. No doubt about that. Maybe she was his best friend too. Zoe had always been there to cheer him on when he was trying and to kick him in the butt when he wasn't. He liked that about her. She always gave it to him straight.

Jack might want to get closer to Shannon and talk

to Zoe, but it was Emily who needed him tonight, and, like always, he'd be there for her.

He sat in his car and waited as he thought of the three girls. Shannon was a warrior who'd fight for them. Emily was afraid to live. And Zoe was a star he feared might one day burn too bright and explode. Jack didn't know if he was lucky or cursed to have them in his life.

Three hours later, the night was moonless. The wind had stilled, as had the flow of visitors in and out of the hospital. He climbed out of the car and walked back to check on poor little Emily.

He wouldn't sleep until he knew she was out of danger.

Thanks to his mother being a nurse, Jack Hutchinson knew the hospital in Laurel Springs well. When the town decided to remodel the old building, his father's company had insisted on Austin stone, so now the building seemed to glow like a ghost against the night sky.

Any patients in critical condition or in need of major surgery were sent to specialists in Dallas. Babies were delivered in birthing rooms on the first floor. All those windows were dark, so the stork wouldn't be dropping by tonight. Those who were terminally ill spent their dying days on the second floor with family lining the hallway during visiting hours.

The building had once been a hotel, so the floors creaked and archways were high and wide. Since the remodel, he thought it stood proud as a way station for coming into and leaving this world. Emily even told him once she could almost see angels in the sun's reflection off the thick glass windows.

After visiting hours were over, rounds were made once an hour, on the hour, unless a patient needed closer attention. Like everything in this town, he doubted the rules had changed since he used to roam the hallways after his mother signed on to her shift and his father was working late. Exploring the hallways was far more interesting than staying home with his big brothers.

He glanced down at his watch as he headed toward the side door marked Employees Only. Five after eleven. Plenty of time to check on Emily.

Jack walked across the grass, knowing he wouldn't be seen or heard from the rooms above.

As he slipped silently through the shadows at the back of the lobby, the low rumble of the vending machines echoed. The reception area was decorated in dull chrome and fading plastic and was as still as a painting.

He marched toward the freight elevator at the far end of the hallway off the first floor. It was used to move laundry, cleaning carts and now and then a corpse. One locked door barred his way. During the day it was unlocked, but required a code to open after five. Jack had learned the code when he was six.

One-five-two-four. The lock opened. How could even a six-year-old forget how to make an X on the buttons of the lock.

On the second floor, rooms circled the nurses' desk.

Jack had to pass only two doors before he was at Emily's room.

Eleven ten. Almost an hour to visit.

When he stepped inside, he pushed the door closed slowly until he heard the click. It wasn't a lock, but at least if someone entered, he'd hear a sound. The lights were low, the blinds blocking any outside light. Blinking machines added an eerie, unnatural glow across the walls. The IV pole's shadow reminded him of a weeping willow made of hanging tubes.

For a while he just stared at Emily Waters. His neighbor. His friend. The first girl he'd really talked to. She was a few inches shorter than Zoe, and so thin she still seemed more child than woman. Shy, vulnerable, afraid of the world.

Shannon Morell and Zoe O'Flaherty seemed older, but somehow Emily didn't appear much different than when he'd first taught her to ride a bike. He'd been five. She was four. Jack still remembered how much wiser he'd thought he was then.

Now she lay curled up as if she were hiding from something. Bone thin. Pale. It was hard for him to believe she'd been brave enough to go away to school for even three months. The long chocolate-brown hair she always wore in pigtails was free tonight. If she were awake, she'd probably say she had Rapunzel hair and was planning her escape as soon as she braided it.

"Emily?"

No movement.

He stepped closer. "You asleep?"

She turned slightly and smiled, but her innocent

brown eyes only half opened. "I don't want to talk, Jack. I just want to sleep."

Jack circled the bed and sat on the side she wasn't using. He leaned back on the empty half of her bed as if he'd just joined her in a double recliner. "Fine with me. I've been driving all day and listening to Shannon rattle on. My ears could use the rest."

Emily turned to him as he knew she would. Pressing against his side, she sighed and put her hand over his heart as if proving he was real and not simply moving through her dreams.

As he always did, Jack circled his arm around her shoulders and rested his chin on the top of her head. He swore he could feel his body heat passing through the clothes between them and warming her.

"I remember the first time we did this. You about scared me to death when you climbed in my window." Jack pulled the thin blanket over her shoulder. "You're the first and only girl who ever snuck into my room, you know."

He felt her laughter more than heard it, before she raised her face up to look at him. "I'll never forget. We'd had a traveling preacher staying at our house. He wore thick glasses and one of his eyes was bloodred. He said it was from allergies, but I thought it was more likely from staring at the fires of Hell. He talked all evening about how evil the world was, and when I asked one too many questions, my mother sent me to bed, telling me to think about where I wanted to spend eternity."

Jack smiled. "I remember. You thought about the

eternal fires long enough to scare yourself, and the last thing you ever wanted to do was see that preacher again."

"So I climbed out my window and ran over to your house. You were in that funny tent bed you had, reading a book with your flashlight. I told you I was afraid and you didn't say a word. You just moved over and let me climb in. Then you read me a picture book version of Robin Hood until I fell asleep."

"You were six and I was seven."

She patted him on the chest. "It was right. You held my hand all night. You made me feel safe. I didn't dream of the fires of Hell. I dreamed I was running with Robin and his merry men."

"You're right, Emily. It was right." Jack closed his eyes, wondering what would have happened if Emily's mother had ever known how often her daughter crossed the street to talk to him. They'd wrap up in quilts and sit out on his patio and talk about every new problem that came along, from first grade to high school.

But her mother never knew of the times she crawled in his window to talk. Or about the times Emily walked the midnight roads when she was worried. Emily had mentioned it once, and Jack had lectured her that, even in a small town, it might be dangerous.

She'd found out for herself one night when she'd been fifteen. A hit and run. The driver never arrested.

After her accident, she said she'd try to never roam the back roads again. When Jack had visited her in the hospital, he'd tried to make sure she was serious, but

Shannon and Zoe were always near, entertaining her. If they'd been alone, Jack might have been the only one she would tell of the dark mood that had driven her out that night.

Six months before he left for college, he suspected she'd resumed her midnight walks. When he confronted her while he was home his freshman year for spring break, Emily evaded his questions. Jack had never forgotten how she'd laughed and told him that a dark angel followed, so she was safe now. She'd said the midnight shadow had always been behind her, watching over her since she'd been hit by a car out on Cemetery Road.

Jack had laughed it off, but he remembered hearing the nurses talk about a 911 call that came in the night Emily had been hit by a car. They'd said a panicked, frightened voice could barely be heard over what sounded like a bar crowd. He'd given Emily's exact location and yelled for them to hurry, and then the phone had gone dead.

When the ambulance had arrived on Cemetery Road, the ambulance driver swore he saw someone move away as his headlights swept over Emily lying in the grass. Her broken arm had been wrapped in what looked like a tablecloth. Cuts ran down one side of her neck and she had two broken ribs. No one saw the Good Samaritan, if he existed, or the car that had hit Emily, but some guessed it was Fuller Wilder, a rough dropout who helped his old man fix cars. Everyone knew either the kid or his dad tested the cars late at night.

Since Emily couldn't remember much, Mrs. Waters claimed an angel must have saved her daughter, and Emily went along with the story.

Because of her injuries, Emily didn't come to talk to Jack anymore, and the few times he'd visited her, Mrs. Waters never left the room.

The night before Jack left for college, she'd tapped on his window to say goodbye.

A few hours later, his mother, always grounded in reality, had opened his door and spotted Emily. They were both atop the covers with college catalogs scattered all around them. Emily had fallen asleep, but Jack was still reading.

His mother had reached for the light, then hesitated before flipping the switch. "Anything going on here?" she whispered.

"Nope. Just helping her look at colleges," he answered. "When I finish, I'll walk Emily home."

His mother nodded and closed the door, leaving the light on. His mom had never been one to doubt her son or look for trouble when none was there.

Jack grinned, thinking hell would break loose in Laurel Springs if Mrs. Waters had found out about that last time Emily had come to his room. She controlled Emily with threats, religion and predictions of trouble.

Jack was glad he'd been Emily's safe harbor and friend while they were growing up. Only now, this time, he wasn't sure what had happened to land her in the hospital. This time she'd hurt herself—by accident or on purpose. "You all right, Emily?" he asked before she fell asleep. "Everyone's worried about you."

"It was an accident," she answered, "but I don't think my mom believes it. She thinks I'm trying to kill myself just to irritate her. She thinks I'm depressed about being scarred, but the lines on my throat are just a part of me. I don't ever think about them unless she reminds me of them."

"I believe you. You wouldn't leave this world without saying goodbye to me, would you?"

"No, Jack. You know all my secrets. I'd have to make you sign a nondisclosure agreement first."

"I doubt I know all your secrets. I've been gone for over a year. No telling what wild things you've done since I left for college."

She giggled and covered her mouth to muffle the sound. "You're right. You might know all my fears, but not my wild side. A girl has to keep her secrets to herself."

"You still got all those stories dancing in your head? I swear, you could be a writer."

"Yep. Sometimes it's like my brain is a TV and I can flip from one story to another with one click. Some story lines are simple, like what I'd like to say to my mother. Others are dark and complicated mysteries where I can't figure out if I'm the villain or the victim."

They were silent for a while. Then he finally asked, "You want to tell me about what happened at that fancy college in New England? Why'd you come home early?"

"I didn't like the people at the school. Everyone was so nice. Too nice. I swear, sometimes I could see the cracks in their perfect act. Everything they did or said seemed practiced, but now and then, I could see the shadow of a tail as they walked away. I tried for almost three months, but it wasn't right. I didn't fit there. I'm not sure I fit anywhere."

"You'll find another school."

"No. Mom's right. I need to stay home and take correspondence courses. I'm not brave like Shannon or wild like Zoe." She gulped down a cry and her big brown eyes rounded in fear. "Only I don't want to stay home. Not with Mom. By the time I was ten, I understood why my dad lived on the road so much. I know she loves me, but she'll argue about anything until she wears me out and I give up. She's the only person in the world who is always right, and she reminds me of that daily. Do you think love can smother someone?"

"I don't know. I don't have much luck with love."

She grinned. "I think I'd like to fall in love with love someday and stay that way forever."

"That kind of love may only happen in books."

She nodded. "Then maybe I'll write about it."

He agreed. "First you've got to get better, Em."

One tear drifted across her cheek. "I know. I'll try. But I think I have to change a few things first, which means I have to discuss one major change with my parents."

"Do you talk to your dad much?" Jack could never remember Howard Waters being any help raising Emily, but who knew—the man might have said something sometime.

"When he was home for one day last weekend, he told me that maybe I should move out. He said if I'm not in school, I need to be making my own way. I thought my mother was going to choke on her objections. Finally, Mom agreed that I am old enough to move out, but only in Laurel Springs, of course, and everyone knows there's no place to rent that I can afford. So Mom wins again."

When Jack didn't say anything, she added, "I just took the pills because I didn't want to think about what to do anymore. It's like I'm running in one crazy circle. If I could just step one step out, I might find a way. If I don't go to college, I can't live at home. I'd have to get a job. If I can't find a job, I can't pay for an apartment. If I don't move out, I'll go crazy with Mother still asking me questions like, 'Did you brush your teeth?'"

"I get the picture. But think about it. What do you want, Emily?"

"Tonight I just want to go to sleep with you keeping watch over me."

"I can make that happen. Close your eyes. I promise I'll stay until you fall asleep." Jack didn't say another word. He just listened until her breathing slowed.

When he heard the nurse making rounds, he slipped from Emily's side and stood in the shadows near the window.

If the nurse had looked, she could have seen him, but she was busy checking on her patient. Once she left, he slipped from Emily's room and retraced his steps back to his car. Five after twelve. Just after midnight.

A shadow crossed in the darkness where the sidewalk curved. Jack thought it looked like a tall, thin man walking with his head down. But then, it could have been an angel. Who knew? Emily could use one right about now in her life.

Jack blinked. The man was gone.

After he climbed into his old Ford, Jack turned toward Main. He drove slowly past the little shops that had become a tourist destination in recent years. He'd heard that folks traveled a hundred miles to buy fresh honey, handmade quilts, and gingersnaps that tasted like Heaven. Each store was filled with things you'd never find in a chain store or even realize you needed until you caught sight of the treasures on a dusty shelf.

Every business was closed now, but the streetlights almost seemed to cast stage lights over the bakery, the café and the new bookstore, while the offices were so dark the windows seemed to be hollow eyes staring out, seeing nothing, showing no life.

When he passed Zoe's mother's bakery, he barely made out two people, wrapped in blankets, on the tiny second-floor balcony.

Jack turned off at a side street, parked his car and walked back. When he tapped on the metal fire escape, they dropped the ladder and he climbed up.

"Evening, ladies." He bowed. "Nice to see you both out enjoying the nightlife in Laurel Springs."

"Shut up and sit down. We heard that rattletrap of a car of yours coming from a mile away." Shannon moved to one end of the bench seat, making room for him.

"I've figured it out, Shannon. You must have rolled

off this balcony and landed on your head, and now you think my name is Shut Up."

"If the name fits," she countered.

"Stop fighting." Zoe wiggled in between them. "We've got to figure out a way to help Emily."

"It was an accident. She didn't mean to take that many pills," Jack said.

"Same thing as before. That car accident started it. By the time she healed from it, she had the headaches. Then one overdose. Now another."

Jack didn't miss the doubt in her tone. "An accident. I'm sure," he said again. "When she's in pain she doesn't think straight. She's got a lot on her mind right now."

Both girls looked at him. "How could you know?" Shannon shot the question first.

"I asked her. She told me her mother wants her to stay home and take correspondence classes. Her dad says if she's not in school by the end of January, she'll have to move out." Jack looked confused. "I swear, the man has lived across the street from me all my life and I've never heard him say anything but 'stay off the grass.' I don't think he even knows my name."

"Jack." Shannon slowed her words as if he didn't understand English. "When did you talk to Emily?"

Smiling, he confessed, "When I snuck into the hospital and talked to her about five minutes ago."

He reached for a corner of Shannon's blanket, but she pulled it away.

"Don't even think about it, Jack. I'm not sharing."

"I wouldn't think of it." Even wrapped up like a

burrito, Shannon was still cold as ice to him. "You're just mad because I talked to her."

"No, I'm not. Sneaking into the hospital seems like something you'd do."

Finally, Zoe joined the conversation. "Stop it. We've got to think about Emily. Maybe she wasn't trying to kill herself. If she had been, she would have swallowed the whole bottle of pills, right? But this was definitely a cry for help. What is so wrong in her world? And why today, the day before Thanksgiving?"

"Maybe it was the sense of failure from dropping out of school," Shannon suggested. "Or having to get a job. I've known college graduates who are so scared to go to work that they sign on for another degree in a field they've figured out they hate."

"Maybe it's moving back home," Zoe answered. "But she's been home for two weeks. Why today?"

Jack stood and looked down at them. "It's the day before Thanksgiving. It's the day you two were coming home. Maybe she knew you'd both be here if something did happen. She wouldn't be alone."

"That doesn't make sense." Zoe stood, as if facing Jack down, ready to fight.

"Think about it, Zoe. Everything she's ever done was with you two at her side."

He had watched the three of them for as long as he could remember. Emily always followed them. She'd danced in the rain one night because Zoe had. She'd signed up for every club in high school because Shannon did. She'd made herself so sick crying once that her mother gave in and let her join Scouts with them.

"You two are her compass. She's lost you both now."

"We don't know that to be a fact, Jack." Shannon shook her head. "Besides, she hasn't lost us."

"You don't know how she thinks." He stood perfectly still and watched. "None of us do. You can't crawl into someone's head. Mom says depression can play tricks with your reasoning. Em needs exercise, good food, coping skills, someone to talk things out with." Jack dug his fingers through his hair. "I don't know. Maybe she needs pills."

Zoe frowned. "We're back to step one. How about we go with Emily's idea. She was going for change when she went away to school. That didn't work. Maybe she'll try again and this time we'll find a way to help her."

The midnight moon sliced milky light in thick bars across the tiny balcony. He felt locked in, helpless. Part of him wanted to go back to the hospital and hold Emily again, tell her all was right with the world. A piece of Jack wished he could shake her hard and yell "Wake up!"

A phone rang inside the apartment. Zoe handed him her blanket as she ran to answer it.

Jack sat down beside Shannon, almost touching. "Can we cut the crap tonight, Shannon? We're both worried about Emily."

To his surprise, she put her hand on his shoulder. "All right, but I'll still be thinking about what's wrong with you, Jack. You'll be hit double time tomorrow."

"Fair enough." He grinned. "How about we kiss on it?"

She poked him in the ribs so hard his heart hiccuped. When he caught his breath, he mumbled, "I'll take that as a no."

nine

Emily

EMILY WATERS LAY on her side and watched the sunrise between the cracks in her hospital blinds. She told herself over and over exactly what she'd told Jack. It was an accident. Only an accident. It could have happened to anyone.

Only, does anyone count out the number of pills left in the bottle?

Part of her felt like a lab rat. How many pills could she take and almost die? One too many and she'd be dead. Then maybe people would say it was an accident. That sounded much better than suicide.

Rolling on her back, she tried to remember how long she'd been thinking of dying. Maybe she just wanted to be like Sleeping Beauty and be awakened by true love's kiss.

Right. She almost laughed out loud.

Her junior year in high school, when she'd recovered from the hit-and-run accident, she'd kissed half the boys in her school, including Jack.

They'd both laughed and admitted neither had felt anything special. When he kissed her forehead and offered friendship, Emily had agreed.

She liked his honesty.

When Jack told her he'd heard rumors that she'd gone further than a kiss with a few guys, she'd shrugged and said, "Nothing special. I'm just testing. When I get bored, or he starts saying dumb things like he loves me, I'll break it off."

Nothing ever felt right for her and she couldn't blame it on the accident. She'd felt that way for as long as she could remember.

She'd admitted to Jack once that sometimes she felt like a toddler slamming her thumb with a rubber hammer, wondering why it didn't hurt. She couldn't feel. And worse, she didn't care.

How many times did she have to fall before she felt the pain? How long until she went too far and hurt someone else? The first overdose two years ago was really an accident. She'd just wanted to sleep. This one was more an experiment. Like walking down the middle of a road at midnight with her eyes closed, or diving so deep she'd have no air in her lungs saved for the journey back up, or holding her breath until she passed out.

Emily had to think. Her mother would be in soon and would begin thinking for her. That was how it always was.

She had no idea who or what started her on this path of self-destruction, but there had to be an off button. She knew her mother loved her, but Emily had heard her whisper to Emily's dad that something was wrong with their only daughter. She wasn't stable. They might need to act before it was too late.

Her dad usually grunted his comments.

Emily knew what she had to do. She had to prepare before her parents came up to visit her. Taking too many pills again might just push them into action, and Emily feared whatever they did would only make matters worse.

She climbed out of her bed. The air was cold on her open backside, but she didn't have time to look for a robe. Her legs were rubbery as she held to the frame for support when she took the first few steps.

Slipping through her doorway, she looked for the supply cart she'd heard rolling toward her room an hour ago. A nurse had pulled it halfway in, unplugged her from the machines and wrapped her hand where the IV had been.

Emily had watched the nurse shove the cart back into the hallway, but she never heard it roll away.

Sure enough, it was parked five feet from her room.

Shifting through the gauze and tape, she finally found what she was looking for. Scissors. Before she could take time to reconsider, she grabbed a handful of hair and cut it off just below her ear.

Coffee-colored curls tumbled onto the tiles as she continued.

Long, tangled hair circles piled around her bare feet as she set the scissors back on the cart and returned to her room.

When the nurse came in with her tray, she said, in a very professional tone, "You've been busy. Everything all right?"

"Sorry about the mess. I'll clean it up. I just wanted to cut my hair."

"No problem. Visiting hours are still thirty minutes away. We'll have time. How are you feeling?"

"Tired, even though I slept solid."

The nurse nodded. "After Jack Hutchinson left, I checked on you every half hour. I don't even think you rolled over."

"Don't tell my mom he came."

"He your boyfriend?"

"Just a good friend. He worries about me."

The nurse watched her carefully as she said, "Does he have reason to worry?"

"No. It was just an accident. I'm not very happy with my life right now and my parents see me as a coward for not lasting a semester of college after they'd paid for the private school. But me, I just wasn't thinking straight. Bad migraine. Took a few extra pills. That's all."

"That why you cut your hair? The headaches?"

"No. I just woke up and decided it was time for a change. But I really butchered the job with those funny round-tipped scissors."

"That you did." The nurse laughed. "We've got an aide who could trim it up for you. I'll send her in when we finish delivering breakfast."

As she moved to the door, the nurse asked, "Anything else?"

"Could you call my friend Zoe? Mom took my clothes. Ask her to bring me up something—anything would be better than this gown. I hate it."

"Everyone does. People fight hard to get better just so they can wear clothes. I'll tell your friend to ring the buzzer downstairs and I'll go and let her in early. That way you'll be ready for company by the time the doors open."

"Thanks."

After Emily had showered and let the nurse's aide tidy up her newly short hair, she barely recognized herself in the mirror. When Zoe showed up, she claimed she loved the new look. After she put on Zoe's clothes, Emily felt like a new person, like she'd shed her skin.

Just before visiting time, Emily whispered to her best friend, "I've decided to change. Not just my look, but me inside. I feel like I've been living in someone else's life. Who I am isn't me. I'm not sure how I'm going to do it, but I'm going to try."

"I'll help," Zoe whispered, "but I think you're pretty wonderful just the way you are."

ten

Alex

"SWEETIE PIE'S BAKERY. HOW MAY I HELP YOU?" Alexandra O'Flaherty answered before she realized it was far too early for a business call. But a dozen citizens of Laurel Springs had yet to pick up their orders. They'd learned over the past three years that Alex would open Thanksgiving morning for those who were too busy to pick up their orders on time.

"Morning, Alex. How's my favorite redhead?" There was laughter in the deep voice. "Cooking as usual? Hope I'm not interrupting."

She recognized Chief Master Sergeant Mack Morell. Always polite. "Morning, Mack. It's a little early for a call, but I guess you know I'm always up early. You still in DC?"

"Yeah, I'll be stuck here another two weeks. And I'm glad you're up. If you're answering the bakery phone, that means you're either still at the books from last night, or you're baking."

"Good guesses. This week was so busy I'm way behind on the books. Also, a few people forgot to pick up their orders, as usual. They'll be banging on the door as soon as it's light. Doesn't anyone bake their own pumpkin pies anymore?"

She heard the low rumble of his laughter. Mack never let himself do anything freely or spontaneously. He was solid as a rock and bled red, white and blue. She'd often wondered if he wore his uniform to bed.

"I guess you know why I'm calling. These days you're more likely to know where my daughter is than I am. Last message I got from her said she was riding home with that Hutchinson kid. That thought haunted my nightmares most of the night."

"He's not a kid, Mack. He'll be twenty soon. His mother's already ordered the cake. They plan to drive up to the academy and surprise him."

"I don't really care, Alex. I just need to know Shannon is safe."

As always, Alex thought. "She's fine. Your daughter and mine stayed up half the night on the balcony trying to solve the world's problems. You want me to wake her?"

"No. I'll call back later. And if it's just the two of them talking that means Emily is in trouble. Did she drop out of that school that sounds like it was named after a hymn? Or did her mom decide to leave old Howard and move in with her in the dorm?" He paused.

Alex was silent for a moment, not wanting to relay bad news over the phone, but he had a right to know. Ever since the girls were five, anything that happened to one affected them all. "Emily accidentally overdosed."

Silence. She knew what he was thinking. Two years ago when Emily had had to have her stomach pumped, they'd all believed it had been an accident, but now, the second time? Before that, when she'd been hit by a car, Zoe and Shannon had camped out at the hospital. Pain passed through all three when one was hurting.

"I wish I could see your face," he finally said.

"Why?"

She knew he was smiling when he answered, "I've known you long enough to tell when you're lying."

Alex closed her eyes and let one tear fall. "I hope I'm telling the truth, but I don't know." She wiped her eyes and added, "I'm glad you called. I wish you were here, Mack."

That was all she needed to say. The master sergeant was used to acting without delay. "I'll catch the next flight out of DC that's heading west. I'll have a car waiting when I land at Sheppard Air Force Base and drive the last leg. Should see you in four hours, five at the most."

"We'll either be at the hospital or sitting down to Thanksgiving."

She could almost hear the smile in his voice. "Am I invited, Red?"

"You know you are, Mack."

He didn't bother to say goodbye. She just heard the click. Since they were both single parents, they depended on each other. Alex had chosen to have a child and loved raising Zoe alone, giving her daughter the childhood she never had. But Mack hadn't had a choice. His wife had walked out on them. As far as Alex knew, neither Mack nor Shannon had heard from runaway mom more than a dozen times since the day she left.

Mack had spent eight years of marriage in the air force traveling around the world. His wife didn't like the constant moving, strange towns, money she didn't understand. Mack mentioned once that after Shannon was born, Sandi insisted on moving back to Laurel Springs with Mack's family nearby.

Apparently, she'd liked staying in one place even less. Since his wife left, Mack had adjusted. He stayed mostly stateside. He did research from home. Worked four long days and had three-day weekends with Shannon when he could.

When duty called, his mother, who lived three doors down, watched Shannon during the week. Mack called his daughter every night.

If he couldn't get home for the weekend, Shannon became the bakery's weekend houseguest. Alex would always laugh and claim two little girls were easier to watch than one. She'd just follow the giggling to find them.

Alex poured a cup of coffee and walked upstairs to the tiny living room. Shannon was still sound asleep.

If Alex were guessing, she'd bet Mack's daughter had stayed up most of the night worrying, trying to make sense of what had happened to Emily. Zoe would be worried too. She'd cry and get mad at the world, but Shannon was her father's daughter. She'd always been the brave little soldier who needed an answer to every problem.

Alex picked up a note by the phone. *Mom, let Shan sleep. I'm going to take Emily some clothes. Will call with report.*

Turning, Alex stared into the shadows of the sleeping room. Shannon still had her clothes on and her curly sunshine hair looked wild.

Come home fast, Mack, Alex almost said aloud. *Your daughter may need you before we learn all the facts.* She took a slow breath. It had been a long week and today promised to be endless.

"I hate to admit it, but I may need you, Mack."

eleven

Jack

JACK WAS RELIEVED when he tried the bakery door and it was unlocked. "Mind if I come in?" he said, already moving inside.

"Of course not." Zoe's mother's voice drifted from the kitchen, sweet as honey scones. "Run the cash register, would you, Jack? I've got to box orders."

"Will do." Jack pulled a clean white butcher's apron from the drawer so he'd look official. He'd worked one summer in the bakery and loved it. Everyone who stepped into Sweetie Pie's inhaled deeply, then smiled.

He'd decided Heaven was probably a bakery.

For the next hour, folks drifted in like a steady stream of sugar addicts. Many had starved themselves of sweets all month so they could indulge on this one day. Most knew Jack well enough to ask how the academy was going. His answer usually lasted long enough for him to ring up their order, take the money and wish them a Happy Thanksgiving.

Alexandra O'Flaherty was a smart woman, Jack decided. She'd left trays of thumbprint cookies in the showcase by the register. The whole place smelled of chocolate and pumpkin pies baking in the huge ovens. Everyone who walked in to claim their order also picked up a few dozen cookies. Appetizers, he guessed. After all, they'd probably skip breakfast while waiting for the big noon feast.

Zoe's mother circled behind him, refilling the trays of cookies. "How many of the thumbprints have you eaten?" she whispered between customers.

"A dozen or so." He didn't bother to look guilty.

"You do know, Jack, that I'm paying you in cookies?"

"It figures, and I'm guessing, at the rate I'm eating, I'll still owe you a few hours when we finally lock the door."

She laughed. "There's always the dishes."

"I'll try to slow down."

Alex handed him a cup of coffee. "Shouldn't you be home with your family? Maybe helping out in the kitchen or catching up on the family business?"

He shook his head. "Since my brothers both married, the daughters-in-law took over the helping-out-in-the-kitchen job. Only problem is, the girls seem to hate each other. I expect blood to be spilled over the corn-bread dressing every year." He took a sip of his coffee. "You'd think the wives of Ben and Harry would get along. They're both married to idiots."

Alex laughed. "So my guess is you're never marrying."

"You got it. I'll serve a few years in the air force, see the world and all. Then I'll hire on as a commercial pilot. I plan to live free as a bird. From the day my brothers married, all they've done is complain about having no time and less money."

The door chimed.

Two of his old high school teachers rushed in to pick up their orders. Both wanted a bag of cookies and both asked him if he'd flunked out of the academy yet.

"Coming back home is depressing," Jack mumbled to himself. "You fight like hell to break out of the ordinary pattern and all people do is ask when you're coming back."

When Shannon stumbled down the stairs still half-asleep, he jerked at the sight of her. Her eyeshadow seemed to have slipped down to her cheeks. Her usually soft hair now looked like a tumbleweed and her sweatshirt was on backward.

He also guessed her bra must have fallen off last night. Women always claim men don't notice things, but Jack noticed that fact. He'd been trying not to look at her body since his sophomore year. If people could have read his mind, they'd have locked him up for being an X-rated minor. Her father would have simply shot him.

"Food," she growled. "I'm starving. I need coffee."

He handed over his half-empty coffee cup and a

thumbprint cookie while his brain forced his thoughts into the PG category. "You always wake up on the wrong side of the bed? If you weren't talking, I'd think the zombie apocalypse must have happened last night and you were patient zero."

"Shut… Oh, never mind. Give me another cookie." After she downed it whole, she asked, "Where is Zoe?"

"If she slept next to you, she's probably drained of blood."

"Morning, Shannon. Zoe's at the hospital." Alex answered Shannon's question as she set the last of the pie orders on the counter. "Did you sleep well on the couch?"

"Are you kidding? Look at her." It occurred to Jack that all women might wake up like this. That would explain why Alex hadn't looked shocked. He had no sisters, and his mother was always up cooking breakfast by the time he woke. Between night shifts at the hospital and raising three boys, there were times he wondered if his mom ever slept.

If women woke looking like this, that might explain why both his brothers looked so unhappy. Go to sleep with the prom queen and wake up with an extra from *Jeepers Creepers*.

"Any word about Emily?" Shannon asked Alex, as she held her hand out toward Jack for another cookie.

"Zoe headed that way an hour ago. Said she'd call me with any news." Alex began boxing the last of the cookies.

Jack grabbed a few, figuring he'd be safer if he kept feeding Sleeping-Not-So-Beauty.

Shannon folded her almost six-foot frame on a step midway down the stairs and drank the rest of his coffee. When she finished, at least her eyes had opened all the way. "I'll be ready in a few minutes, Jack. Can you drive me to the hospital?"

"Sure, but take your time. I'll wait. The way you look, there's a good chance you'll be admitted."

By the time he sold the last of the pies and ate the last of the cookies he'd saved for her, Shannon walked down the stairs looking like the girl he remembered. Light blond hair, bright green eyes and long legs. Those legs had stopped his heart several times before he was shaving regularly.

"You look great," he said before he could stop himself.

Shannon ignored the compliment as she kissed Zoe's mother on the cheek. "Thanks for letting me stay over. I really didn't want to be home alone last night."

"I understand. I'll hold dinner until you and Zoe get back. If Emily is awake, you girls will want to talk. I'm planning a late Thanksgiving anyway."

Jack decided to give it a shot. "Am I invited?"

The baker smiled. "Of course you are, Jack, but don't you want to eat with your family?"

"Are you kidding? My big brothers have been picking on me since I was born and now they have wives asking me when I'm going to settle down, get married, have kids. Dad will spend the day watching them argue and gripe about how much college costs, and Mom will keep patting on me just to make sure I'm real. She'll also keep reminding me I'm her baby. I had nothing to do with that lineup. The minute we eat she'll hand me a to-do list. I saw it on the fridge."

Shannon made a sad face. "Poor baby."

He was tempted to tell her to shut up, but thought it best not to pick on Shannon. After all, she was an only child. She had no idea of the pain older siblings cause. So he smiled at her, winked and said, "I'd rather stay here and let Shannon beat on me, if you've got room at the table."

"We'll make room." Alex laughed as Jack darted out from behind the counter to follow Shannon out the door.

When he started the car, Shannon asked, "Seriously, isn't your family going to miss you?"

"I doubt it. Now that both the sisters-in-law are pregnant, that's all my mom talks about. I don't think Dad's said more than hello to me since I told him I was going to the Air Force Academy. He doesn't understand why I'd want to go off to school when I've got a job right here, working with Ben and Harry. 'Construction is the future!' He always quotes that slogan like he saw it on a billboard somewhere. Once the next generation of Hutchinsons comes along, my folks will probably forget about me. I was a surprise, you know. An accident. At least once a year Mom reminds me they'd only planned for two kids. I'm the product of faulty birth control."

"Me too. Dad wanted me, but my mother didn't think she'd take to parenting. Turns out she was right."

Jack pulled into the hospital parking lot. "You ever hear from her?"

"Nope, not for a couple of years, and that was just a card sent to my grandmother's house. If she never contacts me, I think I'll be fine."

As they walked toward the sliding doors of the hospital entrance, Jack took her hand. A moment later she pushed it away. "Don't feel sorry for me, Jack."

"I don't." He shoved his hands into his back pockets. "Did it ever occur to you that I might just want to hold your hand?"

"Do you hold Zoe's or Emily's hands too?"

"No. I seem to have this terminal disease. I'm only attracted to you."

"Well, get over it."

"Believe me, I've tried."

Zoe stepped out of Emily's hospital room just before they reached the door. "Be careful not to overreact," she whispered. "Emily has decided to change."

"Into what?"

Both girls poked him in the ribs.

Jack held back. "I'll just follow you two in and act like I don't notice a thing."

twelve

Alex

IN BAD TIMES and good, Alex O'Flaherty cooked. She might dream of vacations or even days off, but all she knew was work.

As the day aged she thought of Emily and how she could help her daughter's friend as she made honey cinnamon scones and nutty chocolate brownies with a bit of banana enriching the batter. Yams were baking in one oven and the turkey in another. Wouldn't the world be a simple place if life were like cooking? Follow the directions with care and everything would turn out fine.

Zoe called to let her know all was well, but Emily would be staying at least one more night, maybe two, in the hospital.

Alex told her daughter that Shannon's father had phoned. He'd landed at Sheppard Air Force Base and was driving in as a surprise to Shannon.

Giggling, Zoe promised to keep the secret, then added, "She's already waiting for him. You know how he's always telling her he's not sure he can make it, and then he shows up. Their 'surprises' are as predictable as clockwork."

"I know." That was Mack Morell, Alex thought. He lived by a schedule and had expected his daughter to do the same since she was five. The man didn't even cough unless he'd already pulled the white, pressed, neatly folded handkerchief from his pocket.

She'd wondered more than once over the years if Mack's wife had left him because all their lovemaking was listed in his weekly to-do list.

Alex turned back to her work. She was going to have a crowd for Thanksgiving. Funny how life worked. She'd thought holidays would be just Zoe and her, but it hadn't turned out that way. Friends always seemed to blend in.

The one thing she missed about choosing to never marry was family at holidays, but maybe friends she loved dearly were just as good. She had been raised by a grandmother, her only real kin, who'd passed away while Alex had been in high school. There'd been an old guy who'd lived with her grandmother for ten years when Alex was little. He wanted her to call him uncle, but she never did, not even once. And she'd made a point never to see him when he tried to keep in touch.

After the funeral, Alex walked away from her

grandmother's home with one suitcase. At seventeen she closed her grandmother's bank accounts, took the GED and entered college. She'd lasted one semester.

Maybe it was better walking through life on your own. No one to tell you what to do. No relatives to hate. No gifts to buy for someone you didn't know well enough to even guess what they'd like. Alex liked her independent life. Even the mistakes were hers.

While the girls kept Emily company, Alex set the table, guessing it would be two hours, maybe more, before Shannon's dad made it in. They'd all wait for him. Mack would have stories to tell, and when he and Jack were together there was always laughter. They'd formed a bond when Jack told Shannon's father he wanted to be in the air force, and Mack was a good mentor.

She was pulling the turkey out of the oven when the door chimed downstairs in the shop. Alex was surprised. Jack and Shannon wouldn't be back this early, and there were no more pies to be picked up.

As she walked toward the door she saw a tall figure framed in the smoked glass. Wide shoulders. Slim frame. Waiting as if at attention.

Alex grinned as she unlocked the door. She'd know the build of this man anywhere.

"Welcome home, Mack. You're earlier than I thought you'd be."

He removed his cover and stepped inside. "I caught a lift faster than I predicted I would. It being Thanksgiving, I didn't think much would be flying, but a guy was gassing up when I arrived at the field."

Alex waved him toward the stairs. "I'm glad. I need someone to carve the turkey."

Mack pulled off his uniform jacket and tie, folded and placed them on a corner chair. "Always glad to offer my expert advice." He handed her a box. "I know I shouldn't bring something to eat to a baker, but I picked these up in Belgium. I was there for a meeting last week. Thought you and Zoe could eat them when you watch *It's a Wonderful Life* tomorrow night."

She opened the fancy red box, and the sweet smell of rich chocolate made her grin. "Thanks, Mack. This will be grand. We've seen that movie every year since she was born. She knows every line."

"I'm not at all surprised. Zoe was quoting lines from movies when I met her at five. I used to take the girls to the movies and Zoe would be rerunning dialogue all the way home."

Alex tied an apron around him and laughed when he frowned.

"I'll be your assistant cook, but I could use a cup of coffee first. I've been up since four."

She pulled a cup down that she'd given him a few Christmases ago. He'd left it at her place because he swore such a nice cup deserved better coffee than he made.

They'd cooked together enough to be comfortable and conversation moved easily between them as they worked. She'd never found a man she'd considered marrying, and he claimed to be allergic to women, but they were friends.

By the time the kids got back from the hospital, Mack was putting dinner on the table. Five people crowded around a table meant for four. Zoe talked about New York and how everything in the city seemed to run double time. Jack and Shannon discussed the day-to-day life at the academy.

An hour later, when they passed around pumpkin pie, they were back to talking about Emily. No one mentioned that the overdose might have been more than an accident. But they all agreed they had to help her.

Alex suggested offering her a job at the bakery. Shannon volunteered to search the town with Jack tomorrow for a place Emily could live, just in case Howard Waters really meant to make her move out if she wasn't in school.

"Does anyone think she'd be better off staying at home?" Jack asked.

No one at the table said a word.

Finally, Alex broke the silence. "She was hit by a car three years ago and had to spend lots of time at home, then the overdose two years ago. Now this. I'm thinking she might like some quiet time to herself."

All nodded.

Then everyone stood talking at once. Complimenting the cook, complaining they'd eaten too much.

Mack held the door for her, and Alex moved to the balcony, so they could relax while the kids did the dishes.

The day was chilly, but the sunset was beautiful.

In twilight, Laurel Springs reminded Alex of a picture-postcard photo. For a moment, it seemed the perfect place to live. In her mind, before she'd left home, her world seemed to be in black-and-white. Once she found her way here, she began to see color. Maybe for Emily a change would do the same. Laurel Springs relaxed her soul.

Mack must have felt the same. He leaned out onto the balcony railing and studied Main just as the streetlights blinked on.

A touch of gray brushed through his light brown hair, making him look sun-bleached. She'd always thought him handsome, though she seldom saw him smile, and worry marked his face now. Alex had a feeling work haunted his days even when he was home.

"No matter where I go—" Mack moved to the bench, leaving room for her "—no place feels like home but here. I've traveled all over the world, but like a migrant bird, I always come back where I was born."

Alex nodded. "I found this place by accident, but I feel that way too. I was pregnant, driving across Texas, thinking I'd settle in Arizona or maybe California. When I stopped here for a night, I walked the streets, and knew I'd finally be safe in this place. I think before I came here I was a weary warrior tired of fighting the world."

"Sweet as you are, Red, I've seen that warrior a few times. Once in a PTA meeting. Another time when a drunk yelled at the girls for playing in the park." Mack gave one of his rare smiles.

She grinned at him. "I dropped my weapons when

I settled here. I got a job at a little diner that used to be on Main. The Laradys, who run the newspaper, rented me an apartment upstairs from their offices. They are such a nice couple. They only charged me half the rent if I'd clean the downstairs once a week. After a year, I'd saved most of my salary and all my tips and moved Zoe into our little house over on Miller Street."

Mack leaned back, putting his arm along the bench, almost touching her with his hand. "I was around for the next move when you bought that old diner. The girls were fourteen and helped you change it into a bakery."

She laughed. "It was an easy move and I got triple what I paid for the house when I sold it, so I had the money to follow my dream."

"You happy living here above the bakery?"

"I am. I'm home." She leaned back against his arm. "And the commute isn't so bad either. But, in truth, I could use a little help if Emily is interested. I might have a little free time if I could train another baker."

"Free time? What would you do?"

"Go see Zoe. I've never seen New York. Maybe take a trip somewhere I've never been."

He nodded, and then they settled back to watch the night.

"The meal was great, Alexandra." Mack finally broke the silence. "But this is my favorite time of day, my favorite spot in the world to be, really. Here with you and the kids. All the world seems at peace." He rubbed his forehead, as if trying to erase the problems of the world.

"You ever think of retiring and living in Laurel Springs full-time?"

He shook his head. "Someday. Right now, I've got too much work to do."

She leaned forward, almost touching his knees. "And what is it you do, Mack? You can tell me. I won't tell anyone."

"I cannot talk about my work. Not to anyone. But I can tell you it's mostly paperwork, so don't go dreaming up that I'm a high-flying duplicate for James Bond. I haven't slept with a Russian spy or raced through the streets of Berlin on a bike in years."

"I'm determined to break you." She pulled the clip from her auburn bun and let her shoulder-length hair blow in the cool breeze. "One of these days, Mack, you'll slip and I'll know a few state secrets. There is not an ounce of fat on that body, I'll bet. You don't stay in that kind of shape working at a desk all day."

"Maybe I'll eat another dinner just to throw you off the track of what I really do. I'll never break." He put his hand over his heart.

They both laughed. She'd been teasing him about his job since the first holiday they'd spent together.

Jack yelled from the kitchen that they were taking Emily the last of the desserts. A moment later what sounded like a herd of buffalo pounded down the stairs.

Alex heard the bakery door slam. "Finally, silence at last."

"You want to watch some football?" Mack stood and offered his hands. As casual as old friends do, he pulled her up. For a moment they stood close, Alex within an inch of his six feet. Almost touching.

Usually, he pulled away, but this time Mack just looked down at her. Then, as if it was the most natural thing in the world, he leaned over and lightly kissed her.

Alex was too shocked to move for a moment.

Then he backed away so quickly she felt the wind shift. "Why did you do that, Mack?" He'd never, in the years they'd known each other, made any kind of advance, never talked about it, never even suggested anything that was or could ever be between them except friendship.

"I don't know." Surprisingly he looked as shocked as she felt. "I guess it seemed the right thing to do."

"Well." She pulled herself together. Not angry, more hardening to stone. "Don't ever do it again."

"All right." He turned loose of her hand and took a step backward. "You mad, Alex?"

"No. I know it was nothing. We're friends. But I thought you understood. I don't date. I've never married." When he still looked confused, she added, "I don't touch men and they never kiss me."

His intelligent evergreen eyes studied her. "I didn't know. I've seen you hug the girls a million times. I knew you weren't a hugging kind of person with others, but I didn't think it was some kind of law. I thought it was because you didn't want to have some wife jealous if you patted on her husband." He stared at her until sadness darkened his sharp gaze. "I understand. It won't happen again, Alexandra."

"No, you don't understand, Mack. It's just the way it is with me."

"I understand," he said again.

Alex shook her head and stepped inside. "I don't want to talk about it. Not ever."

She made it all the way to the couch before he came inside and closed the balcony door. As she flipped on the TV and began to skate through channels, he poured two cups of coffee.

For a moment Alex closed her eyes, remembering a time when she was six that she'd tried to forget. It had taken most of her lifetime, but she'd finally pushed the childhood memory to the shadows. One improper touch, like a drop of dye in clear water, shouldn't color her life, but forgetting wasn't easy.

She could hear Mack walking toward her and wanted to scream for him to forget what she'd said. She'd hurt him. He'd done nothing wrong with his gentle show of affection.

She should have just stepped away without any comment. He'd only kissed her lightly, nothing more than a peck, nothing bad.

When she opened her eyes, he was standing in front of her.

"Coffee?"

Alex took the cup.

"Which game should we watch?"

"You pick."

He sat down at the other end of the couch. "How about the Green Bay Packers and the Detroit Lions game? I'll bet you twenty bucks the Packers win."

She knew he was trying to act like the kiss had never happened. He was trying to step back into normal.

"You want anything to snack on?" She was trying too. He'd never understand. He had secrets he'd never tell her about his work, and she had secrets she'd never tell him.

An hour later, Zoe and Shannon came in, both talking at once. The silent little apartment filled with chatter. Jack had just dropped the girls off because his mother called, claiming the least he could do was come home and say goodbye to his brothers, since he hadn't bothered to say hello.

Zoe puffed up. "He said he'd be back in a few minutes, but who knows."

"You know, girls," Mack said, "he's not your personal driver. Friendship should be a two-way street." He stared at Alex, and she knew he was wondering where they stood. Any other woman would have welcomed his gesture and not overreacted.

By the time she made cocoa, Jack showed up. Within five minutes the two men were both yelling at the TV. Alex was laughing at them as if nothing unusual had happened on the balcony.

About the time the game ended, Jack got another call from his mom and waved as he ran down the stairs. The girls disappeared into Zoe's room to pick out more clothes for Emily.

The little apartment was silent once more.

Mack brought the empty mugs to the kitchen.

She kept busy wiping the counter down.

"I was thinking," he said so low no one could have heard him even if they were near.

Alex wanted to scream that they were not talking about what had happened on the balcony, but he simply whispered, "You think that apartment above the newspaper might be available? You know, the one you stayed in when you first moved here pregnant."

Alex relaxed. "I don't think anyone's ever lived there but me. It wasn't in good shape when I moved in, and once Zoe was born it seemed too small for even the two of us. Why?"

"I was thinking maybe, if we cleaned it up, that Emily could live there. The Laradys probably wouldn't mind making the same deal they made you. Half off the rent for cleaning the downstairs office. They're getting near retirement age, and I've heard their son and his wife will be taking over in a few years. Someone said they'd like to start traveling soon. Emily would be doing them a favor watching over the place."

Alex nodded. "I could hire Emily to help out at the bakery in the mornings. Between Thanksgiving and Christmas is my busy time. Then maybe after Christmas she'll have a direction."

"Let's not say anything to the girls until we check it out. It might be too much work." His voice sounded formal. "I'll pick you up and we'll have a look."

"Sounds good. Friday, most people eat leftovers. It'll be a slow day, so I'll close at noon."

After a long pause, Mack asked, "We all right, Alexandra?"

She smiled. "We're good."

He nodded and went back to his seat in her little living room. An hour later they were eating popcorn and watching a Hallmark Christmas movie.

thirteen

Fuller

STANDING ACROSS THE street from the hospital, Fuller Wilder watched the lights on the second floor dim, one by one. Visiting hours were over. The few patients who'd had to remain in care over Thanksgiving were settling in for the night, just like the whole town seemed to be.

He stared at only one window, though. The second one over the back entrance. Emily Waters's room.

He hadn't seen her today, but he'd watched her family march in about noon, then file out twenty minutes later. They hadn't come back. Her friends visited off and on all day. Fuller wished he could visit her. Make sure she was okay. Maybe he'd just walk into her room and introduce himself.

"Hello, Emily, I'm the guy who hit you out on Cemetery Road three years ago." No, that would never work. She'd have him locked up.

If he stood in front of her, Emily would probably scream for the nurse. Or worse, she'd remember the outline of his face from when he'd tried to help her after the accident. Then, with his luck, she'd figure out that he was the one driving the car that hit her.

She'd been walking on a back road. He'd been driving that night. Just an accident. But, if he'd stayed, he would've landed in jail. Make himself an ex-con even if he served his time. No one would hire him. He'd lose the fort, his business. His dad would lose a home.

If he turned himself in, he'd never be able to watch over Emily. That one fact kept him silent more than any other. He'd done all he could that night. But somehow, someday, he'd help her. He'd prove to her and himself that he wasn't a coward.

Fuller backed farther into the shadows of the evergreens lining the hospital property. He couldn't go in. He'd never talk to her. They might both live in the same town, but they lived in different worlds and he knew he didn't belong in hers.

For the past three months, while folks spent time in his shop waiting for Fuller to change their oil or rotate their tires, they'd talked to each other. Sometimes they'd comment that Emily Waters had gone away to some religious college. Small towns keep up with their high school grads as closely as they might a noonday soap opera.

Fuller never said a word, but he listened. A former

teacher of hers commented that Emily had come back a few weeks ago. Too early.

Fuller swore he'd be better off if he'd forget all about Emily Waters. She probably never thought about the night of the wreck. Only he did. His scars from that night were on the inside, but they were there. He'd never forget that he'd almost killed her.

Old habits are hard to break, and he couldn't think of any new habits worth developing. So he still walked home past her house even when he knew she was away.

The oldest neighborhood in town, where she lived, drew him. Each house on Willow Road was different. Bungalows were scattered among the big homes, fancy two-story brick, plantation style, old houses with mission designs, spooky houses about to crumble, all seeming to huddle together in harmony on one tree-lined street that ran parallel to Main.

A few weeks ago he'd seen her car out front of her parents' place and confirmed she'd come home from college. For the first time since she'd left, he felt he could breathe again. She was safe.

Since that night when he'd called 911 and watched over her until help arrived, he'd worried about Emily Waters. They were bound by the accident, by blood, by pain, by sorrow. He'd held her in the darkness as she cried. He'd make sure she was safe from now on. Deep inside, Fuller believed if Emily died, he'd die.

She'd seemed so small that night. His clothes had been soaked with her blood. She'd clung to him so tightly as she cried. He'd been eighteen and never cared about anyone but himself until that night. She'd been fifteen. Just a kid.

She didn't know him. She hadn't remembered him helping her. When he'd seen Emily after she'd recovered, she looked at him with the gaze of a stranger.

But he remembered. He'd almost ended her life.

Creepy, he thought. He should forget about her. She was all right. She had friends, family to keep an eye on her. Hell, if she'd gone all that way to college, she could take care of herself.

If anyone ever saw him watching, following her, they'd probably have him arrested. Since the fourth grade he'd been "that kid," the boy bound to make trouble. The one teachers watch. The one cops question first. The one who gets called in for a lineup.

But none of that mattered. Some nights he just had to know she was out of harm's way before he could sleep.

Three years ago, it wasn't just *a* car that had hit her. It was *his* car. He'd been a dropout looking for an adrenaline rush. Thanks to him she'd had to spend her sixteenth birthday in the hospital.

All she'd done was walk a rarely traveled road.

He'd made the curve too fast.

She had no time to jump out of his way.

Sometimes, deep down, he swore he could still hear the sound of tires sliding on a dirt road. Her scream. The thump of her body against the car's right fender.

When the sounds invaded his dreams, he'd wake, and wish that he could hold her.

Tonight, as he stared up, he wondered who or what

had hurt her this time. Maybe she was just sick. Maybe that was it. Maybe there was no one to blame this time. But she was in the hospital. Something had happened.

A month after the accident, when she'd been carried home from the hospital in the same ambulance, he'd started learning her patterns. Deep in his gut, he knew he had to somehow help her. Pay her back even if he could never say he was sorry.

Fuller sometimes reasoned that if he were in the right place at the right time, he could save her in a snowstorm or tornado. Not likely. Or maybe he'd fix her car so she could get home safely. She might have someone try to rob her and he could step in front of her, taking the bullet meant for her.

Fuller swore under his breath. He was no knight in shining armor. More likely, the cops would arrest him for stalking her. If she ever saw him she'd probably scream.

But he had to watch over Emily, no matter the cost.

A year after her accident, he'd seen her slip from her bedroom window and run across the street. Like a thief, she'd crawled into one of the Hutchinsons' windows. At first he'd thought something was wrong, or maybe Emily and the Hutchinson boy were young lovers. After all, they both came from what everyone called the "old families." They lived on Willow Road, where all the homes were a hundred years old and the streets were lined in trees that met each other in the middle of the brick streets.

Curiosity had driven him to move closer to the

Hutchinsons' window. Emily was talking to a boy who Fuller guessed was Jack. Nothing more. Just talking.

He'd felt like a Peeping Tom that night. A spy. But he didn't move away. She was complaining about her brothers. Jack listened but didn't offer much advice. They were obviously both the youngest in their families, and found comfort in trading stories.

After ten minutes, Jack started telling her about a book he was reading and Fuller figured out she'd just dropped in to talk.

He jumped back a moment before Jack swung out the window and then helped her drop. She looked so tiny next to Jack's six-foot frame.

The Hutchinson kid walked her across the street, then watched as she disappeared around to the back of her house.

Fuller was two years older than Jack, but from that night on, when the kid came into his grandfather's garage, Fuller made a habit of giving Jack's old Ford special care. He liked to think that if Jack gave Emily a ride to school or something, Fuller was, in a small way, watching over her too. Just like Jack.

But Jack was a friend, and Fuller only a shadow.

Another thing he liked was that when Jack Hutchinson bumped into him, he was friendly. Jack didn't act like he thought Fuller was a troublemaker. They might not be buddies, but Jack always took the time to talk.

The night Fuller hit Emily he'd been testing a car he'd just finished overhauling. He'd run a block to a bar, called 911, then ran back to stay with Emily until the ambulance came into view. But, like a coward, he darted to his damaged car and drove away before anyone saw him.

He'd buried the car in his grandpa's junkyard and burned his bloody clothes. He hadn't told anyone. Fuller even lied to the sheriff when he asked if Fuller happened to see a car with one fender damaged.

But Laurel Springs was a small town. People talked. Enough people hinted that the car that hit her could have been driven by Fuller Wilder, or his drunk father. No proof. Just whispers.

Oh, folks still brought their cars to the shop to be worked on, but most people didn't bother to talk to the Wilder family more than necessary. They were grease monkeys, poor folks, drunks, after all. One man whispered that the old man and his common-law son-in-law were soured by war, and *unfriendly* had been passed down to the boy.

But Jack Hutchinson wasn't like that. He'd stand around asking questions as if he were interested. He didn't try to act like he knew about cars. He listened.

Glancing at the hospital, shining old and white in the moonlight, he wished he could stop caring.

Last night, Jack had come to visit Emily after hours. Something Fuller would never dare to do. It would probably hurt her reputation if folks even thought he knew her.

Since the day he'd cussed a teacher out and walked out of school, he felt like he was fading. Becoming less and less a person every year. Most folks just called him "Bill's boy" as if they didn't realize he was now twenty-one and running the shop.

No one liked him, hadn't when he was in school, didn't now. But they'd hate him if they knew he'd almost killed Emily and got away with it.

She had scars. He'd seen them once when he'd sat behind her at the movies. Just before the lights went out, she'd turned, and he'd seen two lines as thick as his little finger running across her throat. He remembered her bleeding from that spot.

Sometimes, when he couldn't sleep, he'd wish he could take those scars from her and put them on his own neck. He'd dream that he'd walk up to her and say he was sorry. But he knew he never would. Her not knowing him was far better than her hating him.

So, for a dozen seasons, he'd stand among the line of old elms and aging cottonwoods where the creek meandered its way through Laurel Springs. He'd watch. He'd make sure she was safe. He'd see that Emily Waters was never hurt again.

It was his self-proclaimed punishment. His quest. Maybe his one chance to do something good.

A shadow pulled the blinds aside on the window he watched. Her thin hand brushed the glass almost as if she were waving at him.

Fuller knew she couldn't see him. He stood where shadows crossed in total blackness.

But he waved back just the same.

With his head down, Fuller headed toward Main. No need to walk Willow Road tonight.

The shops on Main ran only for a few blocks. Fuller rarely went into them. The only one he stepped into often was the bookstore. The owner, Arnie, talked books. Fuller liked pretty much any book that took him out of his life for a few hours. But the bookstore, along with all the other shops, was closed tonight.

One muddy old Audi was parked in front of a quilt shop that stood across the street from the newspaper office. Fuller recognized the car. The Laradys always drove Audis. They passed them down in the family like heirlooms. He'd worked on the brakes of this one last summer so Connor Larady could drive it one more year.

Larady was Fuller's age, and in his last year of college he'd married and had a new baby. Fuller remembered Connor had been worried about the cost of the repairs.

As Fuller passed the Audi, he saw a man, his head so far down that it touched the steering wheel. The engine was off, the window down.

"Connor, that you?" They weren't exactly friends, but Fuller felt like something must be wrong. "You all right?"

Connor Larady slowly raised his face into the streetlight's glow. He didn't say a word. He just stared at Fuller with bloodshot eyes.

Fuller knew drunks well enough to recognize one even in the shadows. The smell of whiskey and vomit made Fuller back a few inches away.

"You drunk?"

Connor was the golden boy of Laurel Springs. Everyone loved him. Hoped he'd move back to town one day. His family owned land, and most of the old buildings on the other side of the creek.

"I don't know," Connor answered. "I don't think so. I stopped and picked up beer and whiskey a hundred miles back. I couldn't eat and I'd already had a gallon of coffee last night. I don't want to think right now. Not about anything." His words were slow, but not slurred. Waving his hand over the passenger seat covered in trash and spilled bottles, he seemed surprised. "I can't be too drunk. I threw up most of what I drank."

"Why don't you drive two blocks to your folks' house? You could sleep it off. I heard your parents were out of town. You need to clean up before anyone sees you like this, Connor." Fuller tried to remember bits of conversation he'd heard. "I heard your folks were up visiting you over the holiday. What are you doing down here?"

Connor shook his head. "No, they are not in Denver. They didn't make it." He gulped down a cry. "My grandmother flew in earlier this week. She is with my wife and baby. They'll drive down Sunday. I had to come back tonight to make the arrangements."

Fuller hated asking. He felt like he knew the answer. "Where are your folks, Connor?"

"They died in a rollover after a truck hit them outside of Raton." His voice sounded hollow, as if all emotions had already been drained, leaving only sorrow. "The funeral home here said they'd go get the bodies. My brother said he wasn't sure he could make it home. I had to drive back to take over things. I have to plan the funeral. I…"

"Move over." Fuller watched Connor crumble, imploding from the inside. "I'll drive you home."

Connor, the man who'd probably be mayor one day, followed orders.

Fuller drove him to his parents' beautiful old house. He pulled to the side, hoping not to attract attention. Then, as if they were friends, Fuller looped his arm around Connor and helped him to the door.

"Breathe," Fuller kept saying. "Just breathe, Connor, but not on me if you can help it."

The kitchen door wasn't even locked, but the place had been closed up. The silence, the stillness, made him feel like death had followed them in.

Fuller wasn't sure what to do. He turned on a few lamps and sat Connor on the couch. When he came back from the kitchen with a bottle of water, Connor was asleep.

Putting his hand on the college boy's shoulder, Fuller promised, "I'll get your car cleaned up and get it back to you in the morning."

As he walked out, Fuller looked around. The place reminded him of one of those pictures in decorating magazines. Everything matched, seemed to be exactly where it belonged. He stopped and stared at a shelf built into the hallway wall at eye level. Three-by-five frames were lined up in perfect order. Connor's school pictures. The last frame held his graduation picture, with Connor in his cap and gown. The tassel from his cap had been looped over one corner of the frame.

Fuller picked up the tassel and stuffed it in his pocket. Then he left, as silent as a thief.

He walked to the Audi, feeling sorry for Connor Larady for the first time in his life.

fourteen

Mack

MACK PULLED ON a black T-shirt and a faded blue pullover.

He was so rarely out of uniform these days that casual clothes felt strange. Like everything in his life, his wardrobe was organized. No garments abandoned in the back of a closet, no single sock left behind by its mate, no shirt with a button missing.

When his wife left fourteen years ago, Mack had thought he might fall apart. He had a job he loved, a daughter to raise and no idea how to make it work. Organizing, following a schedule, a daily routine, was all that allowed him to stay sane.

Looking back, he remembered his wife had excitedly agreed to move back to Laurel Springs, his hometown, so she'd have help with Shannon while he was on missions.

Sandi did use his mother's help: she left Shannon with the retired schoolteacher while she went back to her single way of life. By the time she told him their marriage was over, she'd already rented an apartment in Little Rock and was engaged to a guy who said he'd rather have adventure in life than children.

His wife had cried as she'd packed, claiming this new lover was great, too perfect to turn down. She'd said Mack was a good man, a good father, but he wasn't enough for her. Sandi wanted more.

She hadn't looked back as she'd driven away that day.

Mack knew he'd closed his heart to everyone but Shannon. He swore he'd be more than just good enough for his daughter. He'd be the best father he could.

He also realized that, slowly, others had snuck into his heart. First Zoe, who thought he was a knight, mattered to him. Then Emily, who made up stories about a family of fairies who lived in honeysuckle bushes in his backyard. And finally, Alexandra, Zoe's mom. The friend he could talk to about his daughter. The woman who was thoughtful, always inviting him in for coffee and conversation, always willing to help.

They'd soldiered through the perils of raising children alone.

As he drove toward the bakery the day after Thanksgiving, his thoughts were on Alex and the way she'd reacted to his simple kiss. Surely he hadn't broken their bond with a single kiss. She was his friend.

Hell, she was more than likely the only real one he had.

He'd thought maybe they could have been closer over the years, but it was too risky. He didn't exactly have a good record with women. Alex, on the other hand, was nice to everyone who walked into her bakery, but he doubted she was close to anyone. One more thing they had in common.

Since his wife walked out, he'd been gun-shy where women were concerned. Or, more precisely, wife-shy. The few relationships he'd had were short, mostly physical. As soon as a date started making plans that involved his life, or talking about the future, Mack lost her number. And Alex had made it plain she didn't like to be touched. Clearly, she wasn't looking for a husband or lover. His thoughts rolled around again like a hope, a promise, a wish. She had a gentle kind of beauty a man could settle into loving. If they had time. If she'd allow it. If he hadn't already messed it up before they left the starting gate.

Alex had always been different than any woman he'd ever known. A weekend fling wasn't what he wanted with her. He could talk to her about how to raise Shannon. He could call her if he couldn't locate his daughter. He thought of Zoe and Alex as part of his extended family. Someone you bring gifts to when you travel. Someone to have Thanksgiving with. Zoe even thought he was her cat's godfather. Every time they left town for a market trip in the Hill Country, he had to go over and feed Tigger.

An affair would never be enough with someone

like Alex. But anything more might be too much for them both to handle.

As Mack pulled next to the side of Sweetie Pie's Bakery, he mumbled aloud. "If you were so damn happy with the way things were between you and Alex, why did you kiss her? Hell, why were you even thinking of her that way?"

He could claim it was just a friendly peck. Only, in fourteen years he'd never kissed her before. It wasn't his usual MO.

Or he could claim he was just testing her reaction. What if she'd liked it…? Not very likely. Mack couldn't remember one advance she'd ever made. Not even kidding. No accidental brushing.

The good news was now he knew she wasn't attracted to him. She'd pulled away so fast there was no doubt about that fact.

Maybe he was getting old. He'd been so busy raising Shannon and working he hadn't noticed. Maybe he wasn't her type… Hell, he didn't even know if Alex O'Flaherty was attracted to anyone, male or female. And from past experience, he didn't seem to be any woman's type. He blamed it on the fact he'd been trained to read people, and no woman liked to be transparent. They liked to be creatures of secrets and mysteries. Part of his job was looking for the cracks in people's stories. Sometimes he caught himself staring at strangers and wondering what their secrets might be.

Women had always been harder to read than men. But, on the bright side, they always confessed quicker during interrogation. Get a woman talking and she'd confess before he finished the questioning.

Unlike Alexandra. All she ever talked about was the girls and her bakery. Tea parties were her depth, he'd thought. Until now. He'd seen fear in her eyes last night when he'd touched her. Real fear.

Mack leaned his head back and closed his eyes, finally letting another "maybe" in.

What if she'd been assaulted or abused as a kid?

The flash of fear he'd seen spark in her eyes was a tell. The realization she'd never touched him, another consideration. Maybe this wasn't about him at all. Something could have happened years ago, turning her against all men. Making her afraid.

One question after another popped into his head. Had she been truly, physically hurt, or had some guy simply broken her heart? Was she raped at some point? Had she grown up in a toxic environment? After all, she'd never mentioned any relative.

Mack didn't feel like he had a right to ask. But if she was hurt, or still broken, he'd have to find out. Then maybe he could help.

As he stepped from his car and walked toward the bakery door, Mack washed all emotion from his face. First, before they'd ever be able to talk about the past, he'd have to mend fences, or maybe more like brick walls she'd put between them.

Forcing a smile, he stepped into the warm bakery. As she'd predicted yesterday, the shop was empty.

"Mack?" Alex's voice came from the kitchen.

"It's me. You still want to go have a look at that old

apartment you lived in when you first came to Laurel Springs?"

She pushed her way through the swinging door as she dried her hands. "Did you get ahold of the Laradys? I heard they were out of town for the holiday, something about going to see their new grandbaby."

"Nope, but I asked the bookstore owner, Arnie, how to contact them. Told him what we needed. He said he had a key and handed it over so we could look around upstairs."

"He just gave you a key to the town's newspaper office?"

"I went to high school with Arnie's little brother. Even played football with him one year. It's a small town, Alexandra. The guy knows who I am even if he doesn't know me."

She laughed. "I swear, I'll never understand small towns. You can be completely insane, but if you were born here people think they know you."

Alex tugged off her apron. They walked out, smiling. Mack relaxed. Maybe it wouldn't be so bad for them to just forget the kiss had ever happened.

Only he couldn't get the thought of Alex and him together out of his mind. Like really together, not just talking, but touching. A soldier told him once that when those hungry kinds of thoughts plant themselves in a man's mind, they grow like bindweed.

Mack decided that would not happen. He'd simply go back to thinking of her as just a friend. Yeah, right.

Thirty minutes later they were standing on the second floor of the newspaper office, staring at a mess.

The apartment, or what was left of it, had holes in the walls. Boards missing on the floor. Two windows broken. Water damage everywhere. Birds subletting from the rats.

"You sure you lived here?" Mack asked.

"I was barely eighteen. It was almost twenty years ago." Alex circled the dusty room. "I thought this place was grand. Warm. Big windows overlooking Main. The sounds of people talking and laughing drifted up in melodies made by bits of chatter."

She didn't look at him when she added, "I felt safe here."

Another tap on the invisible wall between them. Another hint to her past. He'd thought he'd known her. She'd said she grew up in upstate New York. Raised by her grandmother. No other kin. Went a semester to college before dropping out, pregnant.

Mack knew he should keep his mouth closed. Don't ask questions. Don't open a wound. If there was a wound? Hell, he didn't know Alexandra O'Flaherty at all. He might as well be talking to a stranger.

He marched in where any man with brains would have hesitated.

"Alex, I don't want you to ever be afraid of me."

Her sky blue eyes widened, making her almost look as young as their daughters. "I'm not afraid of you, Mack. You're my friend."

He took one step toward her. He'd spent a career learning to read the signs people make when they're hiding. "Don't lie to me, Alex. We've always been honest with each other. You don't have to tell me anything, but don't lie to me."

"I…" She straightened. "I'm not afraid of you. I never have been. I never will be." She didn't pretend not to know what he was talking about. "You just startled me last night. That's all. It was dark on the balcony and I didn't know you were so close."

He took another step. "Prove it."

"How?"

"Touch me, Alex. I won't make a move." If she'd told the truth, she'd laugh at the challenge. She'd have nothing to prove. But if she'd lied, she'd take his challenge just to prove her point.

Holding her stare, he added, "We may never be best buddies or lovers. We probably will never be anything more than we are now. Friends. Single parents who depend on each other. But I have to know that you're not afraid."

Alex lifted her arm straight out as though her elbow didn't work. Her hand was stiff as she patted his shoulder. She was proving her point. Taking his challenge, but it cost her. He saw the effort it took. He saw the lie.

She was hiding something. He'd bet his career on it. But he wouldn't push any harder, not today.

Pulling away, she put her fists on her hips and asked, "Can we make this place work for Emily or not?"

He didn't stop her from changing the subject. "It'll take a lot of work."

"Shannon and Jack will be back home in a few weeks. Jack may want to be a pilot, but he cut his teeth on power tools. Find a dozen other kids home for Christmas and give them something to do. I'll feed them. This feels right for Emily."

Mack didn't seem near as positive, but Emily was in a toxic environment. A twisted Neverland where she was never allowed to grow up. The next accidental overdose might kill her. They had to try something. "I'll take a few weeks off next month and help out. Tomorrow we can start by buying a few things we know we'll need."

If nothing else, it'd give him time with Alex. Who knew—maybe he'd get her to talk about whatever fear lay buried deep down inside her.

Whether she confided in him or not didn't matter. He couldn't stop caring about her.

fifteen

Emily

EMILY WATERS STOOD in the corner of her second-floor hospital room, watching out the window, waiting for her mother and father to come collect her.

They were an hour late. Emily had a feeling the staff was ready to clean the room, but she didn't offer to hang out in the lobby. She didn't want to be here. She didn't want to go home. Only the lobby was somewhere in-between, a purgatory, and she didn't want to be there either.

She'd turned nineteen a month ago, but she felt old all the way to the marrow in her bones. You'd think if she kept changing directions, she'd finally turn onto the right path for her life, but it didn't seem to work that way.

The winter sun brushed the horizon and seemed to brighten as it began to die. Do people do the same? If they did, everyone would huddle around the bedside to see their beautiful last glow.

She needed to stop thinking of death. She told herself she wasn't afraid of dying. It was the living that frightened her. Now and then she walked close to death's edge, hoping to get a peek at what lay on the other side, only the curiosity cost her dearly. If she wasn't careful, the price might be her freedom. Mom had hinted that maybe she shouldn't be left alone.

Emily knew what she had to do to survive. She had to act normal.

Funny how life works. Her parents loved her, worried about her, protected her, yet she'd still rather daydream of places in her imagination than talk to them. Sometimes, she almost believed if she slept soundly enough or just stopped breathing a minute longer, she'd drift into an imaginary world in her mind and sail away into another dimension. A place not so very far away, floating just beyond her reach.

She'd never been much of anywhere, but she'd made up adventures and met people who lived only in her mind.

Emily laughed suddenly. If she told her mother her thoughts, they really would lock her up. Oh, the life she'd lived in her mind.

Maybe she should write a few of the stories down. Let them out. Then, if she was very lucky, her brain might rest. Might settle into peace. No one thinks it strange if writers think about robbing a bank, or danger or death or sex.

Emily frowned. The sex part might require a bit of research before she could let her imagination loose on that topic.

Her mother's voice crackled from down the hallway, lecturing her father even before they pushed at the door to Emily's room. That overprotective, loving, disappointed voice: *Stand taller. Think before you act. Try a little harder. Be what you were meant to be.*

Emily grinned. *A mess—maybe that's what I'm meant to be,* she thought. A dancer who didn't hear the music. A writer who couldn't remember the plot.

The minute Anna Waters opened the door, she was all smiles.

"There you are. My little girl. My baby. We're going to take you home and take good care of you, dear. If you insist on going back to that school, we've talked about it and we will help.

"You'll see. By the time Christmas is over, you'll be ready to go back to that college and be a tremendous success. I'll call the registrar's office and I'm sure they'll let you take your finals. I'll explain how sick you are and how much getting a degree really means to you."

"I don't want to go back." Emily turned and faced them as she moved away from the window.

Anna's eyes rounded in shock.

"It wasn't the right place for me, Mom, and neither is home."

Her father remained mute as Anna said, "When you feel better you'll change your mind, you'll…"

Emily's tone turned hard. "I'm not sick, Mom. I just had a headache and took too many pills." Emily stepped into the dying sun's beams and felt no warmth.

Howard didn't even blink in the second it took her mother to get a good look at Emily. Anna redirected her sermon. "I'll never get used to that hair. Oh, baby, it'll take months to grow back."

Emily shrugged. She wasn't prepared for cross-examination.

"What a mess." Anna rushed to Emily as if she were three years old and standing in rush hour traffic.

"I just cut my hair, Mom. Not a big deal." When her mother looked down, Emily added, "And I borrowed some clothes from Zoe."

Anna dusted the jean jacket and distressed jeans as if she could brush away rags. "That child never knew how to dress. Why would you borrow her clothes? I guess the hippie blood of her mother got into her. There is no excuse for holes in jeans or a neckline that is an inch short of indecent."

"I was tired of the hospital gown and Shannon's clothes would be way too big. I like the style and Zoe isn't a child." In a whisper she added, "Neither am I."

"We could have brought your clothes up."

"I don't want any of my clothes. Not the ones I left behind in September. Not any of those we bought for college." If she was redirecting her life, now was as good a time as any to start.

Her mother began to huff as though building steam

like the Little Engine That Could heading uphill. Emily had given her way too many topics to discuss all at once.

Emily took advantage of the silence to glance at her father behind her mother. Standing tall. Looking tired, as always, but she thought she saw a hint of a grin wiggle one side of his mouth.

"What do you think, Howard?" She'd called her father by his first name since eighth grade just because it bothered her mother and didn't seem to faze him in the least.

"You look fine," he answered.

Anna was still huffing.

"Thanks." Emily looked directly into his eyes, the same color as hers. "Would you loan me six hundred dollars for a down payment and first month's rent on an apartment? I'll pay you back."

His "Sure" was drowned out by her mother screaming. "You need to come home. Stop fantasizing about make-believe apartments. Where would you find an apartment in Laurel Springs? You haven't been out of this room in three days. How would you pay him back six hundred dollars? Or maybe a job floated by on the same cloud that the apartment did. You're coming home with us, girl."

Emily shook her head. "I called Amy, who handles most of the rental properties in town. I rented the apartment over the newspaper office on Main ten minutes ago. Amy said it's been up for rent so long she'd forgotten about it. She said the owners will pay for any repairs if I'll do the work as part of my deposit.

As for paying Dad back, Monday I'll be starting the five o'clock shift at Sweetie Pie's Bakery."

"How could this happen?" Anna extended her arms as if waiting to catch her daughter in a lie.

"I have friends who helped me out."

The room was so silent Emily could hear her breath.

The only other sound was Howard's shuffle as he pulled out his wallet and counted out eight one-hundred-dollar bills. He'd spent his life working on the road, and for once the habit of carrying cash paid off. "There's a little extra. You might need it. You can pay me back a hundred a month. No interest. Family discount." Howard barked a laugh.

So did Emily. For her father, that was about as close as he got to a joke.

As she took the money, she looked closely at her father, realizing she hadn't really seen him in years. The man who once read to her. Who taught her to play chess one winter when they were snowed in. The man who was mostly only a scintilla passing through her life.

"Thanks, Daddy."

She turned back to her mother. "Don't worry, Mom. I'm coming home until Christmas. I have to pack." Emily picked up the trash bag full of her old clothes. "Dad's right. If I'm not in school, I need to be on my own. It's time."

Anna settled, resentment tattooed on her face. "You'll change your mind about going. You always back away from anything new. You thought you wanted to go away to school and look how that turned out. I'll believe you'll move out when I see it. Till then, I'm not saying another word about it."

"Sounds like a grand plan," Howard announced as he opened the door to the hallway.

Emily followed, marching out behind her mother.

No one talked on the four-block drive home. The barren trees, twice the height of the homes, seemed to point their bony fingers at her. "Crazy," the wind whispered.

Emily ignored them. She simply stared out the window at the houses on her block. Each one different. Most over a hundred years old. The people who lived in them claimed this one block was the prettiest in town, but Emily wondered about the stories hiding behind the ivy, the gingerbread trim and long walkways through beautifully groomed lawns now dead in winter.

Once they were in the house her grandfather had built, Anna was true to her word. In fact, she talked to Emily only when she had to. Somehow, she thought not talking to her daughter was a punishment.

The three of them ate dinner on trays. Emily barely watched the TV. She was too busy planning. She'd need furniture and dishes. The clothes she did want to take with her could go in one suitcase. If she had to, she'd wash every few days, but she'd take none of the clothes she'd bought for college. She'd pack only what she loved, what she felt comfortable in.

As soon as Emily helped with the dishes, she said she was going to bed.

No one bothered to say good-night.

Emily waited until the house slept. Then she slipped out her window. She needed to walk the night, feel alive, feel reckless, feel like she was a part of the land, the wind, even the cold.

She briefly thought of going over to Jack's window and tapping, but she knew he wasn't home. Her friends didn't know she was getting out of the hospital tonight, and they'd all made plans to drive to Dallas for a concert.

The air greeted her with a frosty breath as she broke the tree line behind Jack's house and neared the creek. She smiled. Her life was a roller coaster chugging slowly uphill then flying down, and Emily never seemed to find direction. Only when she walked alone, with only sounds of nature around her, did she feel free. She loved the dirt roads where no car had stirred the dust in days. Sometimes the creek called to her. The water chattered at her after a heavy rain, and the tall grass near the shore played brush strokes across invisible drums. When she walked, she didn't think of her problems or why her life couldn't be a story worth adventure or excitement or even tragedy. Her imagination would entertain her with stories, as if her life was only the binder that held them contained.

A coyote's howl drifted across the moonless paths and between the trees. Another lonely call answered. Suddenly, a fantasy formed before her, of a shape-shifter running through the trees. Part wolf, part man. Emily laughed. She wished she could stay out here like this forever. Living only in her stories while she walked and dreamed of other worlds.

But the lights of Main drew her away from the wild creek tonight. She wanted to stare up at the second floor of the newspaper office. She needed to study the place where she'd be looking down from in a month.

No one was on the street. It had to be after midnight. She could stand on Main and stare up at her future life.

Curiosity pulled her to the side of the old building. After her eyes adjusted to the deep shadows, she made out the iron stairway that curled up to a second-floor door. The apartment waited for her. Mack and Alexandra had toured the apartment by going inside and up a wide old mahogany staircase that framed the back wall of the newspaper office. But the stairs outside would be a more private entrance, just for her and her guests.

Emily took the first step. The circling staircase creaked beneath her weight, reminding her of an exposed backbone on a long-dead body.

She took the second step. The stairs held her.

The third step. The fourth.

Bolts buried in brick began to protest and the staircase swayed a bit but held.

Fifth. Sixth. She was almost halfway up. Emily told herself she couldn't stop now. With luck, the place would be unlocked and the glow of streetlights through the broken window would offer her enough light to see what would become her new home.

Seventh step. Eighth.

Bolts just above her head broke free and popped like a snap of lightning. The staircase bowed out away from the building.

She screamed. Afraid to turn loose of the railing. Afraid to jump. Afraid to look down. Emily froze.

Her breath came in gulps as she tried not to move. One tiny shift, leaning either way, trying to step down, anything could make the stairs buckle, entrapping her in twisted metal, killing her with falling bricks as the wall gave to the pull of the dying staircase. If the rusty metal twisted as it tumbled, the iron might break her bones even before she hit the ground.

Little hiccups whispered from her open mouth and she feared one deep gulp of air would tip the scales that balanced her on this horror ride.

"You all right, miss?" Worried words floated up from the darkness.

She didn't dare look down. "No," she squeaked, as she felt tears dripping from her chin.

For a moment, all was silent, and she feared she'd imagined the man, the polite inquiry from below.

"If you'll lean back and turn loose, I'll catch you." The calm voice came again.

"I'm afraid."

"I'll catch you, Emily. I promise."

He sounded confident. He knew her name. She had to do something. She couldn't just hold on while the stairs crumbled. He was her one opening. She told herself she wasn't afraid, not now. She didn't have time to panic.

Slowly uncurling her fingers, she leaned back with her eyes closed. If this was her last moment on earth, she didn't want the video to watch in the hereafter.

As she leaned, another set of bolts popped free. There was no time left.

She drifted backward as the stairs tumbled forward. For a moment she felt like she was floating on the midnight air. Then solid arms caught her as though she weighed no more than a baby tossed by a blanket.

A moment later he was falling with her to the ground, her body cocooned against his so nothing would hurt her. She clawed her fingers into the jacket across his shoulders and held on until the knowledge that she was protected could register in her brain.

He held her, letting his breathing calm, then, without letting go, asked, "You all right, now?"

She turned toward him. "I think so. You must be my guardian angel. Nice to meet you."

The stranger sat beside her, now cuddling her gently. "I've never been called that, but I'm glad I was walking by and heard your cry for help. I'm Fuller Wilder. I work on your dad's car, remember? I've seen you with your dad a few times."

Emily had a vague memory of a young mechanic who worked at an old run-down garage her parents insisted was the best in town. The guy she saw there was a few years older than her. Quiet. Maybe shy like her. Usually didn't even look her direction.

He was one of those almost-invisible people in town. She'd seen him around. "I remember you," she lied.

Standing, she faced him. He had to be a foot taller than her and so thin he must have been only muscle and bone. "Thank you, Fuller Wilder."

"You're welcome, Emily Waters." His white teeth shone in the pale light. "You sure you're all right now?"

"I'm fine."

"Would you mind if I walked you part of the way home? I'm going that way anyway. I'm checking on a friend who lives not far from your house."

"You know where I live?"

"I've towed your dad's car in a few times when it wouldn't start." He had a hesitant way about him, a kind of reserve that made her believe him.

"Oh." She couldn't remember that, but it was probably something no one mentioned to her. Her mom hadn't even let her get a license until she was seventeen.

Emily hesitated, then decided her hero probably wasn't the town serial killer. "Can we walk along the creek? I like the way the night sounds out there. Maybe it'll calm my nerves."

He offered his arm. "Of course, my lady."

As they rounded the newspaper building to where streetlights offered a low glow, she saw that his hair was dark brown and his eyes black as coal.

"You walk Main Street often?" he asked.

"No. I'm going to rent the room above the Laradys' office. Once I get it fixed up, I think I'll have a great view of the town. Tonight, I just wanted to have a first look. My friends found the place while I was in the hospital." They crossed a bridge at the end of Main and walked along a path toward the creek.

"You've been sick?"

"I'm fine. Just took one too many pills by accident."

She thought of adding "nothing new" but she didn't want him to think she was nuts.

They strolled in silence for a while.

"You're not afraid out here after dark?" he finally asked.

"No. Are you?"

She saw his smile again as he answered, "Not of anything out here, but I'm scared to death of walking with you."

"I promise I won't change into a wolf or a vampire."

"That's not what I meant. If anyone sees me walking with you, they'll probably arrest me. Folks from my part of town don't mix with the residents who live on Willow Road. The old families. The rich folks."

"I'm not rich. My mom inherited the house. That's why we live there. My dad is on the road six days a week selling business and office paper goods." She glanced his direction and told the family joke. "He's a paper man."

If Fuller Wilder got the joke, he gave no hint.

Emily tried again. "But you probably should be afraid of me. My mother says I'm unstable."

"Are you?"

"Probably. I was back on those old stairs. You saved my life."

"I just helped you down, that's all. You're so small, you were easy to catch."

"I'm not a kid. Lots of women are only five feet tall."

"I know. I remember you being a few years behind me in school."

"I don't remember you, but I was shy and clueless." She laughed. "Guess I still am."

"I was mostly absent or expelled." He stopped to study her a moment. "But I remember you. You always wore dresses and your hair in braids. I saw you then, Emily. I see you now."

"Thanks."

She moved closer, brushing her shoulder against him as they walked. "I'm usually shy, but in the darkness I feel like I can talk to you. You're my shadow angel, aren't you? I've seen you before, following me." Sliding her hand down his arm, she wove her fingers in his. "I feel very stable with you. I can't explain it, but every time I saw your outline in the trees I knew you were watching out for me."

"I didn't scare you?"

"Maybe the first time, but you never moved closer. I like to daydream, and at first, I thought you might be just part of my imagination. Reality and fiction march together in my mind sometimes." She squeezed his hand. "Are you real, Fuller Wilder?"

"I'm real," he answered.

"I'm glad you were there tonight. Why did you come nearer this time?"

"I heard you scream. I knew you needed help."

Emily felt like she'd been waiting for him to come along all her life. As they navigated their way through the paths near the water, she told him all about how lost she felt most of the time. She confessed she hated the school she'd fought so hard to get into. She talked about her parents and her friends and her neighbor across the street named Jack.

When Fuller asked if she loved Jack, she answered, "Of course. We all three love Jack. Zoe is the only one who has dated him a few times, but then, she dates everyone. My friend Shannon doesn't want to date at all. She has a career plan that doesn't include it, so Jack is held at arm's length."

Fuller seemed quieter as they reached the trees at the property line of Jack's house, but he hadn't let go of her hand.

When they stood at the spot where she had only to cross Jack's backyard, then the street, and walk up her driveway, she turned. "Will you walk with me again?"

"Sure."

"I'd like that. There is something else I would like to do, too, if you don't mind."

"Name it."

"Lean down."

He did. And she felt his fingers, still laced in hers, shake a bit.

"I'd like to give you this." She closed the distance between them and kissed him lightly on the mouth. "Thank you, my shadow angel, for making me feel alive. Will you promise to come to see me at the apartment? I'll give you a tour."

"You sure?"

"Positive."

She turned and walked toward her house. When

she glanced back, he was gone. A part of her wondered again if Fuller Wilder was real. Then she knew it didn't matter. Real or only in her mind, he was hers.

sixteen

the end of november

Fuller Wilder
Wilder's Fort

FULLER WOKE A little after dawn, fearing he'd only dreamed of walking Emily Waters home last night. It had been dark. She probably didn't get a good look at him. When she did, she'd run. He was just a grease monkey, the guy who changed the oil in her dad's car. He was nothing to her.

But to him, she'd been that shy kid who'd always stayed in the back seat while he'd worked, her head buried in a book. Until that night out on Cemetery Road three years ago. That night, he'd learned her name.

She was from one of the families who'd settled back

in the 1800s. Not like his old man, Bill, who just wandered by Laurel Springs, looking for a job after he came home from the Vietnam War. No goals, no family, no direction. He'd been paid by the day to clean up around the garage and decided to stay because he didn't have the drive to look for something better.

Once Bill moved up to a steady job working on cars, he hooked up with the dumbest girl in town, Alice Ray Wilder. If her father hadn't owned the garage, Fuller's pop would have probably drifted farther west without giving her a second thought. Bill was forty by then and Alice Ray was a hard-lived twenty-six.

Alice's father, who everyone called Old Man Wilder, didn't even bother to waste his breath suggesting a wedding when she'd announced she was pregnant. Bill just moved into the little house at Wilder's Fort. He didn't give the girl his name, much less a ring.

As it turned out, Alice left for parts unknown a few years later. Her father, Fuller's grandpa, deeded the garage over to Fuller when he turned eighteen, along with a shack on the other side of the garage's junkyard. Grandpa was dying by then, but he told Fuller that if Alice Ray ever came back, Fuller had to offer her a place to stay because she'd probably be dying if she'd abandoned her partying ways.

Bill was a mediocre mechanic, and Fuller eclipsed him in skill by the time he was twelve. Fuller's grandpa passed his knowledge to the boy, not his drunk almost son-in-law. But the old man let Bill stay. Maybe because they both understood war and what it can do to a man.

From his bed on the couch, Fuller looked across to the one bedroom in his shack. His old man was drunk again. Hell, he was drunk so often maybe the news should be announced when he was sober—it was a much more rare occasion. But he'd stayed when Fuller's mother ran, and that mattered.

His dad wasn't lazy. He just didn't care much about life. When he was sober, he worked and ate his meals reading, but drunk or not, he rarely talked.

This morning Bill was spread-eagled sideways across the bed, with one shoe on and the other in the doorway. Some days, he'd wake up by noon and come help out at the shop, but lately he made so many mistakes Fuller spent more time correcting his blunders than working on the cars lined up waiting. But Bill wasn't mean when he drank, just sad.

Fuller didn't remember his mother's face, but he remembered a string of stay-over girlfriends when his dad looked presentable. It didn't take the women long to figure out their new boyfriend might be handsome, but he was heavy into drinking.

Standing, Fuller walked over and closed the bedroom door with a bang, knowing the sound wouldn't wake up Pop. Then Fuller downed a bowl of cereal without milk, drank a Coke and went into the bathroom to shower.

Connor's high school graduation tassel, the one Fuller had stolen, hung on the side of the mirror. He thumbed it, trying to figure out why he'd taken the worthless ornament. The golden strings of thread looked out of place here, but no one would ever see it anyway. There was no need to clean a house that had never had a visitor.

Emily might drop by the garage, though, just to thank him again, and he planned to be presentable. He pulled out clean clothes from a laundry basket. His grandpa had taught him a trick. Never bother with closets, not that the shack had them anyway. Just put two baskets in the bathroom. One for clean clothes, one for dirty. When one gets full of dirty clothes, take it to the cleaners and start on the other basket. No need to worry about washing, ironing or buying a machine. The cleaner traded his services for oil changes.

By eight o'clock, Fuller was in the garage, greeting the first customer. A few regulars commented on how nice he looked. One winked at him and said he looked like a young man who'd got lucky last night.

Fuller just grinned and worked. While his hands were doing his job, his mind was on the innocent girl who'd kissed him last night. She'd said he saved her life. He'd never tell her that he'd been driving the car that hit her years ago. That night, he'd almost ended her life.

When he finally got a break around noon, he didn't light up a cigarette or drink a beer like he usually did.

If she came in, Fuller didn't want her to smell either on him. The fact that he cared one way or the other what she thought shook him to the core. He'd had a to-hell-with-the-world attitude all his life. He did good work because he needed the money. He took care of himself so he could show up to work. But Fuller didn't care what people thought of him.

Until now. Until Emily.

She might never come in the garage. He might never bump into her again. But if he did, he didn't want her to be ashamed that she'd walked with him by the creek or told him all about her friends or kissed him and called him her shadow angel.

seventeen

Shannon

SHANNON PASSED ZOE a new pack of nails and the extra hammer. "We're never going to get this place fixed up. It'll take us through Christmas just to get all the rotten boards out of here. The Laradys own this place, so they should fix it up."

Zoe shook her head. "Arnie said he tried several times to call Connor but no answer. He's got his hands full with his parents' deaths. They say his brother didn't even bother to help."

"In other words, without us no one is going to help Emily? Her mother's still not speaking to her and her father will be 'back on the road,' whatever that means, by Monday."

"It's not just the floors. Don't forget the broken

tile in the bathroom. And the shattered glass. And…" Zoe pointed with the hammer like it was an orchestra's baton. "Too many to name. Larady should pay her to live here."

"I get the picture. We need an army." She looked up at Zoe. "You're not mad about the remodel. You're angry because this time we can't stay around to help her. We've always helped Emily, Zoe, and this time we can't stay. I have to be back at school and you have a flight to New York."

"You're right. But I don't know if this apartment is right for Emily. With the Laradys dead, who knows— Connor may sell the place, and Emily will have to find another apartment even after she does all the work up here."

"Larady won't sell. They never sell anything. One of the boys will move back and take over. Even if they sell the paper, they'll still lease the offices downstairs, and there will still be this apartment upstairs. Emily needs this place. She's excited about being on her own."

Zoe raised her chin and continued, "It's new for Emily. A change. Something she wants. Right?"

Shannon didn't look sold on the idea. "What if she changes her mind and hates living here all alone? What then, Zoe?"

"I don't know."

"She didn't overdose up North at the school. She came home first. Maybe this is right where she wants to be." Shannon knew they were still tiptoeing around the overdose.

Zoe nodded. "Maybe without us she'll make this place hers."

Footsteps stomped up the stairs from the office below. Since the back stairs outside were not usable, Arnie, across the street, had loaned them a key to the newspaper office. Which was nice, but that meant everything they carried up had to go through the maze of counters and office furniture. He'd promised he'd have new stairs installed within a week after he checked with Connor. Shannon guessed whoever took over the newspaper office, if Connor did sell the paper, wouldn't want traffic passing through.

"Anyone here?"

"Em!" Both girls stood and ran to help her as she reached the apartment door, loaded down with bags.

"Where is everyone? I brought food and, of course, tea."

Shannon pulled the first bag off Em's arm. "Dad and Alex drove over to the big lumber yard sixty miles away to get more supplies. Like he thinks we'll run out in the next decade."

Emily looked around, her eyes bright, as if she was seeing what could be beneath all the trash and rot.

Zoe giggled. "They've been working since dawn, and I think we both need a break. Mom said not to expect them for lunch."

Shannon thought it was more likely Alex and Mack wanted to relax. When you're forty, you need to slow down, but it'd probably be another forty years before she'd convince her father of that.

The three friends pushed the tools aside and spread

a beach towel across the scarred bench. Then Emily straightened as if making a grand announcement. "Let's have tea."

She pulled three paper cups from one bag, scones from another, and a thermos from her deep coat pocket. "Forever Tea."

All three nodded. "Best friends forever."

Emily poured. Zoe passed the scones around on paper napkins. Shannon couldn't stop smiling. They'd done this since they were five. Whether it was at a fine teahouse in Dallas or with plastic in the backyard, she loved the ceremony. It bonded them.

As if they were holding fine china, all three raised their cups and toasted.

"To friendship," Zoe said.

"To Em's new home," Shannon added as she watched Emily. Dark circles were under her eyes. She was far too thin, but for once she looked happy.

"To the future." Emily ended the toast. A spark twinkled in her eyes.

All three smiled.

They ate and all talked at once. Making plans. Dreaming about what was to come. Then they laughed about the dumb things they'd toasted when they were kids. Unicorns, chocolate sundaes, and snowflakes landing on your tongue—the year Zoe insisted they have tea as snow fell on the balcony above Sweetie Pie's Bakery.

When the conversation settled on the coming year, they all decided they should concentrate on finding boyfriends. So far, Zoe was the only one who'd dated much, and she had a three-date limit.

As they listed the requirements for a perfect boyfriend, Shannon glanced over at the doorway of the apartment and noticed Jack leaning against the frame, arms crossed, wide grin as he listened.

"Any chance I can join you?" he asked when he noticed her staring at him.

"No," they all said at once.

When he looked sad, Zoe tossed him a scone.

Jack ate half in one bite. "Well, when you ladies are finished with your tea, I could use some help with the windows I hauled over from my dad's workshop. It'll be a lot warmer in here when we get them up."

They downed the last of their tea and reluctantly followed Jack back downstairs. He told them his brothers promised to drop by about three and help with lifting the windows into place. "They both gave me a hard time about not knowing enough to do it right. I didn't bother to argue. I just didn't get the construction gene."

He looked up and noticed none of the girls were listening to him. "Apparently I didn't get the conversation gene either."

Not one answered.

As the four started carrying the first window up, Jack whispered to Shannon, "Wish we didn't have to leave tomorrow. There's a lot to get done if she's moving in by Christmas."

"It'll still be here when we get back in a few weeks." Shannon understood how he felt. All of them working together felt right. They saw progress. "At least if she has lights and windows, she can come up and work on the place anytime she wants to."

"That's exactly what your father said. Even if she just walks around and plans, she'll be thinking forward for a change." Jack hesitated. They both knew what he meant. The possibility of what might have happened hung between them like an unspoken cry.

It was an accident, Shannon's mind silently screamed. *An accident.*

When she glanced at Jack, she swore she could almost hear the same thoughts coming from his mind. But he calmly said, "If Emily thinks she's starting a new chapter in her life, she won't worry about the school she abandoned or how she let her mother down. I heard Mrs. Waters say that Emily had really messed things up this time. Getting in another school won't be easy."

Shannon lowered her voice. "I don't think she wants a school, any school. I think she wants to live alone and read, maybe even write."

Jack nodded in agreement. "When we were kids, Em would sometimes tell me stories running through her brain. They were good."

As they worked, Shannon thought about how she had her whole life planned and Emily always just went along with whatever her mother suggested.

Shannon knew she'd get her degree from the academy, go into the air force as an officer, make good money, and then, when she was about thirty-five, she'd get married and have one kid. Boy or girl, didn't matter. The only things out of focus in her life plan were what degree she'd get and who she'd marry.

She had a feeling picking a degree plan would be easier than finding the right man.

eighteen

Alex

ALEXANDRA O'FLAHERTY PUSHED a rickety cart around the Lowe's fifty miles from Laurel Springs, while Mack tossed in everything Emily might need to get the apartment in shape. Paintbrushes, sandpaper, paper towels, bug spray, work gloves and two boxes of trash bags.

Alex tried to talk to him, but he seemed as distant now as he'd been on the hour drive over. They were like strangers, not two people who'd spent years at soccer games and school plays and graduations from kindergarten to high school.

Strangers who couldn't seem to find their way back to being friends.

She'd often seen the warrior in him. Silent, stoic,

pushing silently through pain, never showing emotions. He was tall, nice looking when he smiled, but except for his daughter, there was often a reserve in his manner. He tackled everything he did as a challenge, never fun. Except for that one kiss on her balcony, he walked a tightrope through life.

But, despite his proper politeness, she knew without any doubt that if trouble came, he'd be the one she wanted standing beside her. She could always count on him if she needed him.

When they checked out and she offered to pay for half, he simply said, "No, I got this."

There was no room for compromise.

Alex tried to think what was bothering him. It couldn't be the kiss. Both had said all was fine between them.

Could Mack be thinking that, since Emily was leaving home, Shannon might pack up and move too? No. That didn't make sense. Shannon was halfway through her first year at the Air Force Academy. She'd been living away from home for months. His daughter had laughed and told everyone that after living with her dad and all his organizing and scheduling, moving to the academy felt more like coming home than moving away.

Frustrated, Alex quit trying to keep any kind of conversation going. She'd seen him sad. She'd seen him worried. But she'd never witnessed him sulky. She had no idea how to cheer up Mack Morell. It wasn't her job anyway.

Alex finally realized she didn't know Mack as

well as she thought she did. He never talked about his work, but she'd got used to that. She knew he traveled often, sometimes overseas, sometimes in danger. She had guessed that he was in interrogation because his daughter said once that he "sometimes talks to bad people." And Mack bragged that he could read most folks like a book. No surprises.

She knew that there were times he worked from home, and Shannon complained he stayed on his computer all day and half the night. Sometimes, she claimed he talked on his phone in another language.

Alex was missing too many pieces of the puzzle to figure out a man like Mack. She didn't know men all that well in the first place. She hadn't kept up with any of her boyfriends from high school. Her grandmother's live-in man was a creep, so no advice there, and the one guy she thought she'd loved had married someone else while they were still dating.

Three strikes you're out, she thought.

She and Mack never talked about his ex-wife, but then, she'd never mentioned anything about Zoe's father. Too far in the past. Too painful to remember.

Mack sometimes related news about his mother, but not so much lately. Shannon's grandmother had been there when Mack needed her. Now she was spending most of the year with her daughter in Austin. Mack's aunts, his mother's sisters, were living in Big D, too, and the three went to quilt shows and movies together.

By the time Mack pulled out of the Lowe's parking lot, Alex had realized that, after all these years, she'd thought of him as her best friend, but she didn't even know him.

He might be able to read people, but she couldn't even read him.

"I told the girls we'd have lunch before we came back. I think the three of them wanted to have their tea party before Zoe and Shannon leave tomorrow."

Mack didn't look at her; he just chuckled and said, "I remember that day you started this whole tea thing. I brought one sad little princess over to your place. It wasn't one of my best days either. Sandi packed that day to finally leave me after she'd been threatening to for three years and I realized I didn't care. We didn't fight. I didn't say a word to try and stop her."

"Didn't you two argue over custody of Shannon?" Alex realized this was probably the most personal question she'd ever asked him.

"No. Oh, she cried when she said 'Take care of my baby,' but she wanted freedom. Her new Prince Charming promised they'd see the world and never live the mundane life of kids and nine-to-five jobs."

"And did they?"

"I heard they separated two years later. He'd been crippled in a skiing accident and Sandi walked away, claiming he'd do better without her—after all, everyone knew she wasn't a nurse. They were in Italy when the accident happened. Husband number three met her there. He was French, I think, but I never met him."

"Did she stay with him?"

"I don't know. I have little interest in keeping up with her, but my mom does for Shannon's sake. Mom said her last name was different on last year's Christmas card. She sent Shannon a hundred dollars inside, but she must have forgotten graduation and her birthday."

Mack pulled off at a lonely, weather-beaten café on the highway. The place didn't have a name, just a blinking Open sign in the window and a billboard that claimed "Best Chicken Fried Steak for a hundred miles."

"This okay for lunch? If we're banned from the tea party we might as well be listening to country music."

She smiled. One thing she did know about Mack: he loved country music.

They walked in through swinging doors made in the shape of seven-foot cowboy boots and took the first table. No other customers were in the place, hinting at the possibility that the sign had lied, but George Strait's "Check Yes or No" was coming through speakers mounted on all four walls. Over in one corner was a rough wood fence surrounding a mechanical bull with what looked like a layer of sand for any unlucky riders to land on.

Mack pulled out her chair, then his. He still wasn't meeting her eyes, but he seemed more relaxed.

"When I was twenty, I rode one of those bulls in a bar in San Antonio."

"Who won?"

"The bull."

Silence settled as their short conversation died.

Alex straightened and decided to step into the stillness between them. Fourteen years of a polite almost-friendship was enough. If he wanted to be closer, it had to start with talk, not a kiss. "How come you've never told me anything about Sandi until today?"

"You never asked. Besides, it's not something I like to talk about, especially around Shannon. If she does ask about her mother, then I'll fill in the facts, but she's never asked. I think she said goodbye to Sandi the day she drove away. The memory of my little girl standing on the couch waving as her mother walked out to her car will always be burned in my mind. She waved and waved with tears running down her cheeks, but Sandi never turned around."

A waitress dropped two menus on the table. She looked irritated that they'd woken her up. "Drink machine is out, but we got coffee and tea. What'll it be?"

Mack didn't bother to open the menu. "I'll have the chicken fry."

The waitress didn't write anything down. "You get a potato side—fried or baked?"

"Fries, of course. Double the gravy. Coffee, black, and keep it coming."

"You want a salad with it, mister? It's only a dollar more."

"Nope." He finally met Alex's eyes and winked. "If I'm sliding into fried Heaven, I don't want anything healthy slowing me down."

The waitress didn't seem to get the joke. She just turned to Alex and waited.

Alex grinned. "I'll have the same thing, only iced tea to drink."

As the waitress grabbed the menus and walked

away, Mack raised an eyebrow. "There is no way you'll eat what you ordered, Alex."

"Want to bet?" She grinned, suddenly feeling younger than she had in a long time.

"Sure. What do we bet?"

She thought about it. "You said I didn't know about you because I've never asked. If I eat as much of my meal as you do, you have to answer ten questions."

He raised his hand. "What kind of questions?"

"Anything. Nothing's off the table."

"Except my job."

"All right, except for your job, but everything else is fair game and you have to answer them honestly."

"But, Alex, you know me. I'm a regular boring dad who goes to work, mows the yard every Saturday I'm home and worries about my kid."

"Afraid to take the bet, Mack?"

"No, because you're not winning. My mom served me chicken fried steak when I was in a high chair. And remember, if you don't win, I get to ask a few questions. Ten, to be exact."

Alex nodded. It occurred to her why the café was empty. The highway strung a dozen small towns together. A hundred cars and half as many trucks must pass by every day. Someone should have stopped for lunch.

"What if the food is terrible?" She wrinkled up her nose.

"Don't try to get out of the bet already, Red. Good or bad, the one who eats the most gets to ask the questions."

"Thunder Road" came through the speakers and they both stopped to listen.

"Springsteen can really write them," Mack said, when the song ended.

She watched him relax while they talked about the songs they loved, but she guessed he was thinking about the bet. If she won, she'd have a chance to really get to know this man. What he thought. How he felt. What he did on those weekends he didn't make it home.

This simple café in the middle of the day, with them both in their paint clothes, somehow felt like a date. Not that she'd had many in her life.

nineteen

Jack

WHEN JACK TOLD his folks about Emily moving into her own place, he wasn't surprised they offered to help. They were both descended from the five Confederate soldiers who'd settled the town. The legend was that all five were still in their teens when they'd signed up with the Georgia troops to fight. They'd been hunting with rifles since they were kids, so they already had the skills needed to soldier. They knew how to survive off the land and how to vanish when they were outnumbered.

At the end of the war all five were broken, scarred and penniless. Two had been captured and, rather than go to prison, they became Galvanized Yankees for a few years. Both had been assigned out West to serve on the frontier as Union soldiers. As they passed through North Texas heading home, they took note of the open land.

After finding nothing back in Georgia, all five pooled what they had, sold their land for pennies on the dollar and headed west to Texas. One married a neighbor girl he'd known before the war. Two married their brothers' widows. One brought along a barmaid he met in Louisiana. Laurel Springs had no record of where the last soldier found his bride, but he fathered ten kids, so the woman known only as "Ben's wife" in records must have existed.

Those in town who descended from the five soldiers considered it their duty to help the town grow.

Of course, Jack had figured out, by the time he'd heard the story every Founders' Day for ten years, that pretty much everyone in town could claim kin to the five boys, or was married to someone who could.

He'd also suspected the first newspaper owner, the grandfather of the present Mr. Larady, may have made up the whole story just to bring the town together. If he had, no one who was alive could remember back that far, and it did make a great story.

So, as soon as Emily announced she was moving out, cousins, almost-cousins and folks married to almost-cousins would begin to offer her their leftover furniture and household goods. The whole thing reminded Jack of a garage sale housewarming party.

Since Jack's father owned the local construction company, he talked to Mack Morell, Shannon's father, on the phone and said he'd sell anything she needed to rebuild for cost and send the bill to Connor.

None of this shocked Jack, but when his dad patted him on the shoulder and told him to keep studying hard, Jack was surprised. Apparently, Mack had bragged on both the academy and Jack hanging in there for a year and a half.

Everyone in town admired Mack Morell. He was a local boy who served his country, raised a daughter alone, was good to his mother and, best of all, had moved back home. The guy could run for mayor and win if he ever stayed home long enough. Once Shannon left for college, he seemed to take more and longer assignments. Jack would be surprised if he made it home for Christmas.

When Mack answered his door Sunday morning, Jack shook his hand and said, "Shannon ready?"

For the first time Mack had to look up at him. Jack had grown another inch. He was now taller than the man he'd looked up to all his life, figuratively as well as literally.

Shannon walked around her father, bumping Jack with her bag. "Why else would I be standing here with my suitcase and pack?"

Mack laughed. "She's all yours, Jack."

Shannon frowned. "Don't go giving me away to the first guy who knocks on the door."

"I won't. I'm waiting for someone who comes bringing something to trade. A horse, maybe even a mule. I'd never just give you away."

Her dad was the one talking, but Jack wasn't surprised when she hit him at the same time she hugged her dad. She then turned quickly and headed toward Jack's old Ford. "Hope this rattletrap will make it back to school."

Mack shrugged. "She hates goodbyes. Just like me, I guess. She'll cheer up after a while."

Jack frowned. All day in the car with Miss Sunshine. He ran toward the car before she left without him.

"We have to get going, Jack." She jerked the car door open. "You can't stand around talking to my dad. We may hit bad weather around Guymon." She tossed her bag in the back seat.

"Study hard, kid," Mack yelled from the porch.

"I will," she yelled back. "See you Christmas break."

Mack turned his attention to Jack. "You got a full tank? An emergency kit? Snow at the top of the Panhandle can come in fast and hard. You know what they say—there's nothing between the North Pole and Texas but a barbed wire fence."

"Yeah, I've heard that. I'm prepared, Mr. Morell."

"We'd better get going," Shannon said, "or Dad will interrogate you for an hour." When they were in the car, she laughed. "I swear, Dad should have cards made. Then he can hand everyone instructions before I get into anybody's car."

Jack pulled away from the Morell home, knowing that Shannon's dad was still watching. "He loves you. Probably because you're so sweet and precious and even-tempered and…"

"Shut up."

Jack drove. All was back to normal. "So go to sleep. I'll wake you when we hit snow."

She kicked off her boots, wrapped up in her coat and took his advice.

Four hours later, he pulled off the highway onto a county road. The rough gravel road woke her.

"What...?"

"I'm pulling beneath this train overpass till the snow slows. Visibility is about twenty feet on the highway right now."

She straightened and looked around. "When did snow start?"

"Half an hour ago. Radio said it's just rolling through. The wind will blow it all to Oklahoma before long. We should be able to move on soon, but it's below freezing. I didn't want to deal with ice on the road and poor visibility. When I saw trucks pulling off, I decided to do the same."

He stared out the windshield as snow drifted over warm glass, making the flakes appear to skate as they melted across. "I've got plenty of gas. I filled up at your last potty stop."

"What about food? I'm starving."

Jack laughed. "You ate breakfast before we left. I could smell the bacon from your front door. We've got trail mix, jerky, two candy bars and a gallon of caramel popcorn my mom always makes me take back to the dorm. Plus, there's that twenty dollars of junk food you bought at the truck stop. We could survive a week."

"Yeah, but what will you eat?" She glanced at him smugly.

"Nothing. I'm following the Donner Logic. I'll let you eat it all. Then I'll eat you."

She raised her fist to hit him and for once he blocked. All at once they were full-out into hand-to-hand combat. Laughing as she attacked and he dodged.

Finally, he caught both her wrists and leaned against her to stop the fight. "We've only been stranded five minutes and we're already fighting over food," he yelled. "Calm down."

"I'm calm. Get off me."

He backed away. "Oh, excuse me for trying to keep you from killing me."

She shocked him by saying, "I'm sorry. I should not try to kill the driver. If I did and tossed your body out, the highway patrol would track me down, since it's your car. Then I'd have to explain how you drove me crazy, which if anyone on the jury knew you, they'd understand completely why I did it. Only I'd still go to jail for littering."

Jack straightened back to his side of the car, closed his eyes and tried to forget the way Shannon had felt beneath him for two seconds. He couldn't keep up with her lecture. Maybe he should just try to sleep.

She finally finished talking and did the same, using her coat as a blanket.

After what seemed like half an hour, he said in a low voice, "You asleep?"

"Yes," she mumbled.

"I got a question, Shan, and I want you to answer it without trying to start an argument."

"Of course," she said too quickly to be truthful.

"Why do we fight all the time?" He turned the car on to let it warm up again. "I think we started arguing in high school when I asked Zoe to prom. Did you want me to ask you? Or were you just mad because I was dating your friend?"

"I don't know," she finally said.

"You hated me then. Now we've settled into a frosty arrangement of almost-friends. Half the time I think I'm trapped in a cold war, and you and I are the only two soldiers left. Even when you're nice to me I know it's just the rest stop between rounds."

"First, I don't hate you. Everybody likes you, Jack. Emily thinks you're great. She claims you're easy to talk to. Best neighbor ever of the opposite sex. Zoe says you're her best boy friend, not boyfriend, that she ever had. Sometimes I think my dad would rather talk to you than me.

"And another thing. Zoe claims you were the nicest boy she's ever dated. Which translates to *no sparks*. She said you never stepped out of line."

Shannon stared out the fogged-up window so long he decided she'd forgotten about him. Finally, she whispered, "Do you feel like we're inside a snow globe?"

"Don't change the subject. We're talking about me."

"Okay. No fights. No yelling. We're in this magical snow globe, and for once, let's talk. Honest and true, just me and you."

"Fair enough. Tell me why every time I step near, you push me away. Whatever it is that turns you off about me, I'd just like to know. I can take it. I'll always take a direct hit to the heart rather than a thousand pin-pricks draining me one drop at a time."

She stared at him as though he'd turned into a complete stranger in a blink.

Jack tried again. "I must have asked you out a dozen times in high school. When we're working together with Zoe and Emily around, it's fine, but when it's just the two of us, you seem to wish you were a million miles away. Like you can barely stand to be alone with me."

"I'm the one you stood up every study date this fall. I could have used your help on the math this semester." For a blink, she met his gaze.

"Right. I didn't make the study dates that you set up. Want to know why?"

"Sure, Jack. The whole truth, remember?"

"I didn't want you to have one more opportunity to push me away."

The heater was still running, but he felt the cold inside the car. She must have felt it too. She pulled her coat up under her chin.

After a while, he asked again, "Why do we fight all the time?"

She stared at the flakes now making tiny rivers down the windshield. Finally she said, "I don't hate you. I guess I'm afraid if I let you too close, I might like you too much. Making it through the academy is very important to me. I'd break my dad's heart if I messed this up. Seven in my class didn't make it the first semester."

He didn't move. After a while he spoke so low he didn't know if she heard him. "Damn, Shannon, I never thought of that reason. I don't want to marry you tomorrow or get you pregnant. I just thought it would be nice to have a date."

She looked like she was about to hit him again. "Forget I said that, Jack."

"I will." He turned to face her. "If you'll kiss me just once. I've been thinking about kissing you since you followed me into high school. Maybe if you kissed me, I'd get over wondering and we could be friends. I got over thinking about Zoe when I kissed her on our third date."

"First, I didn't follow you to high school. There is only one high school in town. And second, Zoe got over you too. She told me you were great, but it was time to move on. She also told me you were a terrible kisser."

"I've practiced since then," he admitted.

"With who?"

"Jennie Lee Flowers."

"Everyone practiced with Jennie."

"Who'd you practice with?"

"Danny Lane."

Jack laughed. "He's gay."

"I know, but we both needed the practice."

Jack nodded as if either of them kissing just to practice made sense.

When the car was silent once more, he said, "Kiss

me, Shannon. We're not home for anyone to see. We're not at school. Let's just take one moment between lives and kiss. Then you can go back to beating on me."

She nodded. "All right. Maybe it will cure us both. I'd like to be friends, Jack. Real friends. You've always been around, but I think there is something between us that keeps us one step from comfortable when we're alone. Now, the academy is so hard we could both use someone we can turn to for help."

"I agree."

"One kiss and then we forget about it. What happens in a snow globe stays in the snow globe. You'll never mention it again."

"Deal," he said as he leaned toward her.

She nodded and moved closer.

Her lips were cold and the kiss was awkward at first. Until she opened her mouth and whispered against his lips. "Kiss me, Jack. Really kiss me. If we're going to do this, let's do it right."

His hand brushed the back of her sunshine hair and turned her head slightly. Then Jack did something he'd thought about for years.

He kissed Shannon Morell.

What shocked him most was she kissed him back.

When he finally broke the kiss, he circled her shoulder and held her against him. There was no need to turn on the heater. They kept each other warm until the snow finally slowed and a watery winter sun peeked at them from the other end of the short tunnel.

He thought of saying something funny, like *we've got to do this every time we're stranded*, or something sexy, like how their bodies seemed to fit together perfectly. But he couldn't. The time had been too special. He knew she had her plans, her life, all organized. The last thing she wanted to do was get involved with a guy her freshman year. He planned to be free too. Marriage, or even falling for a girl, was way down on his list.

She might have said this was a onetime thing. Never to happen again.

And he told himself, as he backed out of the tunnel, that "one time" was all right with him. But he knew, deep down, that there would be more. Someday. This wasn't over between them.

As he pulled onto the highway, she curled up beneath her coat and seemed to be asleep. She hadn't moved away, though. Her head rested on his shoulder and her hands were wrapped around his arm.

He drove, his mind full of what-ifs. He wanted the way he felt right now to stay with him. He didn't want it to fade. But he wouldn't have any part of shattering her dream to graduate. He had the same dream. They'd both worked too hard to get into the academy to toss it away for a slim chance at love.

After a while she asked, "What are you thinking, Jack?"

He glanced at her as sleepy green eyes met his. "I was thinking I should go back and thank Danny Lane."

She laughed and cuddled back under her covers.

twenty

Zoe

A FEW THOUSAND miles from Jack and Shannon, it was also snowing in New York as Zoe stepped off the plane.

This time, she wasn't in a hurry to get back to the city. This time she wished she could stay longer with her friends. There was so much work to be done on Emily's apartment, and Zoe wished she could help her mother out at the bakery. This was her busy time when she worked ten or twelve hours a day and then tried to keep up with the books at night.

She didn't say a word to anyone on the bus as the buildings grew taller. Usually, she played a game of seeing how many people to say one word to. Only the bus was packed and no one met her eyes. The snowstorm rattled the windows and a man near the back of the bus was coughing.

When she reached her stop, Zoe jumped off right into a gutter of icy mud.

The three-block walk from the drop-off was hard. No matter which way she turned, she felt like she was fighting the wind. As she unlocked her door, she hoped that elves had snuck in and cleaned the place, but no such luck.

Zoe turned on the heater and curled up in a blanket to wait for the room to thaw. Her apartment was covered with colorful art she'd bought on the streets, but tonight it didn't make her smile.

About the time she thought she might smell the milk in the fridge to see if it was still good, a tap sounded at her door.

A guy who lived two floors up and was in her theater class asked if she had ice. He'd never spoken to her before, but she'd noticed his haircut, cut short in the front and long in the back.

Zoe gave him both trays.

He grinned. "We're having a Thanksgiving detox upstairs. You want to come?"

"What's a detox?"

"We sit around telling all the bad, boring and bummer things that happened that we are NOT thankful for. After a few beers, everyone's story sounds funny. You want to join in?"

Zoe shrugged. "Sure. My friend back home may have tried to overdose. Doubt there'd be any way to make that funny."

"Save it for the detox."

She followed him up the stairs. He asked her name twice before they got to the party. After several beers and a bag of chips for dinner, Zoe stopped thinking about home. She'd figured out that most of the stories were made up. A few she remembered seeing in movies. So when her time came around, she told about a Thanksgiving where they had ham because no one would kill the turkey. Since she was from Texas, they all thought she was from a farm, so the story went well.

The guy who'd invited her was right. The stories did seem comical. But she didn't tell her real story.

Zoe slept with the guy who'd invited her, but in the morning, she couldn't remember his name, and she didn't care. She hadn't talked to him in class all semester and planned to continue the habit.

Monday was a foggy day outside and in her head. She made it to her drama class and heard about an audition for an off-off-Broadway play. By dinner, she was with her friends from improv class and she was back to laughing and dancing.

They ate at a cheap pizza place half a block from her apartment and all talked at once. These were her people, she thought. They understood her. They were all living life in double time.

They were all going to be stars.

twenty-one

Emily

THE LAST MONTH of the year came in cold and with dry snow that shifted in the streets like thin white waves. Emily's excitement over being out on her own began to fade. Cloudy days and bone-chilling nights kept her inside. No walks along the creek. No strolls on Main. No chance encounters with her shadow angel.

Her mother was still barely speaking to her, which was a blessing. Her father had gone back on the road and all her friends had disappeared. Zoe back to New York. Shannon and Jack returned to the Air Force Academy in Colorado Springs.

They were moving on with their lives while she felt she was hiding out. Dropping out. How could she explain that nothing traumatic had happened at the private college back East? She'd even been making good grades. But she hadn't belonged. She'd been walking on alien ground, breathing foreign air. She'd felt like she wasn't living in her own skin.

Routine was her drug for dealing with these times. And here in Laurel Springs was the best place to be if she planned to find her way back inside her own body.

She was still sleeping and showering at home, but every minute she wasn't working at the bakery, she was at the apartment. The new owner of the paper, Connor Larady, was busy moving his wife and baby back home and dealing with his parents' sudden deaths. Emily tried to help him. She collected the newspaper's mail and stacked it neatly on the front counter. She even answered the phone on afternoons when she was working upstairs and left messages pinned to an empty board behind the back desk. Sometimes people would be so excited to tell someone their story that Em felt like she'd written the whole article before they finally hung up.

She loved listening. A two-headed snake had been found. The Mathis reunion was crashed by strangers but the family planned to invite them back because they won the chili cook-off. The Franklin sisters, who ran a bed-and-breakfast a few towns over, had a niece who sent all the way to France for her wedding dress and it arrived the day after the wedding. The youngest Stone boy's wife had twins two months ago and no one could think of names. Mrs. Stone wondered if the paper would take suggestions.

Emily carefully wrote down all the details.

Working at Sweetie Pie's Bakery was challenging but enjoyable. Alexandra had always been nice to her and now they baked together in an easy rhythm. Alex's favorite saying was "Here, we eat our mistakes." So, Em would either learn to cook or gain weight.

Her boss always insisted she take a break at seven for breakfast, rolls or scones with coffee, and another break after one for lunch. They served a specialty soup and sandwich each day in a small café area with a counter that served eight and six tiny tables set for two. Lunch was always whatever was left over.

Alex hired retired ladies who wanted to work only a few days a week to handle the front in the mornings while she cooked. She was right about being busy. The lunch crowd grew daily. There were lots of parties in need of Christmas desserts, schools ordering cookies, and every business on Main was planning a Christmas open house to boost sales.

It was like people started overeating at Thanksgiving and didn't plan to stop until they started their diets in January.

A baker's day moved into full swing by 5:00 a.m. and slowed a little after one, which was perfect for Emily. She could spend her afternoons working on the apartment and be home by dark for dinner. She'd planned to return to the apartment and continue working into the night, but she was usually so tired she'd almost fall asleep at the dinner table.

To her surprise and her mother's joy, Emily slept soundly every night.

Her mother complained to the same beat so often

Emily could hear the lines in her head even when Anna wasn't close. "You're skin and bone and obviously not eating enough."

"You'll never get that dump of an apartment fixed up."

"You need to think about staying home and enrolling in classes."

Ever since her brothers moved out, her mother had tripled her advice to Emily. Maybe, if her daughter had grown to almost six feet like Shannon, Anna Waters would have let her grow up. Emily had a feeling she'd always be her mother's baby. The only girl. The one child Anna Waters hung all her dreams on.

Though her days passed without adventure or excitement, Emily settled for contentment and letting stories run in her head while she worked. She was sad sometimes—disappointed in herself, lonely—but now she had an ounce of hope. Something about knowing there was a different future coming made even her evening meals at home bearable.

Emily liked the creativity of the bakery. The customers were always happy when picking up sweets. Those who ate the bakery's lunch were usually working folks alone for the noon meal. Emily enjoyed the simple, polite conversations with each one.

She looked forward to the quiet hours when she worked on the apartment. She'd started with the floor in the main room: cleaning, polishing and repairing when she could. Some afternoons, she made it only a few feet across the big, one-room apartment, but she loved looking back and seeing her progress, one board at a time.

When men came and installed the new outside staircase that climbed up to her second-floor apartment, she knew Connor Larady was taking over his parents' businesses and approved of her living above. She still hadn't seen him, but she would in time.

She thought Fuller Wilder might stop by. But most nights she didn't stay late enough, and on the few nights she'd lingered until after dark, he didn't come. Maybe he stayed away because the businesses on Main were staying open late for Christmas shopping. He probably feared someone might see him turning into the alley below her room.

He'd dropped out of school before she got to high school. No one would think she even knew him.

On the second Saturday in December, Emily was bundling up to leave the bakery when Alex asked her if she'd mind working overtime. The bookstore was having an open house and Arnie needed someone to serve the cider and cookies they'd made, the ones that looked like tiny books.

"He says Little Brother will be busy running the register and he wants to visit with the customers."

Emily grinned. "You do know Richard, Arnie's little brother, is the same age as Shannon's dad?"

"I know, but he'll always be Arnie's little brother." Alex grinned, and Emily got the feeling she wasn't thinking of Little Brother for a moment.

"It'll be fun. I'm happy to help him. Arnie's been the go-between for Connor and me. The poor guy is moving back, trying to take finals and running his parents' businesses. I could build a third floor to the place and he wouldn't notice. But Arnie keeps up with me and says I'm doing a great job."

"Connor is lucky to have friends like Arnie who can step in and help," Alex added. "Someone said Arnie even opened the quilt shop that Connor's grandmother owns because a woman just had to have a few things to finish her Christmas quilt.

"Arnie and Connor are probably glad you're keeping an eye on the offices downstairs. Once everything settles, that office will be a lively place again."

Emily shook her head. "It's really one office with half a dozen desks. Near as I can tell, the desktops are covered with stories they were working on. Most of them have two chairs, so I'm thinking Connor's parents probably wrote them together. If they had other employees, wouldn't they be dropping by?"

"I heard they did everything together." Alex wiped away a tear. "They even died together."

"I wish I'd known them. No one ever says a bad word about them or Connor. No one talks about the older son. Did you ever meet him?"

Alex shook her head. "He was several years older than Connor. Someone said he left before Connor started school. Most folks don't even remember his name. I don't think I've ever heard it. The Laradys finally stopped talking about him and people stopped asking questions. I heard he didn't come to their funeral."

Emily felt sorry for Connor. "The newspaper office

is safe with me there. My hammering will frighten a robber away. But a night off from working on my hands and knees will do me good. I'll pass out cookies and cider at the bookstore." She slipped on her blinking Christmas lights necklace and loaded up cider, paper goods and cookies in the back of her car.

To her surprise, three hours later, she was having a great time serving refreshments and visiting with what felt like half the town. Several people asked her for advice on books to buy their relatives. Since Emily had read the children's section of the library by the time she was eight, she felt she could actually help.

Near nine o'clock, when the crowd dwindled and the hot cider was almost gone—thanks to Little Brother drinking ten cups—Emily took the time to glance at the half-dozen books she'd stored behind her. She'd have to buy them one book a week.

Arnie was sitting up front in the huge window display that looked like it could have been modeled after Sherlock Holmes's library. There were two overstuffed chairs with books all around. Arnie's lifelong friend was sitting in the other chair. To no one's surprise, they were talking about books.

Emily nibbled on the last book cookie from the last tray she'd brought.

A low voice drifted between the stacks behind her. "If you haven't eaten too many cookies, I'll buy you a hamburger for supper."

She turned and saw Fuller Wilder smiling at her. A million-dollar smile she guessed he rarely used. Straight dark hair hanging low enough to almost cover one eye. He was handsome in a Heathcliff kind of way, she thought.

"How long have you been watching me?"

"I dropped in earlier and saw you here. I thought I'd wait outside and say hi, but you never came out."

"I'm working. Passing out cookies. You want some cider?"

He shook his head.

She looked at the cookie in her hand. One bite gone. "You want this last cookie?"

Fuller nodded.

Trying to look heartbroken, she handed it over.

Breaking it in half, he passed the biggest half to her.

After a few minutes of silence, she asked, "You need help with a Christmas gift?"

"Maybe. You got any recommendations?"

She turned to the stack she'd hoarded away. "These look good. Maybe one would work."

While he thumbed through the books, she cleaned up the table and took the last cup of the cider to Little Brother.

A few minutes later no one seemed to notice when Fuller walked out beside her, carrying the cider dispenser while she had both hands full of paper goods.

"Good night," Arnie yelled from his perch in the window. "Thanks for your service, Emily. The treats went over quite well, but you were also a big help with the shoppers. If you ever want to stop baking and come to work for me, you're always welcome."

"Thanks. Will you pay me in books?"

"I will."

"Definitely something to think about."

Fuller helped her put her things in her car and pointed at the black pickup parked beside her. "Okay to take my truck? I meant what I said about buying you supper."

"Sure."

He followed her to the passenger side and put his hands on her waist to help her up.

She laughed. "I'm not a child, Fuller. You don't have to lift me up."

"I know, but that's a big step without running boards." He smiled up at her. "I can't believe you're going out with me. I guess I'm a bit nervous."

"It's simple logic, Fuller." She put her hand on his shoulder. "You're feeding me. I'm starving."

"Right." He closed her door and ran around to the other side. "Hamburgers," he said as he climbed behind the wheel. "Where to?"

Emily tried to look like she was giving his question some thought. "There're only two places in town that serve hamburgers this late. How about the bowling alley?"

"Okay," he said without smiling. "But people will see us."

"I hope so, or we'll never get waited on."

"No, I mean people will see you with me."

She leaned back against the seat. "No problem. I have no ex-boyfriends who'll try to beat you up. What about you? Is some old girlfriend going to see me with you and start yelling?"

"Nope. I kill all my ex-girlfriends. Bury them in the junkyard."

"Good. I won't have to watch out for them."

They both laughed.

Moving only inches away from him, she whispered, "If you don't want to be seen with me, I'd understand. My mom tells everyone I'm not balanced. I was voted the most likely to off myself in my senior class."

He pulled to the curb with the bowling alley sign still half a block away. "It's not that I don't want to be seen with you, Emily. I thought you might not want to be seen with me."

She smiled and touched his cheek. "We're a real pair, Fuller. We're both afraid we'll frighten the other off. But I'm up for this if you are. And, just so you understand, this is a date. You asked me out. I accepted."

"A date?" He acted surprised, then took her hand and tugged her out the driver's side. Again, his hand was strong around her waist as he helped her down.

She thought of objecting, but decided she liked it. "That's right—a date, and I expect a kiss on the porch when I get home."

"What if your mother's watching?"

"I'm sure she will be, so after the kiss, I suggest you run."

"Maybe I should take you back to your car and let you drive yourself home after we eat. I'd like to be alive tomorrow to remember this date."

"Coward. But you're right. I can't leave my car on Main."

"Damn right."

Both were still laughing as they walked into the bowling alley and found a table at the Snack Shack that served only nachos, burgers and drinks.

Emily didn't watch the people. She was far more interested in Fuller. He'd cleaned up. No smell of oil. No stains on his hands.

By the time the hamburgers arrived, he'd relaxed. They talked about books. She was surprised how many of her favorites were his also.

After eating, they took the time to walk the length of the alley and watch people bowl.

It was getting late, but she didn't want their time to end. When they walked back to his pickup, she took his hand as she had the night he'd walked her home.

Neither said a word as he drove the few blocks back to Main, now dark except for a few streetlights.

When he stopped behind her car, she asked, "Want to come up and see the apartment I'm redoing?"

"Maybe next time. It's late. You have to be at the bakery at five."

"You keeping up with me, Fuller?"

"Always." He turned in the seat. "All we've got time for is that kiss you said we'd have tonight. I'm thinking that might be a good way to end our first date."

Emily knew she should be polite. Maybe let him take the lead this time. But she'd been timid all her life and she couldn't slow down now. He might be everything her mother warned her about, but she couldn't hesitate.

When she moved into his arms, Fuller laughed, and

for a moment, he just held her close. Then he lowered his mouth to hers and kissed her tenderly.

This guy who was probably all wrong for her did something so right.

twenty-two

Fuller

FULLER WAITED THREE days before he climbed the new staircase bolted to the outside of the newspaper building. He knocked lightly on her apartment door. When she didn't answer, he tried the knob, and wasn't surprised to find it unlocked.

Hesitantly, he stepped inside. The floor was half finished, with a hole in the far corner big enough for a man to drop through. The windows looked new and were freshly cleaned. The tile in the kitchen was cracked and uneven. Someone must have swept away the loose pieces, making the once-white tiles look snaggletoothed. A bare light bulb hung from the ceiling with what looked like new wiring.

Standing in the center of the room, he mentally

made a list of the hundred repairs that would be needed before she could move in. He tried to tell himself that Emily Waters was not his problem. This place belonged to Connor Larady, not him or Emily.

A rattling came from below. He moved to the open door that opened to a landing at the top of the stairs, leading to the newspaper office below. From his location, he could see almost all of the big office downstairs.

Emily banged her way between desks and office chairs, carrying a box half her height.

Fuller simply watched her determination as she took the stairs. Her short chestnut hair was a windblown mess and threatened to blind her, but her tennis shoes gripped the stairs, one step after the other.

When she reached the top, she finally looked around the box and saw him.

"You here to rob me, Fuller?"

He grinned as he took the box from her. "I was thinking about it, but there's nothing worth taking. I searched all those trash bags you've got stacked in the corner. Guess what you've got in them. Trash." He shook the box she'd just brought up. "What's in this, feathers?"

She followed him into the apartment. "Today I decided to move one box over. It's time if I'm going to live here by January."

Fuller set the box in the middle of the finished side of the floor and opened the flaps. "Glad to see you started with essentials." He pulled out a stuffed unicorn the size of a Great Dane.

She grabbed the rainbow-colored toy and hugged it close. "I was in the hospital three years ago and this guy slept with me every night. He propped my arm up so it didn't throb and keep me awake."

Fuller studied her. She might be eighteen, but the child he'd cradled that night out on Cemetery Road was still there. He needed to be very careful. Not get too close. She was fragile. If they became more than friends and she found out he'd been driving the car that hit her, the knowledge might break her naive innocence.

Hell, they weren't even really friends yet. "I just came over to see if you needed some help." He managed to sound casual. "I've got some time on my hands. And I'm pretty handy."

"I can't pay for any help."

"I wouldn't charge you." He didn't know her well enough to say he was just helping her out. One date didn't count for much. He changed directions. "I'm a friend of Connor's." Still a lie, but not much of one. "I thought I'd help *him* out. He's got more than he can handle right now."

"Oh, I didn't know you two were friends. Makes sense, though. You're both about twenty-one. Everyone in town is offering to help him, but most have no idea what to do."

She set her unicorn down and walked around showing him what needed to be done. "The wiring is fine, and Jack's brothers put in the windows. I don't need much heat. When someone turns on the thermostat downstairs it drifts up. A few people who've worked for the paper in years past have started coming in to help out with organizing the Larady files. One told me that the Laradys run several small businesses out of this office. They lease oil rights and own several properties they rent. The family is into a bit of farming. Plus, they print flyers and cards for half the businesses in town. The Mr. Larady who just died took on local ad campaigns and was on the board of every nonprofit in town."

Fuller didn't care about the office downstairs. He wanted to help Emily, and right now she seemed nervous. He wanted to hold her, but that wasn't what she needed. "How many dates did you have last week?"

Her eyebrows rose at his question, but she answered, "One with you."

"Last month?"

She shrugged. "None."

"Last year."

"None." Her brown eyes stared directly at him. Questioning. Nervous.

He smiled. "Me either."

Surprise flashed again. Then doubt.

Fuller rushed on. "I thought if you'll let me help get this place livable, I'd be doing Connor a favor. We'd be finishing a project he doesn't have time for and it would give me and you time to get to know each other. Maybe have another date to celebrate when we finish. Sound good to you? I could come over after I get off around eight or nine and help out. Maybe carry out trash for you. You've got quite a mountain going over in that corner. You could leave it by the back door and I could load it in my pickup."

"That'd be great, but I'll miss you most nights. Since I have to get to work so early, I'm usually in bed by nine."

"Just leave me a note if you need something. Anything I can do to help. Maybe I'll see you on Sunday afternoons? We're both off then."

"Yeah, that would be good."

He wasn't sure, but for a moment, he thought she looked disappointed. Like she thought they might be together more. Like maybe he was here to see her and not just help Connor out?

A bit of his resolve broke. "Who knows—we might even go for another hamburger some Sunday night after we finish. You can buy this time."

"I'd like that. I'll leave a note if I need you to do anything. I'm not very strong. Just moving boxes of tiles across to the kitchen is hard."

"I can handle whatever you need." He tugged off his jacket and hung it over the unicorn's horn.

Emily did the same.

Awkwardly, they started working. He broke up the remaining tiles in the kitchen and bath, then loaded them up in boxes. She worked on the flooring one board at a time, making very little progress.

By the time they carried the last bag of trash down to his pickup, Emily looked exhausted.

"Ready to call it a night?" he asked.

"Yes. Thanks for your help. With you here, I can really see progress."

"I'll come back when I have time." He stood on the other side of the pickup. Part of him wanted to kiss her good-night. She probably wouldn't mind. After all, she'd already kissed him twice.

But reason ruled. This wasn't about getting involved with Emily. This was about helping her. Maybe partially paying off the debt he owed her. Deep down, he needed to admit that girls like Emily didn't date guys like him. Emily didn't need to get involved with him. Hell, she slept with a stuffed animal. Three years difference in age might not seem like much, but it was.

She waved goodbye and climbed into her car.

He drove over to a line of empty trash bins by the park and dumped the bags and boxes of trash. Then he went back to Main.

It was fully dark now, but he had no trouble parking between the buildings and climbing the stairs. He went straight to the kitchen, turned on one floodlight and continued working on the tile.

Over the years, when business was slow at the shop, he'd done odd jobs in construction. Mostly hauling and cleanup, but he'd picked up a few skills. Laying tile was one of them.

Emily had told him Mack Morell had bought the supplies, saying he'd work on it during the weekends he was off, but so far he hadn't been able to get home since Thanksgiving.

Fuller worked until midnight. Prep work, mostly, so the flooring would be done right. Emily probably wouldn't even notice. The kitchen was useless right now, and she seemed to be concentrating on the living area flooring. At the rate she was going, it'd be February before she finished that one project.

Two nights later Fuller returned. He could tell Emily had been there earlier working. A few more feet of flooring were cleaned and polished. Several moving boxes joined the unicorn. It wasn't time to move into the apartment, but Fuller had a feeling that these boxes were more about moving out of her parents' home.

He knew he'd be tired tomorrow, but it felt good finally doing something good for Emily.

twenty-three

Alex

"SWEETIE PIE'S BAKERY. How can I help you?" Alex answered the bakery phone as she pulled off her apron. It had been a long day and the last thing she wanted was another order coming in at closing time.

"How you doing, Red?" asked a low voice she'd recognize anywhere. No one had ever called her Red except Mack Morell.

She leaned back against the counter, crossed her long legs and relaxed. "I've been waiting to hear from you, Mack. The kids will be home for Christmas break in a few days and you haven't been here to help with the remodel. Your daughter calls Emily every other morning to keep up on the progress."

He laughed. "Sorry. I forgot I have another job. Saving the world is taking all my time right now. I'll get back to lay tile as soon as I can."

"It's all right. I haven't been over much either. The tiles might be done. I've been too busy to check the progress. Name a holiday, and everyone heads to the bakery. We'll get Emily's place fixed up after Shannon and Jack get home."

"What about your Zoe? She getting too famous to work?" Mack teased.

"Oh, big news. Zoe got a bit part in an off-off-Broadway play and can't get home till after the New Year. She's only in one scene and the rest of the time she's part of the crew, but she thinks this will be her big break."

"I'm tied up until after Christmas too. Maybe longer." He sounded sad.

She smiled. "You're in a play?"

"Something like that." When he laughed, a bit of the tension left his voice. "Tell Shannon I wouldn't miss Christmas if it wasn't very important. She'll understand. She's an airman's daughter. I've tried to call her, but she wasn't in her room, and I don't think she carries her cell. She's probably pulling a few all-nighters studying at the library." He paused, then asked, "Can she stay with you over the holiday? My mother will want her to go to Dallas with her, but I know Shannon will think she'll need to be home to help Emily move."

"Of course. You know she can, Mack. It'll help me not miss Zoe so much. We'll pal around. Maybe go shopping. She'll be fine."

"They're growing up, Alex. Before long they won't need us anymore."

"I don't want to talk about it. It seems about the time I get parenting figured out, the job's over."

"I know. I feel the same. What should we talk about? I need to hear a friendly voice. How about the bakery? What's cooking?"

"Very funny." She lowered her tone, as if there were someone in her empty store that might hear her. "How about I ask you my first question? I never got a chance on the way back home from Lowe's. We were too busy talking about the kids."

"I thought you forgot about that bet. I still can't believe you ate that entire steak."

"You lost the bet, Mack. You have to answer ten questions." Maybe this conversation would allow him to step away from his job and his worries for a few minutes, she thought. Maybe she didn't know much about him, but she could hear worry and exhaustion in his tone.

"All right, ask anything you want. I'm ready. I don't have a dishonest bone in my body. I swear, I'll answer with nothing but the truth."

Alex knew she was stepping into uncharted territory with Mack, but she was too tired to think of another question. She'd have to ask the one that often popped up in her mind. "Mack?"

"Yes, I'm waiting," he answered. "Go ahead, hit me with whatever you want to know about me or men in general. From birth to today, I'm an open book about anything but my job."

"All right. The first question. Do you ever think of me as a woman?"

"Of course I do, Red. I noticed the day I met you that you were a woman. Taller than most. Slim. Great red hair and laughter sparkling in your blue eyes. And you always smell good, like sugar and spice. You're lucky I don't lean over and take a bite out of your neck just to see if you taste as good as you smell." He sounded proud of himself. "How's that for noticing?"

"No, Mack. No kidding. Seriously, do you ever think of me as a woman?"

She waited, fearing the phone had gone dead. It was a dumb question, she decided, but it had been so long since any man looked at her. Really looked at her. Most days she felt like a mother, a baker, a friend, but no one saw her as a woman. She just needed to know that once in a while a man thought of her as a female.

"Yeah." He broke the silence so suddenly she jumped. "I've thought of you as a woman. What guy wouldn't?"

She held the phone so tightly she knew her knuckles must be white.

Finally, he added, "A man would have to be dead not to be aware of you as a woman. But, Alex, that's as far as it'll ever go. We're friends. A few daydreams won't change a thing. And you don't have to worry about me stepping out of line."

Alex nodded to herself. "I understand. I just needed to know if you see me like that once in a while. I sometimes think I'm invisible to men, all men. If I robbed a bank, the witnesses would say, 'Yeah, I saw the robber. A baker, I think.'"

He swore, obviously reading between the lines. "I wish I was there and could see you now. I have no idea what you want me to say."

"It's all right, Mack. You were honest. That's what I wanted." She failed miserably at keeping her voice even.

He was silent for a few heartbeats. Probably trying to figure out what she wanted.

When he spoke, his tone was low, apologetic. "I will not try to change anything between us. You don't have to worry about me ever making a pass again. You know I'm not that kind of guy. If you don't want to be touched, I can respect that. I don't know what I was thinking when I kissed you Thanksgiving."

She couldn't breathe. He was saying too much.

"Alex? You still there?"

"I'm here."

"Talk to me. You're upset and somehow it's my fault."

Closing her eyes, she charged ahead. "What if I wished you were that kind of guy? Maybe just once? What if you're not the only one who has thoughts about us becoming more than friends? What if we took it slow and you did touch me, kiss me, make me feel alive? I had someone hurt me when I was a kid. No one believed me, not even my grandma. So, I might hesitate, but that doesn't mean I don't want you. Only you, Mack."

She thought he must have dropped the phone, but she could hear mumbled cussing coming in rapid fire.

Static through the phone and then he was back on the line. "Listen to me carefully, Red. I've got to board a flight in an hour. It may be a while before I get back, but if I could, I'd be taking the first flight back to you. Do you understand what I'm saying? We need to be having this conversation face-to-face."

"You're not coming home. I already know that. I understand."

"Right. But I will be. It may be months, but I will be home."

She could hear him trying to find the right words.

"Look, Red, when I do get back, we need to talk. Just me and you. No one else around." He let out a long breath. "You need to understand something. I'm coming home to you, Alex."

He hung up without saying another word.

She sat in her silent kitchen for a long time just thinking about what he'd said. She'd started something, and she wasn't sure how she'd handled it.

He'd reacted far more than she thought he would.

A nervous little laugh bubbled up in her. Maybe right now, in her life, it was time for far more. She'd had nothing for so long that just a little would never do.

Alex grinned. What would Mack do when he heard the next nine questions?

twenty-four

Emily

TWICE IN THE following week, Emily noticed Fuller eating lunch in the tiny café area of the bakery. He sat alone, his clothes stained with oil and dirt. No one joined him, but a few people nodded toward him in a silent hello.

When she brought him his soup, he managed a low "Thank you."

Emily decided he must just be helping her with the apartment for Connor's sake. Just doing a favor for his friend. He probably ate at the café just to try the food.

But deep down, she'd hoped he was helping her, not just Connor. She liked seeing him, talking to him, maybe even becoming friends.

He'd said that helping with the remodel would give

them time to get to know one another, but if they were never at the apartment at the same time, that wasn't likely to happen.

"Thanks," he said when she refilled his coffee as the lunch run slowed.

She smiled at him, but he still wasn't looking up. "I like the pattern you put on the kitchen floor. It makes the small space look bigger."

"Yep." He stood and walked toward the cash register.

One of the retired teachers, Miss Margaret, stood waiting to ring up Fuller's meal. She asked about his father.

"He's fine," Fuller said, without emotion.

As the woman handed him his change, Emily blocked Fuller's path to the door. "You forgot your cookies."

Fuller finally looked up and met her eyes. He hadn't ordered any cookies, but he'd have to talk to her if he wanted to explain that.

She smiled, daring him.

"Thanks." He took the cookies as he fought down a grin.

"You're welcome, Fuller Wilder." She held the door open for him to pass. "See you later."

"See you, Em." His words were too low for anyone else to hear.

Emily smiled as she walked back to the counter. Could it be possible that Fuller was shyer than she was when people were around? They'd talked easily on their date.

"You know Fuller's dad?" Emily asked Miss Margaret as she walked past the counter.

"I do. My last year teaching was when Fuller was in the first grade. When he had trouble reading, his father came up every afternoon and sat beside his son as I worked with Fuller. He might not have been completely sober some days, but he was there to make sure his son learned."

"Did you ever talk to him?"

"Not much. Fuller's dad was a man who lived in his memories, and I never saw him say a single word to his boy. He was handsome, like Fuller is now, but he made little effort to talk to anyone as far as I know.

"Maybe the memories kept him going. Maybe they haunted him. I have a feeling he barely knew his son was around most of the time, but it was important to him that Fuller could read." She grinned. "He always took the time to thank me when they left, and for a year after that every time I had work done on my car the old man would come out and tell me that Bill said there'd be no charge for Miss Margaret."

Emily thought about what Margaret said. Emily had been overprotected all her life. She couldn't imagine how silent it must have been for a little boy with no mother, no brothers or sisters.

That night she was still working when Fuller stepped into the back door of the apartment, his arms loaded down with supplies.

"You're still here," he said as if simply stating a fact. "I figured you'd be home by now."

She stood. "Is it a problem that I'm here? I thought we could work together tonight."

"No problem. I just thought you'd be gone by now. It's a little late for you early birds."

"I took a nap today. I plan to work a while longer. I'll try to stay out of your way." She went back to work but yelled, from the other room, "How were the cookies?"

"Great."

He moved into the bathroom to work. The saw he'd brought made enough noise to end further conversation.

Three hours later, she brought him a Coke. "I left you a note on the bar of what I need."

"I'll take care of it. I know where I can pick up a used sink. It's not new, but it'll look better than the one you've got. If I switch out the tub for a shower it'll give you more room. It wouldn't take much wood to build you a few rows of shelves."

"Sounds good." This wasn't the way she wanted to talk to him, but at least they were talking.

She pulled on her coat and waited as he walked the few feet to the bar and picked up her note. For a long moment, she wondered if she'd made what she wanted plain enough.

Finally, he looked up as he tapped the note on his open palm. "This all you need?"

"Yep." She echoed his one-word answer.

Walking straight toward her, he slid his hands inside her coat, circled his arms around her waist and lifted her off the ground. "One hug coming up."

She wrapped her arms around his neck and held on tight. Tears ran down her cheeks. This, just this, was all she needed.

Finally, when he lowered her back to ground, he saw her tears. "You all right?"

"I am now."

He wiped a tear away with his thumb. "I guess some days everyone just needs a hug."

"No, Fuller, I needed one from you." She pulled a few inches away. "I know you don't want to date me, and that's all right. We can just be friends. I..."

"You're wrong." His hands brushed her shoulders.

"About what?"

"I do want to date you. Hell, I want a lot more than that, but you can do better than me, Emily. You need to forget about anything ever happening between us. A guy like me would never be good enough for a girl like you. Just ask anyone in town."

She jerked sideways, releasing his gentle hold on her shoulder. When she turned back, her free arm swung full force, landing her open hand against his jaw so hard that the sound echoed off the walls.

He was unprepared for the blow. He stumbled backward a step before he regained his balance.

"I'm through with people telling me what to do. Even you, Fuller Wilder." Her breathing was coming so fast it sounded like rapid-fire hiccups. "Don't you tell me what is good for me. I will not stand for it."

She couldn't tell if Fuller planned to fight or run. She didn't care. All the rage since she'd come home had been building inside her. Everyone she knew wanted to hold the reins on her life.

When he took a step toward her, she braced for a blow. She'd never hit anyone. No one had ever hit her, but if she was going to survive in this mixed-up world she had to feel, even if it hurt. She'd had enough of being protected, pampered and sheltered from life.

His hand rose, but the blow she'd expected was a gentle touch against the side of her face. Just before he lowered his mouth over hers she saw a fire in his eyes that had nothing to do with retaliation.

She stood as he took his sweet revenge. This wasn't a light kiss of a first date, or even the tender play of exploring. This kiss was far more. One kiss that seemed to overtake a lifetime of longing. One kiss telling her exactly how he felt.

Emily melted against him, taking all he offered.

When he finally broke the kiss, he whispered against her ear. "Now do you have any doubt how I feel about you?"

"No."

He kissed his way down her throat. "Can you handle this, my shy Emily?"

"I don't know."

She felt his laughter. "We'll go slow. But I don't just want to date you. You got to know that, Em. We're not kids." He pressed his lips against the pulse in her neck and she melted closer. "If I can't convince you to step away from me, then I'll never have the strength to push you away."

"I'll fight for what I want, Fuller, and right now I want to be closer to you."

He rubbed his warm cheek against hers. "I know. I can still feel the burn of that slap."

Pushing her hair away from her face, he added, "It woke me up. Only, let's face it, neither of us has any idea how this works. We'll probably do it all wrong. I don't want to hurt you, Em."

She pulled his mouth to hers. "We'll figure it out." One quick kiss and then she pulled away to add, "You know, I think you just might be the one person in this world who will help me. So save me, Fuller. Teach me to feel."

Part II: Spring 2004

Jack's last academy journal entry before graduation: May 17, 2004

Tomorrow I graduate from the Air Force Academy. Time to stop writing to myself.

I loved my years here. I feel like all the studying and hard work has prepared me for life.

P.S. I think I'm in love with my best friend.

twenty-five

Jack

JACK WALKED OUT of Fairchild Hall and headed toward the parade ground for the last time. He could have taken the bus, but he needed the walk. A light rain was falling, giving a chill to the day, but four years of memories kept him warm. The sound of taps seemed to echo in the air. The beat of forty squadrons marching. Even the pink glow of Pikes Peak at dawn would stay in his memory forever. Jack had a feeling he'd go back to this place in his mind for the rest of his life.

He was decked out in his dress blues beneath his rain slicker and feeling every inch a second lieutenant. After four years, he was ready for duty.

His parents and brothers were standing next to Shannon Morell, near the entrance. She looked so slim in her uniform, her golden hair tied up in a bun. He grinned. She also seemed out of place bookended by Hutchinson men. They were tall, like Jack, but both had put on fifty or sixty pounds while Jack was in school. Both had more than ten years on him and were starting to look like they'd been run over by middle age.

Jack nodded at them. They nodded back. The limit of most of their conversations.

"Where's Mack? I mean Chief Master Sergeant Morell?" Jack asked Shannon. Mack would have to salute him now. He'd be a lieutenant. An officer. Shannon's dad had already said he wanted to be the first to pay his respects.

Shannon smiled at Jack, knowing the game they played. "He's finding us just the right seats. You know my dad. Everything has to be in order."

Leaning down, Jack kissed his mother on the cheek, then shook hands with his dad. He wasn't a man who said much, but pride was about to pop the buttons on his Hawaiian shirt.

While Ben and Harry watched the crowd, Jack turned to Shannon and also kissed her cheek. "I'm glad you came too." He knew he wasn't supposed to even think it, but he always noticed how great she looked in her uniform, or in anything else, for that matter. He loved her athletic build that she carried with grace.

Over the past few years, they'd developed a comfortable friendship. A few times a week they ran together before dawn. Now and then they'd studied together and even eaten meals next to each other. Jack considered them in a holding pattern during this time of their lives.

"Wish Zoe and Emily could have come." He shook his head. "Correction—I wish I could be in New York for Zoe's performance tonight. I heard Alex even made the trip for opening night. She says Zoe thinks this play might be open more than a week."

"I would like to have gone, but I was already here, so I picked watching you walk. I'm glad you're happy I traveled all two hundred yards from Vandi." She gave him one of those looks that said she couldn't believe he was graduating without any living brain cells.

He continued to stare at her, wishing he could see behind those green eyes. Two and a half years ago, they'd made out under a railroad bridge. It had been snowing too hard to travel. They hadn't been really involved, but both had been in an odd mood that strange Thanksgiving break. For an hour, in the middle of nowhere, halfway between home and school, they'd held one another.

Jack had the feeling that if he'd pushed just a little, he and Shannon might have gone all the way that day in their snow globe rendezvous.

But he hadn't. So many people in the world looked for instant gratification, but he and Shannon were both made from different cloth. They planned for what they wanted. Set goals. The *them*, if there was ever going to be a *them*, could wait for the right time.

Since that night, they'd both pushed their feelings aside. Both wanted careers, and getting involved with anyone before graduation would only cause trouble.

Jack had tried to talk to her about that snowy afternoon a dozen times, but Shannon seemed to forget it ever happened.

"You need a ride back home tomorrow? I'll be heading out in the morning," he asked. "I've got a week before I report in for a briefing."

"I was planning to drive home with my dad. He said he'd rent a car, but he got a call and has to rush back to DC as soon as your graduation is over. Something big, I'm guessing. The worry lines on his forehead are chiseled in."

She looked troubled. "Dad's hair is longer too."

"I hadn't noticed." The chief master sergeant's hair was not of any importance to Jack.

"It means he's going undercover somewhere in the world. He won't say anything to me, but I know." One tear worked its way down her cheek.

"Maybe your dad's just been busy, Shan. Hasn't had time to get to the barber."

"No. There are other signs. He's told me twice not to worry if he's out of pocket for a few weeks. Last year, when he was *out of pocket* I didn't hear from him for two months. Yesterday he dropped a few thousand in my bank account for summer expenses. I'm not in school. When I'm not at a camp training, I'll be living at home. Eating over at my grandmother's place. What do I need money for if he's only gone two weeks?"

Jack's mother wiggled between them. She couldn't seem to stop patting on him. "You're welcome to ride back with us, Shannon. One of Jack's brothers can travel with him to keep him company."

For a moment Jack almost laughed. Shannon looked miserable. She had never talked to his parents for more than five minutes in her life. She might not want to ride with him, but traveling with his parents would be hell. Mom could go on for hours about her grandsons. He was starting to believe she'd had kids only so she could get the grandkids.

"I don't mind riding with Jack," Shannon said. "I need to ask him some questions about senior year."

"Of course. Maybe we can caravan, stopping at the same time? Jack's father likes to leave early. How about we pull out at six and drive a few hours before stopping for breakfast?"

His mother missed the look of pure pain on Jack's face.

Before Shannon could answer, Jack added, "Sure, Mom. Sounds great. We'll be waiting in the hotel parking lot at six. If for any reason we're late, I'll call the hotel by 5:50 a.m. Then you can drive on and we'll catch up."

Shannon's father arrived, herding the Hutchinsons into the stands. In full uniform, Chief Master Sergeant Morell looked like a great warrior herding sheep.

"Thanks," Shannon whispered to Jack just before she joined the line. "We will be late, right?"

"Right. I'll wake up before six and make the call, then pick you up at eight."

To his shock, she kissed him on the cheek. "I'm proud of you, Lieutenant."

Her smile almost made him forget there was nothing between them. She had a way of doing that. Except for that one time, that snow globe moment, when he'd held her close.

She disappeared into the crowd and he walked toward his place in line. He should be thinking about all that would be happening in the next few months. No more school. He was a pilot, an officer. An aeronautical engineer. His exciting life was about to begin. But his thoughts drifted back to Shannon like they always did. The drive home might be their last chance to be together. She'd signed up for summer training at the academy. He'd be taking on his first duty. They'd be hundreds of miles apart.

The next morning, Jack sat in his car watching the sunrise. He'd called his mother at 5:55 a.m. and said he was running late and not to wait. Then he'd packed his gear for the last time and decided to simply sit in the car and wait for Shannon.

He wanted to watch the sun come up over the academy one more time. This place had been his home for four years. He'd become a man here. "Off we go into the wild blue yonder" would always play as the background of his mind when he walked toward a plane.

After all the panic surrounding graduation, Jack needed to take time to breathe and think. His mind kept drifting like a space traveler between two planets. Jack wanted to live a life of service. He wanted to be a good person. And, Lord help him, he wanted Shannon. He always had. He always would. It didn't matter if he was fourteen or twenty-two.

When she walked out of her dorm thirty minutes

early, he wasn't surprised. Her dad once said she was born early and expected the world to simply catch up.

"I tried to call your room." She shoved two bags in the back of his old Ford. "When you didn't answer, I figured you were probably already waiting for me."

Jack took the time to stop and take one last look at the Cadet Chapel that shot one hundred and fifty feet into the sky. A wedding party was just leaving the church. Swords arching over the bride and groom as they ran out. The last sword swung down as they passed, almost swatting the bride, and laughter echoed.

Jack turned the car toward I-25 and continued their conversation. "I couldn't just sit in my room thinking about how some other guy will be looking at those four walls come fall. I feel as if I'm being kicked out of the nest."

She smiled at him. "But, Jack, you can fly."

He nodded. "I can, can't I?" He'd soloed his junior year.

They drove off campus, both lost in their own thoughts. A few miles down the road, he stopped for coffee. Neither seemed in any hurry. There was no chance of catching up with his parents.

"How come you never brought a car up here? You could last year."

"I liked having you to drive me or Dad flying up to get me if he was home. I like passing through the open country between my two lives. You have that feeling too?"

"I do." Jack glanced at her, not the least surprised

she was smiling. She was now a senior. "So, I was your personal driver?"

"You're mine, period, Jack. Don't you know that Em and Zoe argue that you belong to them, too, but you're really mine?"

He frowned. "I'm not a puppy, Shan, and next year I won't be around to be your driver. You'll have to find someone else or start putting some miles on that three-year-old car of yours."

"No, idiot. I mean now that you've graduated, we can stop pretending there is nothing between us."

"I never pretended that. I wasn't pretending two and a half years ago when I kissed you on the snowy day. Though the memory faded. You've made it plain a dozen times that that kiss would never be repeated. By the time I was a junior, I gave up and accepted we'd just be kind of friends."

"I told you we had to wait. We couldn't get involved while we were both at the academy."

"Fine. We followed that rule, right. Your rule, not mine." He glanced at her and was not surprised her cheeks were red with anger. "Shan, a guy just doesn't hang around forever. Half the time you act like you don't want to even speak to me. Now all of a sudden you've picked this last ride home to suggest we start something. Well, maybe I'm not ready." He thought about it a few seconds and added, "Just exactly what are you hinting that we start? A friendship? We got that. Dating? That won't be easy with you here and me in DC. A long-distance affair? That's not much better than putting up with us being just friends."

Deep down he still ached for her, but damn if he'd admit it. She'd turned him down one too many times. Now it was time to follow his plan. Serve his time in the air force. See the world.

"Pull over and I'll show you how it could be between us." She glared at him so hard he wasn't sure what she had coming, but something told him he'd walk away with bruises. "I see no point in you having to guess—we can skip all the guessing and wondering."

Driving a few more miles, Jack found a rest stop where he could pull over. This time of morning, no one else had stopped to enjoy the view.

He turned off the car, swiveled in the seat and took a drink of coffee, preparing for her explanation.

"Jack, do you love me? One simple question. You should be able to handle it."

"I've told you three girls a dozen times I love you all. I've known Emily since birth, Zoe and I have been best buddies since she slugged some guy who was picking on me in grade school and you are a crush I can't cure." He lifted his cup in salute. "But none of you own me. And you, Shannon Morell, do not have the right to boss me around or tell me how to live my life."

"Put your cup down, Jack."

He did as she suggested, guessing she was about to hit him. Since junior high, that seemed to be her favorite way to touch him. Only with combat training she was becoming deadly. She'd accidentally kill him one day, and all he'd do to defend himself was duck.

She leaned over, placed her cold hands on either side of his face and kissed him.

It might have been two and a half years since she'd kissed him, but damn if it didn't feel as familiar as yesterday. He'd kissed her, made love to her a million times in his mind.

He deepened the kiss and she followed his lead for once. When he dug his hand into her hair and kissed her hard, he probably bruised her lips, but he didn't care and she didn't back off.

It crossed his mind that a hundred kisses should have led up to this one. The hunger was raw. Passion pounded in the silence and still she didn't pull away. All the need, all the wanting came back, slamming against his senses, blinding him for a moment to anything else.

She suddenly pulled away, gulping for air. Staring at him, as if she'd never seen him before.

Jack felt anger inside him that he couldn't understand. Was she playing him? Or had she felt this way always and hidden it so well from him? If so, he felt cheated.

"Why'd you do that?" His words were so hard he could almost feel them hit her.

"Because I don't know how or when it's going to happen, but I think we're going to be together, Jack. Maybe forever, or maybe for a one-night stand that will haunt us both. We've had this primal need for each other even before we were old enough to understand it."

So that was what it was for her, a primal need, nothing more. She didn't love him or care if he loved her. And she'd just proved her point. He had the same need. But for him it was far more.

He straightened. "Shan, you don't have a romantic bone in your body. A kiss, or even sex, shouldn't be dispensed like a handshake." He didn't have to think deeply to confirm his theory. Not one time came to mind when she'd flirted with him. If a girl wanted a guy, you'd think she'd at least wink at him. "Maybe I'd be more comfortable with it if you acted like you were attracted to me before you kissed me like that. You could take me out to eat and we might even talk. Maybe you could tease me with a few accidental brushes before you dictate who's going to be on top."

She lifted his hand and put it on her cotton shirt at breast level. "How's this? If we're going to be together, at some point we'll have to start touching each other. So, start now. You might as well know, I'm not the least bit top-heavy."

"Not romantic," he said without bothering to remove his hand. "And I don't care how big your breasts are. Believe me, I've looked at your body enough to have already guessed that fact."

"But I have great legs."

"I know. I've seen you in shorts. If you didn't— now, that would be a deal breaker. But you're still not romantic."

She raked her fingers into his hair. Too hard. Too quickly.

He retreated a few inches.

She pouted.

He grinned, knowing if she kept on this attack plan, he'd probably lose the battle. "Your breast feels nice." In truth he couldn't feel much except her bra and a real sensation that his scalp might be dripping blood in a few places.

If she was trying to turn him on, the electricity was definitely off.

He moved his hand away. He knew Shannon. Raised by a father. She'd spent the past three years proving she was as good as or better than any one of the guys. She ran straight into any challenge, and apparently, he was her new conquest. At school she'd wanted to be the best at everything she tried, and all of a sudden, she wanted this. He was this week's project.

Jack touched his head, testing for a wound. He wasn't even sure what "this" was. An experiment? An attack? A way to push him away? If so, the plan was working.

A truck drove by and honked at them. Jack thought of ignoring this, whatever it was, that had just happened. Nothing felt right.

"I can't just have sex with you on the side of the highway, Shannon. That's not how love works."

"Who said anything about love? My parents loved each other once, and what a mess they made. I've heard Mom keeps falling in and out of love, and I don't think my dad will ever touch another woman. They're both messed up. I plan to keep it simple. We're adults. Our bodies seem to need each other."

"You make it sound as simple as the lottery. Pick a number and take your chances."

"Why not? I'll finish school in a year. You're already out. If this works out, we'll date a few years, maybe get married and travel the world. We both want the same things, Jack. Someday we'll want other things, but right now we both want to serve our country, have adventures and have sex. I thought this summer would be a good time to start on that. I've already covered the birth control part. You could stay over when I'm home and Dad's not. Maybe I could fly up to where you're stationed for a weekend. Or we could meet halfway, get a hotel, but that sounds weird. Like we're doing something wrong."

"I don't just want sex. I'm sure it would be great but..." Jack could not believe he was saying the words. "I want more."

"More what?"

"I don't know, but I'm starting to feel like a lab rat. We finish school. We have sex. We marry and have 2.5 kids."

"I only want one."

He studied her. "It's not that easy."

"Sure it is. You'll get fixed after I give birth."

"No, not that. Life is not that easy. Love, dating, marriage isn't that easy. You can't just map it out. Life doesn't work like that."

"I know, Jack. There are a million variables, especially in our careers. I've lived this way all my life with my dad. I remember when I was five and started school. He walked me the three blocks listing all the what-ifs that could happen. I was prepared for everything from a dog bite to the apocalypse before I could read." She frowned. "Then, when I got home from school that first day, he was gone. Called to duty. I had to wait a month to tell him how my first day of school went."

Jack had always known this side of Shannon. She'd always been the one to come up with a plan. The one who thought about every scenario. But he thought that once they started dating, she'd fall hard in love. He'd kind of been looking forward to cuddling on the couch and watching a movie while they touched under the covers, or lying in bed just getting to know one another. Maybe stealing kisses and touching when no one was watching, or standing in the rain because they couldn't pull apart long enough to run inside. He'd dreamed about having mind-blowing sex, sleeping awhile and doing it again.

But nowhere in his plan had he ever thought they'd just come up with a strategy and put it into action as if it were a battle plan.

He closed his eyes. "Say something nice about me, Shannon."

She thought a moment. "You are the best guy I know. You always have been, Jack. We have the same values. We're from the same town. I'm attracted to you physically."

A van passed, honking wildly, then pulled off the highway.

"What was that about?" Shannon turned to look back.

"That's my parents. Apparently, they didn't leave early either."

Five minutes later, Jack was hearing all about the flat his dad had and how hard it was to find anyone open to fix it properly.

His mother chimed in. "The good thing is we found you. Now we can caravan."

Jack looked straight at Shannon. "You're right, Mom. How about my brothers ride with me so Shannon can enjoy a visit with you?"

His mom looked delighted as Ben and Harry rolled out of the back seat looking like they'd just received an early release from prison.

Shannon gave him an "I'll kill you later" glance as she climbed in with his mother.

Jack hated to sacrifice her, but he needed time to think. His two older brothers would talk so much he'd have time to himself. Sure enough, they spent an hour complaining about their wives and how there was no time to even go fishing since the babies came. One said if they had another kid he'd have to clone himself just to get any sleep. The other claimed he and his wife were too worn out to even think of having sex, so they didn't have to worry about another kid.

Finally, Jack asked them if they had it to do all over again, would they get married?

Both said yes.

"Why?"

Both were silent. Then Harry answered. "It's life, man. I love my wife. I'd die for my kids. It's a messy time, but I don't want to miss it."

To his surprise, Jack watched them change. They started talking about all the things they loved. Holding your kid for the first time. Knowing there's someone to hold your hand if you get sick. Building a home with another person. Not just construction, but a life.

When his parents' van pulled off at a Denny's for breakfast, both his brothers called their wives while they waited for the food.

Jack felt like he'd just spent four years studying and had stepped from school into his first lesson on how to live. Maybe Harry and Ben weren't as dumb as he thought they were. They worked hard all day long and went home to families they loved.

He reached for Shannon's hand under the table and he wasn't surprised when she pulled it away. The only thing that made him feel good right now was, if possible, she was as naive as he was about how any relationship worked.

Another fact he chalked up as new. His two dumb brothers knew something he didn't know.

One other crazy thought came to mind as everyone ate and moved with the flow of a rambling conversation. Jack wondered if Shannon would be all right if he felt her breast again. That was the only part of their fight he'd liked. Except the mind-blowing kiss that left him feeling like he had a hangover. A moment later he thought of slamming the Denny's platter into his face. After that kiss, he'd turned her down and now he was thinking about touching.

Grow up, Hutchinson, he almost said aloud. No matter how old he got, Jack had a feeling part of him would always be in junior high when it came to Shannon.

twenty-six

Shannon

WHEN THE HUTCHINSONS dropped Shannon off at her darkened house, Jack's mom asked if she was all right going in alone.

Shannon almost answered that she was always alone. Even when her father was home, he was often working. She was an only child with one parent and one part-time grandmother. Alone was her reality.

Thanking them, she grabbed her suitcase and bag. "Tell Jack congrats one more time. You must be very proud of him."

"We are," Mrs. Hutchinson said. "And of you, dear. Only one more year to go and you'll be off on your own. Jack said you're studying computers, not planes. I'm sure that will be a fascinating career." Her lack of enthusiasm hung like humidity.

Shannon tried to smile and managed a wave as they drove away. *On my own. Nothing new. And when I graduate, I plan to spend ten hours a day with a machine.*

She unlocked the door, dropped her bags in the living room and grabbed the house phone. There would be no contacting her dad this late. He was either in DC by now or already on a flight to his destination.

She dialed Zoe as she looked around her black-and-white house. Dad couldn't match colors. Even her clothes had been black-and-white until she started shopping for herself at eight.

"Hi, Shan." Zoe's bubbly tone made Shannon smile.

"Hello, Zoe, how is the Big Apple tonight? Wish I was there with you and Emily tonight. We could do the town. We could stay up all night talking. We could find someplace to have tea."

Zoe's bubbly laughter came through the phone. "Emily and I were just talking about you. Wishing you were here, but glad at least one of us made it to Jack's graduation. How'd he look in his dress blues? Handsome enough to eat, I'll bet?"

Shannon smiled. Talking to Zoe was always like jumping into the middle of a conversation. "Is Emily beside you? Can she hear me?"

"She just stepped into the shower. We have to go out on the town. It's New York, you know."

"Good." Shannon kicked off her shoes. "I need to talk to someone and I don't want to worry Emily with my problem."

"Got you, sister. I'm here."

Shannon relaxed. Zoe might have a butterfly's attention span, but she was always there. No matter what the problem, she was on Shannon's side, whether it was celebrating or confessing.

"I think I've finally screwed everything up with Jack." Shannon straightened as if she was about to testify before a court.

"Impossible. He's always been crazy about you, even when you beat on him. Masochistic complex, if you ask me. Jack's your someday fellow when you get around to turning his direction." Zoe giggled. "I always figured if you ever got tired of picking on him, I'd invite him over to cry on my shoulder, or any other body part he liked. Surely someone's taught him to kiss by now, so we could've moved on to the fun stuff."

"Go ahead. Invite him up to New York. I think if he ever did like me, I killed that spark. Take my advice—don't waste time telling him what's going to happen. Just surprise him."

"You explained the plan of attack, Shan?"

"You know me, Zoe. I have to live in order. All that falling in love mush never applied to me. I just told him it was time we got involved."

"What else?"

"I told him we should start having sex."

"Sounds like something he'd like to hear. What else?"

"I put his hand on my breast."

"With clothes or without?"

"With." Shannon closed her eyes, wishing she could live the day over, starting with him picking her up and ending with not having to listen to his mom for four hours.

"Not good," Zoe whispered. "I think men usually like to do that themselves."

"I thought I'd save time. We were parked at a rest stop and there wasn't much privacy."

Zoe laughed. "Shan, you've got to read a few of those romance books I keep sending you."

"It's too late. Jack and I are over. If he'd wanted to ever talk to me again, he wouldn't have had me ride with his mom and dad all the way back home. I would say it's over between us, but I think, more accurately, it never began. We've always had school and the air force, but if the time hasn't been right by now, it never will be."

"But we all agree Jack was meant for you. You balance each other. You're both smart. He makes you laugh and you ground him."

Shannon refused to cry. "I know, but I pushed him away for too long. He's got a good soul, Zoe, but he'll match better with you or Emily. Not me." She almost added that she was meant to be alone, but that just sounded too sad. "I want to be single for a while, then marry someone like my dad."

Zoe's voice came through in a whisper. "Jack is like your dad."

"No, he's not. It's over, Zoe. He doesn't love me."

The phone was silent for a long minute. Then Zoe asked, "How can I help, Shan?"

"Talk to Jack. Make sure he's all right. He always tells people you're his best buddy. Someday I'll tell him I'm sorry for all the hell I put him through, but he's better off without me. I've got to work on being me before I start being a couple."

"You're sure?"

"I'm sure."

Zoe's tone lightened. "I raise my teacup to you, Shannon Morell. To what might have been and wasn't and to what will someday be."

Shannon grinned. "Always a poet and a good listener."

"I agree. I'll tell you all about Emily's and my time in New York later, but right now, we have to get ready to go to a party. I plan to get smashed and Emily can't wait to meet the playwright who wrote the production I'm in. She says she wants to talk to him about plot. Which is strange, since I couldn't find one in this new play. But, on the upside, he's a corner sitter like her. They should get along fine, and when we leave Em can help me find my way home."

Shannon laughed. "Take care, Zoe. Don't go too wild."

"Take care, warrior. Brighter days will come."

twenty-seven

Mack

MACK'S FLIGHT WAS delayed in Denver. First, because of a storm off the western coast, then because of scheduling problems. He arrived late to DC and learned other members of his team had been held up at LAX. The departure for the mission was on hold, but he had been told to stand ready.

He had rushed from Jack Hutchinson's graduation to make it back to DC to board an overseas flight, and now it might be two days before he left the States.

He'd tried to call Shannon a little after dawn, but guessed she was driving home from the academy with Jack. The cell phone he'd bought her must be out of range. It would take a day to fly back to Laurel

Springs, and before he could unpack, it would be time to come back. He was stuck in DC.

Midafternoon, he called Alexandra in New York, just to talk, but when she heard he was alone and frustrated in DC, she said she'd call him back later. They could talk into the night. He'd tell her all about the graduation and she'd tell him about Zoe's tenth play in three years. Most closed within a few weeks, and the ones that hung on never made enough to pay the rent.

He remembered the Christmas Emily moved into her tiny apartment over the newspaper office. Zoe had only stayed a few days to help, but she'd sent decoration suggestions to Mack for weeks.

That holiday was when he felt like he'd really found Alexandra. She'd been a friend because their daughters were close, but that winter, he'd discovered there was far more to Alex than her sweet smile and her talent as a baker.

They'd gone far beyond friends with few words cluttering their relationship. Neither talked about a future together. They'd both traveled that road before with another and barely survived the crash when it ended.

Somehow, in the silence, what they had was crystal, beautiful and fragile.

Mack was restless as he waited for Alex to call. He didn't care what they talked about. He just wanted to hear her voice tonight.

The hotel room boxed him in. The assignment worrying his mind. Thanks to the weather, he had time to sleep or plan, but uncertainty would keep him on edge.

This assignment was supposed to be simple, a cleanup operation. Collect the statements from all involved; get the facts all lined up. He'd be home in less than a week. Two, at the most. If all went right, it'd be two weeks and he'd be holding Alex and, as he always did, he'd have to learn the feel of her all over again.

When he got back, maybe he and Shannon would have a couple of days, too, before he had to fly off to the next assignment. His daughter was quickly becoming a headstrong woman he was very proud of and he wasn't surprised that she seemed to love the possibility of a career in the air force as much as he had twenty years ago.

They'd get together and maybe go hiking up near the Garden of the Gods, if her off time matched with his. If he got home fast and all in one piece. The assignment might be easy, but the location wasn't.

Nothing new, he told himself.

Mack went down to the bar, his cell phone in his pocket. For once, he didn't want to be alone, and having strangers around might take his thoughts off the bad feeling he had about this "easy" assignment. One fact, one tiny piece didn't add up.

Hell, maybe he was getting too old for this kind of work. He'd go to fifty, retire and buy a fishing pole.

A few beers and the mindless roar of half a dozen TVs all blasting different games finally dulled his worry. He ordered a sandwich to go, knowing the kitchen would be closing soon.

An hour later, he was watching the end of the Texas Rangers game when Alex walked into the bar. Her long legs looked great in black pants tucked into soft leather boots and a white sweater with one shoulder bare, showing freckles. She looked cute, stylish, and as always sexy as only a redhead can look. He sometimes had a hard time believing she had a daughter the same age as Shannon.

Damn if he didn't love seeing her smile. Every time he saw her, whether they'd been apart three days or three months, that smile drew him. And tonight he saw a hunger in her twinkling blue eyes when she looked at him.

"Hello, Red. I had a feeling you'd catch the first train out of New York heading to DC."

"You know me well. The girls were going out to eat with cast members, then to a party tonight. They invited me, but it's not my kind of crowd. The play went great last night. She did her few lines like a natural, and she wanted to celebrate on their one night off."

"Does she have any idea where you disappeared to?"

Alex shook her head. "Nope. The party will last all night and she and Emily will sleep all day. I told her we'd go to dinner tomorrow night."

Mack slid his hand down her back. "We've got time, then. Almost twenty-four hours."

He took her carry-on bag as he slid off the bar stool.

Alex picked up the takeout still in a plastic bag. "For me?"

"Just in case you came." He grinned. "I figured you'd be hungry."

The first time they'd got together circled in his mind.

Their daughters had been staying overnight at Emily's apartment, and he'd asked her to go grab a bite after they'd bumped into each other on Main. They'd decided to walk to a café, even though a frost hung in the early spring air.

It had taken a while, but they were finally alone, with nothing but time on their hands. She'd told him what she wanted over the phone a few times, but while they'd been working on the apartment, they'd had no time to meet. Or, more accurately, act on her suggestions. Both had been waiting for the moment when they had no one around. He was rarely home when Shannon was in school. He saved his days for the weekends and the breaks when she left the academy. But then it seemed the girls were always with them.

Finally, three months after she'd asked him if he saw her as a woman, they'd found themselves alone in a local bar that served the worst Mexican food in Texas. Somehow, he'd managed to keep up with the conversation while he studied her. Neither seemed to want to waste time flirting or teasing. When he'd paid the bill, he took her hand and she held on tight.

As he'd started toward his car, she'd pulled him around. "We can walk to the bakery. No one will be there."

He threaded her arm around his and they strolled slowly down Main. When she unlocked the bakery door, they stepped inside without turning on any lights.

Slowly, testing his way, he slid his hand inside her jacket and put his arms around her waist. "You all right with this?"

"Yes," she answered, but her body seemed frozen in place.

"We can talk, Alex. I don't want to rush you."

"No. I don't want to talk about this. Not at all. Not ever. I just want you."

"But it'll change things between us."

She moved closer and whispered, "Make love to me, Mack. It's as simple as that."

He had no idea what was going through her mind. All he understood was that she wanted him to think of her as a woman and he'd done that ever since the day he'd met her.

Leaving their coats on a chair by the door, they walked in shadows up the stairs to her small apartment, and without a word, he silently gave her what she'd asked for.

And more, Mack thought. He'd left his heart behind when he slipped out of the bakery door at dawn.

Things hadn't changed much in the three years since, Mack thought as he stepped off the elevator. Every time they met was like the first time, the best time for both. And they got together whenever they could. Sometimes in Laurel Springs. Sometimes in DC, when she'd fly up to see Zoe in New York and stay over an extra day or two. Or he'd politely ask her to pick him up at DFW and they'd stay the night before driving back home.

He loved those drives. They'd agreed on only one rule. The driver couldn't take his, or her, hands off the wheel. But the passenger was free to do whatever she or he wanted.

He could count the times on his fingers that he'd been lucky enough to hold her all night, but for him, it felt like they'd had a lifetime. And tonight, they'd have hours. It was never enough, but he'd take Heaven in small slices.

Once in the room, only the lights of the city view guided him as he slowly undressed her. She came easy to him now, and he knew her body better than he'd ever know her thoughts.

They'd talk later, while he held her. She'd tell him about the girls. He'd ask questions about everyone in Laurel Springs, but Alex wouldn't talk about herself or about why she needed him.

That was all right for Mack. It was enough just to know he gave her what she wanted. She could be a mother, a friend, a baker everyone loved, but now and then, she needed to feel like a woman. His woman.

He was a man who figured people out for a living, but he didn't understand her, which disproved his theory that a man had to understand a woman to truly love her.

The first time he'd held her, Mack had known she was broken. She might never tell him the details of how she'd been abused as a child or why her first boyfriend hadn't cared enough to stay with her when she got pregnant at seventeen. But Mack made sure she knew that every time he touched her he cared deeply.

So deep he'd never hurt her. So deep he'd never leave her.

They could tell the world or keep it secret. It didn't matter to him. All he wanted was to love her.

In the silence of his hotel room, in a city neither would take the time to see, Mack lifted Alex in his arms and carried her to the bed.

As she settled in, he whispered what he'd always whispered. "I don't care where we are, Red. If I'm with you, I'm home."

She laughed and whispered back, "Me too."

twenty-eight

Jack

By the time Jack had been home three days, he was ready to leave. He thought of calling his commanding officers and asking if there was any chance a war had started somewhere in the world. His mother was either trying to kill him with sweets or pat him to death. Both brothers had talked him into babysitting the second night he was home, and his dad wanted to drive around town, showing him all the buildings they'd remodeled or built while he was away at school.

If Emily hadn't invited him to dinner at her apartment on his fourth night home, Jack might have made up some reason to leave. His mom insisted on sending food, a dessert, homemade rolls and two jars of jelly.

Jack felt like a confused Santa arriving six months early to the hidden apartment.

Em's place was beautiful in a quirky kind of way. Colorful, mismatched furniture and books everywhere. Stuffed animals and cowboy sayings like "Don't squat with your spurs on" were tucked into any open space.

Within three months after she'd moved in, Connor, her landlord, had hired her part-time to write for the paper. She still worked for Alex at the bakery three mornings a week, wrote articles in the afternoon, and ran the bookstore for Arnie on Thursday nights and Saturday mornings if he'd had a late night square-dancing.

On the rare occasion she wrote Jack, her letters were filled with local news and her love for the town. Emily rarely talked about herself, and unlike Zoe, she never called. In an odd way, her letters reminded him of the nights she'd crawled into his window when they were kids—the talks bonded them then as the letters did now.

For a shy girl who never talked in school, Emily had moved into the center of everything happening in town, and she obviously loved it. Now, two and a half years later, she had her own weekly column, and Zoe had told him Emily was writing a series of children's books about a family of fairies who lived above a newspaper office.

She'd told him once that if she could ever get all her stories out on paper, maybe her head wouldn't hurt. Who knew—it might have worked. Jack hadn't heard her complain of headaches since she'd moved into the apartment.

Jack had been so busy lately he felt like he wasn't keeping up with her. He also feared he may have lost his job of worrying about her when he saw Fuller Wilder standing in her kitchen.

Jack stepped through the door at the top of the winding staircase off the alley and forced a smile when he saw the mechanic. Dark hair, black eyes, and a solid build, obviously from working hard. Fuller might be a few inches shorter than him, but Jack wouldn't want to challenge the guy.

"Hello, Jack. You're early." Wilder grinned and lifted a hammer. "Em told me to have these hooks up before you and Shannon arrived."

Jack froze. There were so many things wrong with what Fuller said Jack started a list.

One, what was Fuller doing in Emily's apartment?

Maybe he'd come in the unlocked door as Jack had. Jack needed to talk to Emily about locking her door.

Two, since when had Wilder become a handyman? Jack was home. He could have screwed in a few hooks. Em should have called him.

And three, why in the hell was Fuller calling her Em? That was Jack's name for her.

Wilder didn't seem to notice that Jack was mute. "Want a beer?"

The guy actually reached into Em's fridge.

Jack stood, staring. He didn't have anything against Fuller, but the dropout and Emily didn't go together. A blind man could see that.

Maybe Jack should cut him some slack. Maybe Connor had hired him to fix stuff in the apartment, and Em was being nice to him. She was nice to everyone.

She'd probably offered him a beer before when he worked. But that didn't mean Wilder should just help himself.

Jack felt guilty. He hadn't been home more than a few days this year. The academy had taken all his energy. He should have made time to watch over Emily. It had been his job since he'd taught her to ride a bike.

Shannon bumped into him from behind. "Get out of the doorway, Jack. You'll let flies in." She laughed when she saw Fuller.

Jack watched Shannon walk to one of the stools facing the pass-through to the kitchen. "Evening, Fuller. Good to see you. You cooking tonight?"

"If you mean putting the frozen lasagna in the oven, yes, I'm cooking. You want a beer? I asked Jack if he wanted one and he turned to stone. The question must have been too hard for him."

Shannon glanced back at Jack. "Oh, don't worry about Jack. He always freezes rather than make any decision."

Jack ignored the jab. Maybe Wilder had helped Emily get her apartment together, maybe he did repairs around the place, but as near as Jack knew, none of them were friends with him. Em would have mentioned it in her letters. What would a guy like Fuller have in common with Emily? She'd dreamed of being a missionary when she was little. She slept with a unicorn. Fuller's mother had probably fed him beer in a baby bottle.

But, hell, what did he know? He'd spent the last four days trying to figure out what had happened between Shannon and him on the way home from the academy. She had kissed him, put his hand on her breast and then hadn't even said goodbye to him. "We're finished" was still a silent scream between them.

She was smart, beautiful and a great friend to everyone but him, it seemed. She'd never known how to talk to him—or turn him on, apparently, if that had been her plan in the car. What had she thought? Since she mentioned the word *sex*, they should do it right there.

Jack managed to walk a few steps and put his bags down. He gave up worrying about Fuller when he realized he couldn't figure out his own life. "Hello, everyone. Sorry about that. I've got a lot on my mind."

He passed the rolls to Fuller. "Mom had me wait for her rolls to cool before she locked them up in Tupperware. Which makes no sense to me. I doubt they'd dry out on the way over here. The jam's for the rolls, and the dessert is, well, the dessert. If we need one, of course."

Jack only had to glance at Shannon to know he was rambling and making no sense.

He forced a smile and gave all his attention to Fuller. "How you doing, Fuller?"

"Fine." Fuller watched Jack as if he thought Jack might burst out in a song at any moment. "Congratulations on your graduation. Em told me it's what you've always wanted."

Shannon, mutinously, moved to Fuller's side. "Jack flies jets. The air is thin up there, but we all love him despite the damage to his brain."

Jack was considering leaving when he heard someone's feet tapping up the stairs from the office below.

Emily flew in. "Sorry, I'm late to my own dinner party." Plopping a backpack down on top of a bookcase, she rushed over to Jack.

"You're finally home. It's been forever. I'm sorry I missed your graduation, but I had to make Zoe's opening night."

He swung her around. She always seemed so young, so little. She might be twenty-one, but she was still the little girl he watched over. "I missed you, Em."

"Me too."

Glancing toward Shannon and Fuller, he noticed both were smiling. No jealousy there. But when Em pulled away, she rushed into the kitchen and kissed Fuller's cheek as she thanked him for starting the lasagna.

A little too friendly toward the cook, Jack thought.

So much for wondering if the mechanic was staying for dinner. The card table by the window was set for four.

Shannon barely talked to Jack while they ate. He asked about her dad. She said she hadn't heard a word, but Jack could tell she was worried.

Zoe called from New York halfway through dinner. After she talked to Shannon and Emily, she asked to speak to Jack. He wasn't surprised when she invited him to come up and spend his last few days of freedom in the city. She had a bit part in a play, nothing big, but she'd love him to see it.

Jack didn't mention the invitation when he returned to the table. He thought about going, but Zoe's life was so different than his. Jack felt like a foreigner. Her town was New York now. He seemed to belong nowhere.

During the dinner party, Jack felt everyone was trying too hard to be happy. His friends were drifting away from him. When Em placed her hand over Fuller's, Jack knew she'd never crawl into his window to talk again. His childhood was fading before his eyes.

Emily talked about how she liked the bakery, but she loved helping Connor out downstairs. The young Larady had settled into what had been his parents' lives. He ran the paper, managed property, kept his grandmother company. Rumor hinted Connor's wife wasn't so happy, but Em said she'd learn to love Laurel Springs.

Shy Emily shone as she described all she'd seen in New York. "The three days seemed like a grand adventure. We saw everything."

Jack tried to act interested, but Shannon's obvious silence bothered him. Usually, when they argued, she'd be the first to try to make up, be friends again. But not this time.

To add to Jack's dark mood, it started raining as Emily shared Jack's mother's dessert. He noticed Shannon didn't even attempt to eat hers.

He'd asked her twice what was wrong, and she'd simply shrugged and said "Nothing."

While Wilder helped Emily clear the table, Jack leaned closer to Shannon and tried again. "You all right?"

"Can you give me a ride home? I walked over."

"Sure." Jack stood and turned toward the kitchen. "Em, this was great, but Shannon's waiting for her dad to call. How about we make it an early night."

As he said good-night to Fuller, Jack noticed how tightly Emily hugged Shannon.

Something was wrong.

Shannon didn't say a word as he drove her home. After their argument on the way home from school, he wasn't even sure they were friends. He pulled up to her dark house and simply waited.

"You want to come in and watch the news?"

"Sure." She wasn't yelling at him or trying to plan his entire future, so maybe it was safe.

They walked up to the door. He waited while she unlocked the house. The Morells were one of the few families who locked their doors. Without a word, she got two Cokes out of the refrigerator and he turned on the TV, then muted the news.

"What's wrong? And don't say nothing again, Shan." He thought he'd try the direct approach.

"Dad didn't call. Not all week. Not to let me know he got back to DC. Not when he left on some mission. He always calls from the airport."

"He's all right, Shan. He knows how to take care of himself."

She shook her head. "You don't know that."

He moved close and held her while she fought to keep from crying. "Promise me something, Shan. If you ever think I'm missing, you have to swear you'll keep believing I'm okay."

She nodded. "I just don't like the feeling of being out of control. I've always hated it. I'm proud of my dad, but I hate this one thing about his job."

"I know." Jack kissed her cheek. "Believe me, I know."

There were a dozen reasons he was mad at her. She'd acted like he didn't matter to her, then all of a sudden wanted to have sex. Not fall in love. Not talk to each other about the future. Just have sex. Then, if it worked out, she'd decide they should be together.

He was hurt, but he couldn't leave her alone, not tonight. So, he flipped through the channels, found an old movie and stayed.

At dawn, he woke to find her cuddled into his side. Pushing back the mass of straw-colored hair, he kissed her lips, which parted in invitation. Once, twice—he stopped counting and kept kissing. His hand slid beneath her T-shirt and covered her breast. No bra to block the feel of her. He caught her sigh as he kissed her deeper.

She returned his kiss for a moment before her eyes flew open completely and she shoved hard against his chest.

"What do you think you're doing?"

"Kissing you." Jack hadn't thought there could be much confusion about that fact.

"Well, stop."

"You liked it, Shan. Five days ago, you were the one who suggested I start sleeping over."

"I've changed my mind."

"No surprise there." He stood. "You're twenty-one. One of these days you'll grow up and stop driving me mad. Only when you finally do figure out what you want, you'll look around and I won't be there."

He started for the door.

"Where are you going?"

"I'm going to New York."

He was out the door before she had time to react. He was tired of being attracted to a woman who ran hot and cold. This was the beginning of his career. A new life. The one he'd been thinking about since he'd first heard Mack Morell talk about the air force.

Before he reported for duty he needed to have some fun. Zoe had offered him a party, and he was about to take her up on it.

In a few days he'd fly to Washington, DC, and report for duty. Tonight, he wanted to feel alive.

twenty-nine

Jack

LIEUTENANT JACK HUTCHINSON landed at JFK International Airport at dusk. He took a cab to Zoe's apartment, not wanting to waste time trying to figure out the subway system.

As he stepped out of the cab, amid all the noise of New York, Jack heard Zoe scream his name.

She bounced down the stoop she'd obviously been sitting on as she waited for him. As always, she seemed to be made of energy. If they'd been outlaws in the Wild West, she'd be the leader riding full-out into chaos. And Jack would be right behind her, because, after all, what are best buddies for?

Zoe, his wild, crazy, talented best friend since the second grade, jumped into his arms.

"You came, Jack! You finally came for a visit!"

Jack felt like he'd stepped off the plane and landed in confetti as he hugged her fuzzy vest and layers of beads. Holding her felt familiar, like stepping into a party. Like acceptance. Like joy. "Hello, slugger."

He found it hard to believe this small woman had once fought his second-grade fight against a third grader and won.

Everything around him was colorful, exciting, new, and Zoe was his guide as he entered Oz. They ate dinner at a little Italian café, then took a carriage ride around the park just because, Zoe swore, everyone had to do it once. Then they stood in the middle of Times Square and watched people.

Her curly red hair bounced around her shoulders, and she seemed to dance beside him. Every place she showed him made her smile, as if she was seeing it for the first time too. They stopped in a few bars, mixing with people who didn't seem to even notice they were standing next to them.

He ordered drinks he'd never heard of, while she told him all about her new play. All the actors sounded more interesting than the characters they played and Zoe loved them all.

Jack couldn't stop smiling. Her world was so different. The air seemed heavier here, spicy with smells he couldn't name. Different languages floated in the air, whispering of places he'd yet to see. And then there were the lights. The buildings that touched the sky. The sounds. They linked arms and he shortened his step so they walked in an easy rhythm. Jack felt like he owned the night.

The evening shadows melted into midnight, and the people on the streets still seemed to be in a hurry. Zoe tugged him toward her apartment, already planning their tomorrow.

"We'll have to ride the Big Bus and the subway. We'll go to the zoo and you have to see Radio City…"

He stopped listening. He didn't care where they went. Jack felt his senses go into overload as the heartbeat of the city matched his own.

Jack loved the easy way Zoe seemed to melt against him. The way they never had a pause in the conversation. The peace of not worrying about what he said or how he said it. Zoe didn't question life; she simply lived it.

"Don't you have to work tomorrow?" Jack put his arm around her, and for a moment thought it was the only part of the evening that didn't feel just right. She didn't fit into his side like Shannon did.

Zoe looked up at him with her huge blue eyes. Her hair hid half her face. Red curls bounced. "How are you and Shannon getting on?" she asked, as if it were a casual question, a simple one.

"We're not. I've got to get over this crush I've had on her since my voice lowered. I have a feeling we'll never be right. I used to think she teased me and picked on me because she was crazy about me. She's so beautiful, but she doesn't see it. And she's easily twice as smart as I am. She reminds me of that fact often. But… she rations out feelings."

Zoe turned into her building. "She's the best friend I've ever had. Kind. Honest."

Jack laughed without humor. "Yeah, I know. But I'm not what she wants, Zoe. Not really. I've got to get over her before we destroy each other." Zoe was the one person he knew he could be honest with. And besides, he'd had way too much wine to lie.

Zoe unlocked her apartment door on the third floor. "Come on in, Jack. I know the cure." She winked at him. "It's about time we finished what we started on prom night."

Jack didn't bother to argue. He'd had enough arguing for a lifetime. Right now, all he wanted to do was live. Tomorrow, he'd go back to being serious.

thirty

Alex

ALEX WOKE WHEN the phone sounded. It had been a month since she'd seen Mack in DC. For a moment, she was lost: it was too dark to know if it was midnight or dawn. Popcorn on her chest. One shoe on, one off.

She was home above the bakery. Alone. Zoe in New York. Mack somewhere working as always.

Stumbling over a blanket and one of the couch pillows, she managed to make out the time on the oven door. 2:15 a.m. Zoe never called this late. Mack never phoned when he was on an assignment. Even if he got back stateside, he wouldn't call this late, and surely one of her June brides wasn't calling this late to let her know their wedding was off and they no longer needed the cake.

As she felt her way to the wall phone she thought about how much she hated wedding cakes. But what kind of baker would she be if she posted a sign that said *No Wedding Cakes*? And added, *Also, no more* Sesame Street *birthday cakes.*

Are bakers allowed to hate decorating? Maybe she could cut her hours to something reasonable if she didn't decorate?

"Hello," she answered, already thinking how the cake she'd cooked yesterday might be turned into a princess cake. Just pull off the bride and groom and stick in Barbie at the top.

"Sorry to call so late," said the low voice she loved hearing. "Just called to see how you're doing, Red."

"Mack! You're back."

"Not yet, but I should be home soon. I just got a secure line and had to hear your voice, honey. This job is finally wrapping up and I've been gone too long this time." He paused. "I hate to admit it, but I had a bad feeling about this assignment, and it turned out to be routine. We're starting cleanup now. I'll be home by the end of next week. How about meeting me in Dallas for a night before you drive me home?"

"I'll think about that." Mentally, she was already packing. Every time they separated, she missed him more.

"You do that, 'cause it'll probably be all I'm thinking about until my plane lands in Texas. I never thought I'd miss a woman the way I miss you."

"It's only been a few weeks since we spent twenty-four hours in a DC hotel together."

"That was you?" he said, with laughter in his voice. "And it's been a month."

"It was me, Mack. I still haven't caught up on my sleep." The memory of their night was still thick in her mind. She loved the way Mack made love. She'd had sex before, obviously, but she'd never known what making love meant until Mack. "I've got another question for you." She giggled when he groaned.

"Hit me with it. It's got to be the last one. I know I've answered nine by now. That last one took me two months to figure out. I'd never thought of a bucket list."

Just as she started to speak, she heard a racket on the other end of the phone. Static.

In broken words, Mack shouted, "Have...go. Will call. Tell Shannon not to worry."

Noise flooded the line, but she thought he said, "It may take a while."

Then the phone went dead. Alex had no idea where he was or how to call him back. Maybe it was just a bad connection. Maybe he was somewhere in a storm.

Maybe all was fine.

Only Mack had never told her to tell Shannon anything. Alex knew he usually called his daughter before he talked to her because Shannon, if she was in town, would mention something about his call the next time she saw Alex.

His daughter might not know they were lovers, but she had to know they were friends.

Alex set the phone down and curled back into her nest on the couch. She wouldn't tell Shannon anything. Not yet. *Mack will call back tomorrow*, she tried to convince herself. And if he didn't…his message wouldn't comfort his daughter.

Forcing herself not to worry, Alex let her mind go back to when they'd first started.

At first there had been something exciting about keeping their encounters secret. Alex loved having this private world with just the two of them. She liked to think that she saw a side of Mack that no one else had ever seen. She teased him about his underwear and the way he folded his clothes neatly.

As they grew comfortable, he'd make her laugh at little things, and spend so much time explaining anything from the remote control to the microwave she'd fall asleep as he talked.

They agreed that telling the girls would complicate things. But Alex had a feeling Mack feared their attraction wouldn't last. After all, his last one hadn't.

If that happened again, they could both walk away without having their friends and daughters take sides.

But now, after three years, she knew she'd love Mack the rest of her life. It wasn't the fun, secret affair she craved. It was the man. She didn't care if the world knew she loved him, but at the beginning, she'd convinced him that they'd act on their feelings and not just talk about them.

They'd agreed to talk about everything except forever. And he'd stuck to the rules she'd set.

Alex didn't want to glimpse a future that might never be. She'd done that once before, and been shattered to learn none of the talk had been real. Her one lover had vanished, claiming it was all a game to him.

He'd been the hunter, and Alex, at seventeen, had been the prey. He'd left her in a hotel room a hundred miles from home. He'd run, and she'd walked away pregnant.

It took her years to risk her heart again. If she hadn't asked Mack that first question, she might never have known a great man. Or love.

Tears rolled unchecked down her checks. Deep down, she knew Mack was in trouble. Something had happened.

She also knew that she'd face this worry alone. Nothing of his was in her house. Nothing of hers was at his place. No pictures or love letters. No lovers' gifts exchanged.

An ache spread across her heart and throughout her body. An affair wasn't what she wanted. It wasn't enough. She wanted all the messy clutter of a life together. She wanted pictures and notes, people to link their names together as if they were one word.

She wanted Mack, only she'd been the one who'd set the rules three years ago.

As her cheeks dried, she watched the sun rise over Main Street.

The last of her ten questions had now changed, and she knew when he answered it her world, one way or the other, would never be the same.

Part III: January 2005

thirty-one

Fuller

FULLER WAITED UNTIL the shops on Main Street were closed. Few people were around when he walked across the road and into the alley. All seemed quiet in the world tonight. He'd been friends with Emily for four years, but they'd kept their feelings a secret from the world.

She'd always talked to him when he came in for lunch at the bakery, and he usually passed time in the bookstore on Thursday nights, but except for Shannon and Jack, no one knew they were a couple. It was a fact that just belonged to them.

Now and then, she'd whisper that she loved him when she was cuddled up in his arms, both reading different books. But they'd never gone beyond passionate kisses.

Now and then, it worried him that maybe she loved him the way she loved Jack. Friend love.

Damn, he'd hate that. He told himself that going slow was proving how much he cared about her, but sometimes he ached to show her in another way.

Fuller knew that she was too fragile to push. He'd let her take the reins on this. He never wanted her to feel like she'd been hurried into anything. She could do a lot better than a mechanic, so he promised himself if she fell for someone else, he'd be happy for her.

That was a lie, but lying to himself was a common pastime for Fuller. He told himself his dad would sober up one day and start taking some of the load. He thought that if he kept saving half the income from the shop, eventually he'd have enough to build his own house. He imagined that if he kept reading books, he'd be as smart as the friends of Em who'd gone off to college, like Shannon and Jack.

As he climbed the stairs, he thought of how it used to be before Emily woke him up. Looking back, he realized he'd just been drifting like his dad had done all his life. Not really living, just wandering through the days as if nothing ever mattered.

If nothing and no one mattered to him, he couldn't be hurt.

He didn't dream of what life might be like until Em kissed him that night he'd walked her home. Knowing her made him want to be a better man. He'd classed up the garage a little, made repairs on the house behind the junkyard, even painted it. He'd also talked his dad into working after hours. That way he didn't have to deal with customers, and he had less time to get drunk in the evening. His pop seemed to like the silence of the shop and the cool evening. Some nights he'd haul a radio out and listen to a ball game while he worked.

Not big changes, Fuller thought, but progress.

He silently opened the door of Emily's apartment, just as he always did.

The room was in shadows, but he could make out a tall man in a uniform wrapped around his girl.

Neither heard him come in.

"Jack, turn loose of my woman," Fuller said calmly.

"Not a chance. I'm never turning loose of her. She smells like strawberry scones." Jack lifted her off her feet as he turned to face Wilder. "I don't see a ring on her finger, Fuller, so I'm taking her. Finders keepers."

Fuller saw the change in Jack since he'd graduated months ago. He'd filled out a bit. He looked more sure of himself. He wore his officer uniform well.

Emily giggled. "Put me down, Jack. I have to hug Fuller. I haven't seen him all day."

"You haven't seen me since last year."

Fuller crossed his arms so his clenched fists didn't show. He'd thought of flattening Jack Hutchinson a dozen times, like every time he hugged Emily, as he was doing now. But Emily would just get mad at him. Not so much because he hit Jack, but because Fuller didn't believe that she could care for him more.

It'd take fifty years before Fuller would fully believe that she could love him as much as he loved her.

Jack was right. He should put a ring on her finger, but he couldn't until he told her the truth. One lie couldn't stand between them for the rest of their lives. But if he told her he'd been the one who hit her out on Cemetery Road that night, Emily would leave him, and Fuller couldn't live with that.

Laughing, Jack let her go, and, like Fuller knew she would, she ran straight to him. She hugged him first, then kissed him on the lips—a quick kiss, but a real kiss. Then she whispered, "I love you."

"I love you too." Fuller nodded toward Jack. "Why'd you let this bum in?" With Emily cuddled under his arm, Fuller extended his right hand. "Welcome home, Lieutenant."

"Thanks. I'm only here for a few days." The three moved toward a sitting area in the center of the room. "My dad thinks he's having a heart attack over the new zoning laws going in north of town. I flew in to make sure he's all right. 'Change' isn't in his vocabulary."

Fuller got the picture. Two years ago, Emily had started helping Connor Larady get the town's paper in shape. And now everyone in town, including Jack, who lived in Washington, DC, knew she'd have the facts. Jack's dad wasn't the only one steaming over a big company coming in to buy up land.

The local companies, like Hutchinson Contracting, couldn't compete.

Fuller motioned for them to take their seats. "How about I cook dinner and listen? You two talk."

No one argued as he unloaded groceries in the

kitchen. He watched the two talking, their heads almost touching as they peered over a map of the town.

"We want the town to grow," Emily said. "But by families, not cracker box housing developments and strip malls."

As they ate, Jack kept asking questions. He might be flying all over the world, but he still cared about his hometown.

Fuller remained silent. In truth, he was simply waiting around until Hutchinson left. Maybe because Jack was everything he wasn't. Smart, college educated, good family, great career. Fuller didn't see a real friendship happening between them, but Jack was Em's friend, and that mattered.

When the conversation switched to Zoe, Fuller paid more attention. He'd met Zoe only half a dozen times, but she was a firecracker. She was always rushing from one job to the next. From one man to another. Em told him Zoe wanted to taste everything in life.

"You know how Zoe is, Jack," Emily said. "She's as wild as they come."

Jack nodded. "I'll stop by and see her when I get back to New York. How's Shannon holding up? It's her last few months of school."

Emily looked sad for a moment. "The last I heard, her dad was still in Germany or wherever he is. We all thought he'd be home by November at the latest. Zoe's mom even planned a big party for him, but he didn't make it in. He did call and talk to Shannon a few minutes, then asked her to pass the phone to Alex. We were all there watching."

"What happened?"

"I don't know what he said, but Zoe's mom started crying. She must have been more worried about him than the rest of us. Shannon's dad seems like a man who can take care of himself, but Alex is a worrier. I should know. I've been baking next to her for three years."

Fuller watched Jack. The airman didn't do a very good job of hiding his emotions. "How is Shannon?" he asked again.

Em shrugged. "Her dad's never been gone this long. She said he was wrapping up a problem and just told her to study hard like it was no big deal. Jack, you should call her."

"I will," he said, but Fuller heard the flat tone of a lie.

After dinner, Jack shook hands with Wilder and kissed Emily's cheek. Then he surprised Fuller by saying, "I swear, you two seem so perfect together. Treat her right."

Emily grinned. "He does, Jack. You can stop worrying about me."

Jack nodded once and started down the stairs.

Fuller listened to his steps tapping down the back stairs before he turned to Emily. "He's a great guy, Em. I'm not sure he likes me, but he cares about all three of you girls."

"I know. We love him too."

"More than you'll ever love me, maybe?" As dearly as he wanted Emily, Fuller wanted her to be happy too. "I can understand why you'd want him."

"That's not true, Fuller. Jack is my friend, nothing more."

"What have I got that he doesn't have in spades?" Fuller knew this day would come.

She wrapped her arms around him. "I'll tell you what you have that Jack doesn't. Me, silly."

Then she pressed her slender body against his and kissed him. With her lips still touching his, she whispered, "I want to be more. I want to be closer to you. I need to show you how I really feel about you. Only you."

His knees almost buckled when she moved against him, allowing him to absorb every soft curve in her body.

He pulled away, tried to slow his heartbeat and took her hand. "We need to talk about something first. I'd like nothing more than for us to be together, Em, but we have to be honest first. I have to tell you the truth about something." He felt like a fish on the dock. He couldn't breathe, and his gut was being sliced open with a blade.

She threaded her fingers through his as they sat across from each other at the tiny table. "This is serious, isn't it?" She smiled. "I love that I'll know your deepest, darkest secrets. You have always been a man of mystery to me, but don't you know by now that you hold my heart in your hand?"

"Just one secret is all I have, but it eats at me that I haven't told you." He'd had a hundred opportunities and he'd always hesitated. One more day, one week, one more month before she had to learn the truth.

He hated that he was about to erase the sparkle from her eyes, maybe obliterate their friendship as well. "Remember when you were fifteen and got hit by a car one night?"

"How could I forget? It took me a year to heal and my mother took over my life. My dad was right to have me move out. In my mother's eyes everything I did was a problem she had to solve. The saddest part was, I didn't realize that she was suffering as much as me."

"Going back to that night." He closed his eyes, not wanting to see the hurt the truth would bring. "I was the one driving the car. I hit you, Em. I almost killed you that night."

She pulled her hand slowly away from his.

He kept his head lowered. There was nothing else to say. "I'm sorry" would be a poor offering in exchange for all the chaos he'd caused.

Finally, she whispered, "You were the one who held me that night too. You were the one who called 911. You waited with me until they came."

"I was the one who caused you all that pain." He wanted to touch her throat. He wished he could kiss the scars and let her know they didn't matter. She was so beautiful to him, to everyone she met. No one but Em saw her scars.

But Emily had turned to stone. She couldn't even look at him now. She was shy, an introvert who had only a few friends, and she'd just lost one.

Fuller stood. Part of him wanted to run as far away as he could. He wanted to ask her to forgive him, but he hadn't simply caused a few breaks and scars.

He'd changed the course of her life. Who knew—she might be as wild and free as Zoe if the wreck hadn't happened. Or she might be brave like Shannon. She might not talk of death sometimes as if it courted her in the shadows.

"I'll go," he said simply, guessing his face was the last one she'd ever want to see again.

"No," she said as she rose and finally stared at him, her brown eyes full of tears, her hands shaking at her sides. "If you want us to be honest, totally honest, I have to say something about that night."

Fuller didn't know if he could stand to know how much pain she'd been in or how she'd lost so much in a blink. But she had a right to tell him. It might not help with easing her pain, but she could share it. No matter how heavy the stone she threw, he'd carry it with him the rest of his life.

"You were driving fast that night. You were making a curve. I was on the shoulder, among the rocks, not the pavement. You had enough room to pass me, and I glanced back in time to see that even going fast, you'd stayed in the lane. You didn't run onto the shoulder."

"But?" She couldn't mix up the facts of that night. If he hadn't turned wide, he wouldn't have hit her.

"Fuller. It wasn't your fault. It was mine. I never told anyone, but I stepped into your lane a second before you hit me. I stepped in."

Em wrapped her slender arms around her body as if she were suddenly cold but had to deny herself his warmth. "It wasn't the first time I've walked close to death. I'd done it by the stream a few times and only ended up with a cold. Once I stared down a train, but the whistle's blast startled me and I fell backward, off the tracks. When I was in grade school, I jumped off the roof of a garden shed just to see what would happen. I broke my arm that morning, and my mother declared I was clumsy. Who accidentally jumps off a roof?"

She held his face in her hands. "Do I need to go on?"

"No." He didn't want to hear more.

"You don't want to get close to *me*, Fuller. Death sometimes calls *me*. It did before the accident, and it has a few times since."

Fuller gripped his forearm hard enough to bruise to keep his hand from shaking. "The pills those times. That was not an accident."

"Yeah. I was just trying to walk as close to death as I could. If I don't die, I win that round." Her voice was so light it came out in the whisper of her breath. "My mom's right. I'm not stable."

He scrubbed his face, hoping to rub off reality. "When was the last time?"

"Three years ago, when I had to be hospitalized. They ran all kinds of tests, but I'm good at pretending to be normal."

She moved beside him. "You didn't hurt me that night. You saved me. You held me. All my life, I've felt this numbness inside. That's when I flirt with danger. But that night, when I was fifteen, you held me. You wouldn't let death come calling."

"That's why you asked me to hug you that first time

here?" She wasn't wanting him to love; she was simply needing to hide from the darkness.

"At first," she admitted.

He opened his arms. He didn't care about the why. She moved against him. For a long while he held her tight. Finally, he said, "I believe you, Em. I always will, whatever secrets you want to share, but I wish it had been my fault. I could deal with that, even if you hated me. But this flirting with death frightens me."

"I'm better, Fuller. I haven't danced with death since that night you walked me home and let me kiss you. I saw it in your eyes in the streetlight's glow. If I'd been hurt on the falling stairs, it would have hurt you. We're tied together somehow. I have to be careful because I matter to you."

"More than anything, Em." He kissed her head. "What can I do to help you to believe just how much?"

"Stay with me. Just stay with me. I haven't thought of death in a long time. I'm busy. I'm happy. And most of all, I have you. Stay."

"Tonight?"

"Forever."

Fuller smiled. "Are you asking me to marry you or just move in?"

"Both."

"You could do better, Em."

"So could you, Fuller. I'm not an easy woman to live with. My college roommate said I was moody. She said I was lower than mold on the fun level."

"I can live with that. When you're down, I'll hold

you till dawn. But we get married right away. I don't want the town talking about us."

"I'll call Shannon and Zoe. They were coming in for our Valentine's tea party. We could be married in the preacher's office after we have tea."

"So I come in second, after the tea party?"

"Of course."

"I can live with that." He kissed her like he'd always wanted to, like they belonged together.

"Promise me one thing," he said, much later. "Promise if those dark thoughts come, you'll let me walk the dark side with you. If you lean in, I'll be right with you."

"I promise," she answered.

thirty-two

Alex and Mack

THE LAST WEEK had been a kind of hell she'd had to go through alone. She and Mack had agreed years ago to keep their affair private. She didn't feel like she could break the code. They'd kept it light. Two friends having fun, enjoying each other's company. Two lonely people, afraid to care too much.

Only she hadn't followed the rules. She did care. Too, too much.

For the first few days after his strange call weeks ago, she heard nothing. If she told Shannon about her father's phone message, that would simply mean one more person worrying, not knowing. That served no purpose. There was no way to get a call through to him.

About the time Alex was about to break and call

Shannon, Mack's daughter called her. "A rep from the government called me," Shannon said too loudly to be calm. "Said Dad was recovering from an injury. Details will be forthcoming."

Alex didn't breathe as she listened. A part of her had been expecting something like this, but it wasn't as bad as she feared. Mack was alive. Recovering. That had to be good, right?

"Alex, you there?"

"I'm here."

Shannon continued, "The man said Dad told him to remind me to call his friend Alexandra. She'd want to know."

"He's okay?" Alex held the phone so tightly.

"He will be fine, the guy kept saying. I think he thought it would calm me, but it only made me more nervous. Dad says if a man tells you a fact once, it's true, but if he says it three times, he's lying."

Shannon took a breath and rushed on. "So, I'll relay all I learned and hope it's true. Dad was in an accident. He's in a naval hospital in Germany," she said between gulps. "It's not bad, Alex. He's doing fine. The guy said Dad doesn't want me to leave the training seminar I'm in. Exact quote was 'Tell her not to come. She'll just have to sit around waiting like I'm doing.'"

"Where is he hurt?" Alex cut in, when Shannon sounded like she was crying.

"Dad told him to tell me that the worst thing about it is he'll be on crutches for a while." Shannon's voice lowered. "That's not too bad, is it, Alex?"

"No. That's good." Alex ran through facts. No head

injury. He was in a hospital. Mack was sending messages, not calling.

Alex asked for more details, but Shannon didn't know any.

"He's all right," Shannon said, sounding like she was trying to convince herself. "Just wanted you to know he might be longer coming home than he thought."

Alex could understand why Mack would play down whatever had happened. He wouldn't want his daughter to worry. Only Alex had been on the phone with Mack when whatever happened had started. She knew something unexpected had happened. She'd heard the panic in Mack's voice. If it was nothing, why had it taken him so long to call back? And if he was sitting around in a hospital, why didn't he call her directly?

"Alex, should I worry?"

"No. I'm sure Mack would be mad if we wasted worry when he's told us he's fine. You know your father. He never tells more than the facts. He's just telling us that now."

"Right." Shannon's tone relaxed. "I should stop worrying."

"Right. How about we call each other every day to remind each other of that. I think Mack would be all right with that."

"That sounds like a plan. Oh, I almost forgot to tell you the other news. Emily called and is planning to get married. Can you believe it?"

"You're kidding!" Alex was relieved that the conversation had moved away from worry.

"No, for real. I like Fuller and all. He's always helping out, but I didn't think they were serious. Like, getting married serious."

Alex tried to follow the conversation, though her
mind was still loaded with thoughts of Mack. "Fuller
has eaten the same soup at my café twice a week for
three years, and he always talks to Emily while he's
there. It didn't take me long to figure out it wasn't the
soup bringing him in. I had a front-row seat to watching them fall in love. He's crazy about her, and she
beams every time he walks in."

"I guess. But do you really think they fit?"

Alex grinned, guessing Mack's daughter would say
the same thing about Mack and her. "When is the
wedding?"

"Three weeks. Emily says she can't wait longer.
With my luck, it'll probably be the same weekend my
dad is coming home. If he's on crutches, how's he
going to drive from Dallas? I can't miss her wedding,
but I'm all Dad's got. You don't know him, Alex—
when he gets sick or hurt he's a bear. The one time he
had the flu I threatened to run away from home. Nothing I did was right. I'm thinking I'd rather transport a
dozen possums than Dad on crutches."

Alex stepped in to help, as always. "Tell you what.
If your dad does come in at the same time, I'll pick him
up and babysit him while you girls do all the wedding
stuff. You and Zoe are going to have your hands full
organizing a wedding, and if your dad comes in, he
won't want to go to a wedding on crutches."

"Thanks, Alex. You're the best weekend mom in the world."

"Glad I can help."

As soon as they said their goodbyes, Alex walked to the door and flipped the sign to Closed. If Mack had someone call Shannon, this stranger would be calling her next. She knew Mack. He'd wanted Alex to talk to his daughter, calm her down. That was why he'd told her to pass the message.

She made a cup of coffee, pulled her apron off, found a notepad and waited.

Twenty minutes later, a tired-sounding chief master sergeant called her himself. "Hi, Red." His voice sounded rusty, as if he hadn't talked in days, and she could hear the pain. "I had the doc call Shannon, but I had to call you. I had to hear your voice."

"Hello. Not as easy a mission as you thought, right?"

He coughed a laugh. "I just broke one of my rules. Never step into the line of fire. It's an easy rule. You'd think I could remember it."

She stopped breathing as she waited. He sounded so broken and alone.

"It wasn't as bad as it could have been, but I wasn't able to call for a few days. Blood kept dripping out of me. I was so doped up I was out of my head half the time and asleep the rest."

"Eight days, Mack. Eight days I worried."

Another silence, and then he added, "Thanks for not telling Shannon. It was enough that I caused you pain. You did right." He swore. "Eight days, was it?"

"Tell me what's happening now."

"I can't go into details, but looks like I'm going to be stuck with a limp. Everything else will heal, but I don't want Shannon to see me like this."

"When you're able to fly, I'll pick you up in Dallas and drive you home."

Another long silence. "That's just it, Alex. I don't want you taking care of me. I never wanted anyone to have to do that. There's a great place in DC where I can rehab. When I see you again, I want to be standing when I hug you."

She simply listened. He was hurting. He wouldn't have called if he hadn't had something he had to tell her. Something he couldn't pass along through Shannon.

"I love what we have, Alex. Every hour, every minute we've had together. Once I'm well, there are a few dozen places I'd like to take you. I've always thought I would."

He coughed again.

"Maybe you should rest, Mack."

"No. I've got to say this. I don't even want you worrying about me again. I know we agreed to keep this light, but we both know it's a hell of a lot more than an affair, even if we've never said the words. I've had time to think between sleeping pills. I came to one conclusion. I don't want to ever put you through what I had to do this last week. We can't go forward, Red. We can never take what we have to the next step. I won't make you a widow."

"I've never said I would marry you, Mack. I never said I had to have more."

"I know. But just once we have to say what can't be. I don't want either of us thinking it can ever be more."

Alex was too hurt to argue. "It's all right, Mack. Don't worry about me." She bit her lip as she lied. "I'm just glad you're safe and healing. What hospital will you be at when you hit the States? I'll send you those scones you love."

He seemed to relax. "That'd help. They're flying me stateside tonight, but it'll be weeks before I'll make it home. You sure you're okay?"

"I'm fine. The hospital?"

He gave the name, then asked, "If it's all right, I'd like to call you in a few days, once I'm in the States?"

"All right. You can talk me to sleep." In her mind she shouted, *You can tell me nothing about what you do or where you go. You can never say any words that hint of commitment or even love. You can set all the rules and I'll play along. For now.*

Two days later, when Mack settled into his room at Walter Reed hospital, he couldn't wait to call Alex. He'd been afraid that she'd be mad when he'd made it plain that what they had wasn't going to lead anywhere. He was married to his work. He always had been. Even if he thought he was in love with her, he couldn't put her through the odd hours, the being gone for weeks, and always the possibility that one day he wouldn't come home at all. He couldn't, wouldn't do that to his Alex.

He was giving all of himself that he could to her. Maybe, if he made it clear, she'd understand that he was doing it for her. The last thing he ever wanted to do was hurt Alex.

As the bakery number rang, he pictured her running to answer it. She always loved their late-night conversations. She'd be alone in her little apartment over the bakery.

Three rings. Maybe she'd been baking late and had to wash her hands.

Four, five. Maybe she'd fallen asleep. He loved how she slept so deeply in his arms, then came wide awake and stared at him a moment, as if trying to figure out if he was real.

Six, seven, eight. No answer.

He let it ring as he tried to think of every reason she wouldn't be by the phone. She knew he was going to call. She never went out after nine. Not Alex. She was a morning person.

Ten, eleven, twelve rings.

One last reason came to mind. She didn't want to talk to him.

The possibility that he'd lost her slammed against his chest ten times harder than the bullet that had sliced through his leg.

Mack hung up. He closed his eyes, realizing he'd just screwed up the best thing that had ever happened to him. He'd lost Alex.

He wasn't sure when he finally fell asleep. Maybe when the nurse shot a cocktail of who-knew-what into his IV.

He thought of buying Alex a cell phone. Then she wouldn't have to be around the bakery phone. He could reach her anywhere. If she'd pick up.

In an hour, they'd come get him for more tests. He'd be trying to walk a few steps soon. The chaplain would come in to remind him he might still die from one of the wounds left in his body.

Mack had nothing to look forward to.

He felt the warmth of the sun on his cheek and opened one eye. To his surprise, he saw red hair hanging out of a blanket on the chair next to his bed.

"Impossible," he whispered.

Alex stretched. "What?"

"How did you get here?"

"I know a pilot. He flew me in last night and convinced the doctors that I needed to be in your room when you woke up. Said it was a matter of life or death."

"Hutchinson."

"Right."

"I'll have a talk with him later."

She wiggled out of the blanket. "He's already gone. Plus, you don't have time. The chaplain will be here any minute."

"I know—he comes every day. Why are you here? I didn't want you to see me like this."

Alex leaned over and kissed Mack's cheek. "You're forty-three, Mack. It's all downhill from now on. So I guess, even battered and bandaged, I'm looking at you in your prime."

"What am I? A piece of beef?"

"No. You are the man I love. There, I've said it whether you ever do or not. Now I have one last question for you. I've put it off long enough."

"You came halfway across the country to ask me one question?"

"I did. Mack Morell, will you marry me?"

"What, are you crazy? I thought we just agreed to keep things like they are between us. I explained how I feel. I care too much to ever put you through a marriage to me."

"Question. Do you love me?"

He closed his eyes and swore for a while. When he opened one eye, she was still waiting. Damn it, he couldn't lie. "Of course I love you, Red. How could anyone not love you?"

"Then we're getting married. That's what people do who love each other and want to, for better or worse, spend the rest of their lives together. Besides, they wouldn't let me stay in this hospital with you if we're not married."

He raised an eyebrow and felt the pain of a bruise on his forehead from the first time he'd hit the floor a week ago. "So, let me get this straight. You're marrying me so you can visit me in the hospital?"

"Right, you idiot."

His head had gone from hurting to pounding. "We can talk about this later."

"No, we'll talk about it now. Do you love me?"

"I've already told you, Alex—I love you. I have for years. You're the first person I think of when I wake up and the last person I want to talk to before I fall asleep.

I've only had two women even think they loved me and one of them walked out on me. She couldn't stand this life. It was too hard. I can't put you through that. But I think I'll lose my mind if I thought you were out of my life forever."

The memory of how the night had seemed so dark when she hadn't answered her phone last night washed over him. If he could have, he'd have crawled out of his bed and headed toward Laurel Springs.

"I'm not leaving you, Mack. Not now, not ever. You're the one man, the one for this lifetime, and I'm not letting you think you're doing some kind of favor by leaving me."

Before he could continue the argument, she turned her head to the door. Two men in uniform stood beside a doctor. All three were smiling; they'd obviously heard everything.

"What are they doing here?" Mack frowned.

"Those two are either witnesses to the wedding we're about to have or referees to the fight. The doctor is here to make sure you're sane enough to say 'I do.' We'll fill out the license later."

Mack surrendered.

thirty-three

Zoe

AFTER WHAT SEEMED like a lifetime, Zoe finally got a part in a new play that she loved. It was made for her. The character was full of life, running through one exciting adventure after another. Zoe got to dance and sing in one scene and fall deeply in love in another.

On opening night, she danced across the stage like the professional she was. She said her lines perfectly. She never missed a step.

And as the curtain fell, all the audience cheered.

All thirty of them.

There was no curtain call. Backstage, all was silent for a moment. Zoe straightened and, with a smile, she thanked everyone.

She skipped the after-party and walked home alone

for a change. She didn't want company. She couldn't stand the idea of almost-friends telling her how great she was and how the play closing after one night was not her fault. They'd say the promoters hadn't done their job. The producer was just looking to fund a play that flopped so he could have a write-off. It wasn't her fault. She'd be a star next time.

When she stepped into her tiny apartment, she knew what she had to do. It was after midnight. She had plenty of time.

Zoe stripped off her jacket and tossed her shoes in a corner. Then she pulled all the ingredients from the shelf over her stove and began to bake. Almond-cranberry scones, just like her mother made, with a strip of icing on top. Thumbprint cookies like Jack loved. Lemon pound cake that Mack always had to have two slices of.

She made Emily's date bars and Shannon's peanut butter brownies in bite-sized bits. They'd be perfect for a tea party.

By dawn, every table in her apartment was loaded down with sweets.

Zoe covered each one before dropping into bed. Later, she'd box them and send them out, but right now, she needed to sleep and think of home.

The next day, the afternoon sun warmed her apartment as she cleaned the tiny kitchen. Emily called as Zoe poured herself a cup of tea. For once, quiet Emily had so much to talk about that she didn't ask about the latest play. Zoe smiled as she nibbled on a few date bars and helped Emily plan her wedding.

"You've got to come."

Zoe laughed. "Turns out I can. My next few weeks have opened up."

"And Shannon's got to come."

"Of course." Zoe felt her duty to get serious if only for a moment. "You sure he's the right one for you?"

"He's the only one. I think I knew it when I first kissed him."

"Then you've got to marry him. Sounds like you kissed a frog and got a prince on the first try. And me, I've kissed half the frogs in the pond and I'm still looking."

"Do you really want just one prince?"

Zoe laughed. "No. Maybe I've got just what I want, too—variety."

An hour later, when she turned on the lights and closed the shades, Shannon called to tell her that Mack was wounded and in a hospital, and Zoe's mother had flown out to be with him.

Zoe felt like she'd celebrated with Emily and now she worried with Shannon.

At eleven, the hall pay phone rang again, but the connection wasn't clear. She thought she heard her mother say that she was staying at the hospital with Mack. He'd been hurt, but was recovering.

"That's nice, Mom." Zoe felt worn out. "I've got to get some sleep, Mom. I'm glad you're sitting up with Mack."

Alex hesitated. "I love Mack, Zoe."

"I know, Mom. I love him too. You watch over him."

Her mom laughed. "How about we talk about it

later, honey. You sound so tired. Just tell me how the play went."

Zoe smiled. "I'll get it right next time, Mom."

"I know you will, sweetheart. There's always next time."

"Mom, one last thing—I'll mail you my new scone recipe. It's better than you make at the bakery."

"We'll see." Zoe could almost see her mother smiling. "Did you put a secret ingredient in them?"

"You know I did, and this time it might just work."

"It might." There was silence for a minute before she added, "You know, no matter how bright your star shines, you'll always be a baker's daughter."

"I know. I'm very proud of that. Love you, Mom."

"Night, princess. While you're home, help the girls keep the bakery open."

"Will do." As she hung up, Zoe decided to leave tomorrow, help Emily plan and help her mom by watching over the bakery. With nothing on her calendar, she had time to spend a few weeks back in Texas.

Maybe she'd dance to a few slow songs for a while. Then she'd return to New York and jump back into double time.

thirty-four

Emily

EMILY STOOD IN the bedroom she'd grown up in. Her mother was fussing with her hair, and for once, Anna Waters looked happy.

"Fuller seems like a nice boy, but it's just too soon. I'm not ready for my baby to get married. You're only twenty-two." She grinned. "Same as I was, I guess."

"We'll be fine. This is what we both want, a small wedding with only family."

Anna Waters stopped long enough to blow her nose. "I know. He told us when he came to the house to ask our blessing. It's the marriage, not the wedding, he said. I was all ready to ask a few questions when your father just stood up and shook Fuller's hand like it was a done deal. There was nothing left for me to do but welcome him to the family."

Emily grinned as she silently thanked her dad. "Why don't you and Dad go on a cruise to celebrate how much money you've saved?"

Anna raised her double chins. "We might just do that."

Emily grinned. "I'm happy, Mom. Relax. Be happy for me."

"I am." Tears dripped down her cheeks as Emily's mother added, "I truly am."

Emily decided she'd better move on fast. "Zoe flew in from New York last night and Shannon drove home from Colorado. I'll have my best friends standing beside me. Isn't that grand?"

In her mind, she was already at the tiny chapel next to the Baptist church. She had a feeling the only person she'd really see today was Fuller.

Half an hour later, her dream came true. Her father walked her down the aisle and her mother cried.

Connor Larady and his family sat on Fuller's side because Connor said Wilder had saved his life once. The rest of the guests were on the bride's side, but it didn't matter.

Fuller looked too nervous to care who was there. His gaze never left her face. In his new black suit and with his midnight hair cut a bit shorter, she thought he was the most handsome man in the world.

As they walked the three steps to the preacher, he whispered, "I got what I wanted in this life. I get to watch over you, Em. I don't think I even had a heart until you came into my life."

Emily smiled, realizing that for this moment there were no shadows hiding in the corners of her mind. Maybe being happy, being content, was simply finding someone to love. She drifted through the ceremony and the reception without turning loose of Fuller's hand.

At his side was where she wanted to be.

Zoe's mother didn't make it to the wedding. She'd left for DC to welcome Mack back to the States. He'd told Shannon she had to be there for Emily, and if anyone thought it strange that Alex had flown out to meet him, they didn't comment.

Fuller's dad showed up to the reception at the bakery. He said he couldn't find his watch, which Fuller mumbled was as good an excuse as any. Bill was relatively sober, but Emily saw the uncertainty in his watery eyes as he awkwardly kissed her hand.

Bill seemed a bit lost. With his son getting married, his world was about to change.

Fuller, as he'd obviously always done, calmed him. "It's all right, Dad. You stay in the house on Wilder Fort for as long as you like. It's your home now. I'll make sure groceries are delivered there every Monday. Emily and I plan to live in her apartment for a while, and then I want to build her a house on the only lot left on Willow Road."

Bill nodded. "I'll help you paint the new house. I'm good at that."

"Thanks, Dad."

Fuller leaned closer to whisper to his dad. Em was near enough to listen. "She thinks of our new house as a someday dream. I didn't tell her that I've already paid cash for the lot and by this time next year I'll have enough to pay the Hutchinson brothers to frame up the house."

"That's great, son." Bill glanced at Em. "I won't say a word."

"Thanks, Dad. I figure I got my dream of forever today and I want to make sure Emily has hers."

As Bill wandered toward the punch bowl, she whispered to Fuller, "I love you. You're good to him."

"It took me a while, but I realized maybe life never gave him a chance. He had no family. His almost-wife left him. The war broke him down. I'm all he's got."

She laced her fingers in her husband's and added, "He's got us both now."

Five minutes later they were running down Main to Fuller's pickup. He lifted her up and set her on the seat. "We better get going. We only have three days for a honeymoon."

She laughed. "No, Fuller, we've got the rest of our lives."

Part IV: Summer 2013

_____

Journal entry: Somewhere over the Rockies

There are times in life when you drift through the years as if floating on a river. You weather the currents and sleep during calm waters while somehow the world changes and you remain the same.

As I began my tenth year of flight, I realized I was passing over life, looking down from 40,000 feet, not living it at all.

It was time to change my course, but I seemed to have lost my compass.

Captain Jack Hutchinson

thirty-five

Jack

HIS HOMETOWN HADN'T changed much over the past nine years Jack Hutchinson had been in the air force. The few days he spent there over Christmases and now and then to attend a wedding or funeral hadn't given him much time to look around the place.

He'd heard the big housing development had failed. No one wanted to commute over a hundred miles a day just to live in a small town.

Only today something had changed. He could almost feel it in the air as he drove toward the house he'd grown up in.

Today, Dad wouldn't be there. Or at his office. He'd never answer the phone saying, "Yellow." As if he thought it was a joke.

John Hutchinson had been sick several times last year. A cold that moved into pneumonia. The flu that lasted two weeks. Chest pains that they thought might be a heart attack. He'd seemed to be moving from one illness to another.

Jack's brothers took over the construction and Mom made it to the office most mornings to do the book-work and ordering. John showed little interest in the company he'd started as he slept through most mornings. Jack's mom would drive him out to the construction sites, but the last few times he didn't want to even get out of the car.

A few weeks ago, Jack had talked to him. His dad had complained that he had a cough and his knees were bothering him, but not enough to bother a doctor with either complaint.

The last thing he'd said to Jack was "Keep flying, boy. The view's always better the higher you get. I should know. I've spent most of my life digging."

Jack hadn't called his parents last week. He'd seen on his sister-in-law's Facebook that the family was planning a picnic. He'd been in flight while the rest of his family were cooking out.

A week later, when Jack heard his mother crying as he picked up the phone, he knew his father was gone.

Jack flew home, dressed in a black suit he rarely wore. Today, he'd stand around while all the arrangements were made. Tomorrow would be the funeral. Everyone in town would be there.

Everyone but Dad.

Jack was thirty-one. John Hutchinson had been

sixty-two. The possibility that Jack had lived half his life sobered him. He felt like he was treading through waist-deep water. Just keep moving.

The visit to the funeral home and the talk from the preacher weren't comforting. An hour later, he was polite when he had door duty. Letting people in and out. Taking neighbors' food, thanking them, collecting the cards when flowers arrived. Putting up with everyone hugging him and saying words of wisdom, like "this too will pass" and "at least he didn't suffer long."

Finally, the doorbell stopped ringing and the family sat down to a feast no one wanted to eat.

"Jack," his oldest brother started, "Harry and I would like to talk about the business sometime while you're here."

"Not now," his mother said as she left the table without eating a bite. "It's time to round up the children. They've had a long day and tomorrow will be the same." Both daughters-in-law joined her, but the boys remained.

Jack stared at his brothers. "What's the division now on the business?"

"About the time you graduated, Dad cut us in as partners, but he made it clear that when he died, you were to step in as the third partner if you wanted the spot."

Studying them closely, Jack saw the worry. A partner not working for the company would cost them. If he said he didn't want any part of the business, he'd insult them. They both had families, and Jack doubted a cut would be welcome.

"What about Mom?"

"She's got social security and the house is paid for. If she needs anything, we'll watch over her. A while back she said she might take the weekend shift at the hospital when Dad got better, but he never did. At sixty-two, a shift on her feet won't be easy. She's never let us pay her a dime for doing the books."

Jack looked straight at his brothers. "You two are the reason Dad was able to keep the company going. I've watched you both take over and grow what he started. If I move back home, I'd expect to be offered a job. Paid for the work I did, that's all. But right now, I've got a commitment to Uncle Sam and you can handle things here."

They still stared as if waiting for the other shoe to drop.

"I've thought of a split that I think would be fair to us all. How about Dad's share of the profits goes to Mom? She'll need it just to keep up with all the grandkids' birthday gifts. She'll feel better knowing there's money in reserve. If she doesn't have to go back to work, maybe she can still help out at the office. I think she's always liked being a part of the team."

Both brothers nodded.

"Great idea," Harry said. "Ben and I are both worthless in the office. We were worried about having to hire someone."

"One other thing," Jack added. "When I move back, you two build my house at cost."

Harry smiled. "Only if you get your hands dirty and help every day till the carpet goes in."

"Fair enough." Jack stood and did something he'd never done. He hugged his big brothers, and, to his surprise, they hugged him back.

As he turned, he saw his mother standing at the door, crying and smiling at the same time.

Jack felt sixteen again. "Since I don't have any homework, Mom, you mind if I go over and see a friend?"

She lifted one finger. "You be home by midnight."

Jack kissed her cheek. "I will, Mom."

As he stepped out of the house and walked toward his rental car, Jack smiled. He'd done the right thing. Logic told him he'd never move home. He'd never join the family business. But he'd left the door open. That was the way they wanted it, and he did too.

As he drove down Main, Jack noticed the lights of the bakery were still on. The place was so cute, someone should shrink it down as a Christmas ornament.

Circling, he parked out front. He saw Zoe moving tables around inside the bakery. For a moment she looked like a kid again, working in her mother's shop. Her wild red hair was tied up in a square that was probably one of the lunch napkins, and her T-shirt was so long it could almost be a dress.

He tapped on the glass and she looked up. For once, she didn't run to hug him when she opened the door. She waited.

"Sorry about your dad."

"Me too." He stepped inside and, as always, the wonderful smells surrounded him. Only something was new, different.

"Want to talk about it?" Her big blue eyes were blinking back tears.

"Not really. What's that smell?"

She backed toward the counter, pulling him along with only her fingertips. "It's a new tea I'm trying. Lemon Jade Sencha. Green tea, marigold petals and lemon peels."

"Got any coffee, slugger?"

"Jack, you've got to try the tea."

"All right, but, Zoe, you've got to tell me what you're doing in your mom's shop making tea. This is a bakery, you know."

"I've come home to stay awhile, and Mom suggested I try some new ideas out on her customers. Over the years, I started dividing my time between here and New York. It's fun to help Mom out. Calming after the city. Only this time, I packed up my apartment before I left."

"You left New York? Why, Zoe?"

"I'm not really sure I have a plan. It just seemed time. Maybe I was tired of dancing in double time. I was losing the lease on my apartment anyway, so living here is better than being homeless. I'm a butterfly, remember. I can live anywhere.

"Mom's gone to Dallas to pick up Mack. They always spend a few days alone before coming home, like they're newlyweds. So, I decided to try serving teas in the afternoons. I rearranged her shop. Coffee shops are everywhere, so maybe it's time for a teashop."

He looked at the mess of tables and chairs. Double what Alex usually kept in the small place where she served lunch. Raising one eyebrow, he stared at his friend.

She rolled her eyes. "Let me explain it, flyboy. If we move this counter back three feet, we can get in more tables. Now that it's summer, there's room for half a dozen on the walk, and the balcony above will offer some shade."

"And why are you doing this? In a few weeks you'll be gone, and Alex will have to clean up the mess."

"I told you. I'm staying awhile. Mom seems run-down. I'm doing her a favor by taking over while she gets some rest. She's been sleeping late while I've been home. I may not be as good a baker as Mom, but I can handle the business while she rests."

Jack studied Zoe. She was thinner than usual. Her eyes had dark lines beneath them. Maybe New York had finally worn her out. "Your mom's not the only one who looks tired."

"I'll be fine, Jack. You know me. I'll bounce back. In the meantime, I'm having fun here and helping out."

He decided to play along. "So, tell me our plan for this place."

"Mom has always worked from five to one. After that, this place is dead. I was thinking I could open a teashop with hours only from three to five. I'd serve her great scones and muffins. Then I'd have teas from all over the world. I'd have special teas for the different seasons and this wall—" she pointed to the side wall that had no use "—I could stock all the stuff that goes with tea. Teacups to go. T-shirts that say Tea Shirts. Little teapots."

He grinned at his wild friend. "Zoe, folks in this town drink coffee, sweet iced tea or beer."

"If I build it, they..."

"I doubt it." When she looked disappointed, he gave in. "All right, give me a cup of your tea and I'll help you plan. If you move the door over three feet, you'll have space for another two tables."

She hugged him. "When I have it all planned out, I'm going to tell Mom the grand plan. Not before. As for now, I'm staying in my old room upstairs, telling her I'm saving money while I work here."

As she poured two cups, he remembered the night he'd dropped by her place nine years ago. They'd slept together that night and woke up at noon with bad hangovers. He also remembered she'd taught him a few things about making out, but they never had sex. He thought he'd passed out, and when he asked her how it was, she'd laughed and said that when neither partner is sober enough to remember, it doesn't count, so they'd have to do it again. But both of them knew there would never be a rerun. What he'd needed was a friend to go wild with before he stepped into his career, and what she'd needed was to know he cared about her.

After that, she'd known he'd always be her friend, even if she didn't make it on the stage.

"Since Mom lives with Mack now that they're married, she said I could stay here for as long as I like. I think I've figured out that I don't need the bright nights or the parties. I just want to be around people I know."

Jack kissed her wild hair. "You used to say you

wanted to walk down the street and have everyone know your name. You got that here, Zoe."

She giggled. "You're right, Jack. I do."

"You need to rest. Right, Zoe?" For as long as he could remember, she'd always run full-out until she stopped. Her mother would pick her up and carry her home, always saying, "Zoe needs to rest."

He'd asked his mom about it once, and she'd said some folks were born to live in a full run, but Zoe needed to take care.

He looked at her big blue eyes now and saw a deep exhaustion. "Lots of rest, I'm guessing."

"Something like that." She shrugged his unspoken question off.

He lifted his cup. "The tea is good."

"Thanks." She patted his hand. "About your dad. Don't you know when you die, you just fly away to the next life?"

Jack nodded. Zoe's saying made as much sense right now as any other he'd heard. "Open the teashop, Zoe. I got a good feeling about it."

"Me too. I'll tell Mom all the details next week. She'll be against any change, but Mack will be on my side. Who knows—she might give me the bakery. Mack wants to travel with her. At their time of life, they need to enjoy and have a few adventures."

"Do you think of Mack as your father?"

Zoe shook her head. "No. He's always been my knight in shining armor."

thirty-six

Alex

ALEX STRAIGHTENED AND forced a smile when she saw
Mack step off the plane at DFW. He'd carried the limp
for eight years now. His reminder of breaking his one
rule: *stay out of the line of fire.*

But Mack Morell was still the most handsome man
she'd ever known. The only man she'd ever loved. Her
husband. She touched the gold band on her left hand.
How could two people so right for each other take so
long to figure it out?

They'd waited until Christmas that year he'd been
hurt before they told the girls they'd married in DC,
right after he'd made it back from the mission that almost got him killed.

When they stopped sneaking over to each other's

homes and just pretending to meet accidentally at restaurants and told their daughters the truth, they'd discovered the whole town knew about the wedding.

Apparently, Jack had heard it from a friend just assigned to JBAB—Joint Base Anacostia-Bolling. The friend had heard the story from a buddy assigned to the Walter Reed hospital.

The story went: A chief master sergeant from Texas, just back from a dangerous mission, had got married as soon as he was shipped stateside. His redheaded bride never left the hospital until they loaded him in the ambulance to be transported to the airport.

Jack said he knew the information was correct, because the whole staff claimed he was a bear of a patient and the wife was sweet as apple pie.

Alex had seen Mack at his worst that first month, she decided. Spending the next forty years with him would be a breeze. Now, even after eight years of marriage, he still took her breath away.

Mack spotted her and waved as he took the stairs, right leg first, every step. He'd been gone only a week this time. No more dangerous assignments. Now his assignments were teaching at bases all over the US.

The only time he left the States was on their yearly cruise trips. He often told Alex he'd seen all the ugly places before he'd found her, and now all he wanted was to travel with his wife to all the beautiful sites.

Alex pushed all her worries aside. What she had to tell him would wait awhile. She wanted more time with just him. There would never be enough. They'd waited until he was forty-three and she was forty to marry. Both knew they'd probably never see their fiftieth anniversary, so they had to pack more into every day they were together.

"Hi, Red," he whispered as he kissed her cheek. "I missed you." The kiss was gentle, but the hug showed that he was hungry to be close.

"Not as much as I missed you."

Mack grinned. "Zoe's home again, right?"

"Right. I think the magic of New York has finally worn off. She says she's feeling run-down. Just wants to rest awhile. I told her she could have the apartment over the bakery. We never stay there anyway and I love having her come down and work with me."

They walked toward baggage claim. "Any chance we can get a hotel here and drive back tomorrow?"

Alex shook her head. "I'm worried about her. I've never known her to be sick two months. She's lost weight."

"All right, we'll go home and take care of our Zoe. She may be thirty, but she still needs her mom's chicken soup."

"I think she's just exhausted. She's in a strange mood. Can you believe it? She claims she just wants to hang around the bakery for a while. Then she told me she was heading upstairs to take a nap yesterday. I've never seen her do either of those things."

Mack relaxed while Alex drove home. For a while they were silent. Him winding down from the week and her smiling at him, silently saying she was glad he was back.

Finally, he broke the silence. "Any chance you

could ask Emily to help Zoe with the bakery for a few weeks? I thought we might fly to London."

Alex shook her head. "Emily is in her last month of pregnancy. Fuller barely lets her walk to the mailbox without worrying about her. After three boys, they're finally going to get their girl."

"Fuller will be building onto the house again. I swear, if they have many more kids, his little house on Willow Road will be as big as all the others."

Alex pulled off the highway. "I thought we'd stop for a chicken fried steak."

"I'm not really hungry."

"I'm starving. Do you mind watching me eat? We could talk. I've got a question to ask you."

Mack grinned, knowing she was thinking about how a question had started their affair that they planned to make last a lifetime. She'd be fifty in a few more years, and he still planned to chase her around their home. The eight years they'd had of marriage wasn't nearly enough. A hundred years wouldn't be.

"I'll talk. You eat," Mack suggested.

The dump of a café didn't look like it had changed much. A new sign outside now read Best Chicken Fried Steak in the World. Country music was still rattling from the speakers. The only difference was now a dozen tables were full.

He pulled out her chair as always, then took the seat next to her. Across the table just seemed too far away. "I see that mechanical bull is still here. Looks like one of his ears is missing."

"Probably landed in some fool's skull. Those things are impossible to ride."

"I tried it once."

She giggled. "You told me. Four seconds, was it?"

"Five. I almost made the bell."

When the waitress passed, he ordered two dinners, coffee for him and tea for her. It felt good that the place, no matter how bad, was still the same.

"You remember that morning in the hospital when I talked you into marrying me, Red?"

She laughed. "I think it was the other way around."

"Might have been. I was on drugs. Anyway, it was the best idea I ever had."

"Me too." She rested her hand on his arm. "When I flew to that hospital, I didn't know what was going to happen. I just knew I wanted to be beside you. Good times or bad."

They listened to a few songs, but the crowd was too noisy to really hear. When the food arrived, she ate and he watched her.

"You said you had a question. Maybe you should ask it. I plan to take a nap when we climb back in the car. I must be turning into an old man—the time changes get to me lately when I fly."

"You're not an old man, Mack. You're barely into your fifties."

"Yeah, but it won't be many years before the air force pushes me out the door. I had an offer to do some private consulting. A kind of two weeks on and two weeks off for about the same money I'm making now.

When the time comes, I think I'd like that. When I'm not fishing, of course, and traveling with my bride."

"Mack, you're not too old to do anything."

"Right." He raised an eyebrow. "Maybe you should ask your question, Red. I got a feeling there's some adventure you want me to take. I know you've been looking for a partner at the bakery, but I'm really not interested. You'll have to find another way to cut your work time. I'm the eater, remember? You're the cook. Besides, I don't think I'm that big of a risk taker."

"What if we can stay home on this adventure?"

"I'm in."

Alex looked him straight in his intelligent eyes and asked him, "How would you like to do it all over again?"

"What? Marry you? In a minute. We could have a big wedding. Invite the whole town. Have someone else make the wedding cake."

"No. I was thinking more about starting a family over again."

His eyes lit up. "Is Zoe pregnant? Is that what this is all about? She wants us to help raise her baby?"

"No. As far as I know, Zoe is not pregnant. She hasn't even mentioned a boyfriend in months." Her grip tightened on his arm. "Mack, it's me. We're pregnant, Mack." Just to make sure he understood, she added, "You and I are going to have a child in less than five months. I thought I was just going through the change of life." She smiled. "Turns out I am. A big change."

Mack still looked blank, like she was speaking another language. "Alex, are you asking me a question? Is this some kind of game?"

"It's not a game. But I am asking you a question. Do you want to go along on this journey with me?"

"I'd go to Hell and back with you, but we're too old to have a baby."

"Apparently not. The doctor says I'll be feeling it move soon."

She sat back and ate a few more bites. He'd need time to process. This didn't fit in his organized life.

Without a word, he finished his coffee and paid out, never even touching his food.

When she headed for the door, he let go of her hand and turned back. She thought he must have forgotten something, but when she looked around, Mack was swinging his bad leg over the rough wooden fence in the corner of the café. The mechanical bull was staring at him and the waitress was laughing.

"Crank him up as high as it goes. Here's my five bucks in case I don't have enough sense left to pay. I'm taking the ride."

Before Alex could scream, Mack was on the bull. All heads turned to watch.

"No," she whispered. "No."

The waitress plugged the bull in and the bucking began.

Everyone cheered once, twice, three times. Then they all groaned as Mack flew off the bull and hit the fence. He crumbled like a cheap water bottle tossed in the sand.

A few men near the entertainment stepped in to

help him. Mack stumbled forward, blood on his chin and a goofy smile on his face.

Alex would have slugged him if he hadn't looked so beat up already. "You lost again? How many times does it take to learn?"

He put his arm around her and pushed his bruised chest out. "No, I won. I stayed on six seconds this time. I'm almost there."

As they walked across the gravel parking lot to her car, she smiled. She knew him. "That's the craziest thing I've ever seen you do, Mack. You always think everything out."

"You haven't seen nothing yet. In five months I'm going to be a father." They both laughed until tears flowed.

When they climbed in her car and drove off the parking lot, Mack leaned over and kissed her cheek.

"I'll be in my seventies by the time he graduates from the academy. Everyone will think I'm his grandpa." He frowned suddenly. "We've got tons of work to get done in five months. A nursery. Car seats for this car and my truck. A swing set. We're all settled into the house, so everything will need to be moved around. There's no room for a baby. Maybe I should follow Fuller's lead and build a room on."

"Mack, we can do this."

He let out a yell as if he was riding broncs again. "You bet we can. We've both been parents before. We know what we're doing. I say we go for it, Red. Any chance it'll be twins?"

She laughed. "I don't think so, but it may be a girl. You can't talk it into being a boy."

"I know. I tried that once. Thought I'd be disappointed if a girl came out. But a minute after I saw Shannon, I wouldn't have traded her in for a dozen boys."

thirty-seven

Jack

JACK ALMOST DIDN'T recognize the number when Shannon called. Since they'd broken up after his graduation he'd had maybe four calls from her in nine years. Usually, she was simply passing on news. She'd hurt him so badly he never tried to contact her, but he kept up with her through friends.

He'd been in Germany when she'd graduated with top honors. She probably wouldn't have wanted him around anyway. Zoe flew in and Emily and Fuller made the drive. Mack told him the three girls had decided to have tea on the parade grounds at midnight, and amazingly, no one had caught them. They'd told him a few years later that she was working for OSI

(Office of Special Investigations) in the computer research division.

Jack was proud of Shannon, but the girl he'd spent all of high school and college crazy about no longer existed. She was a captain, moving up fast in DC. She used her programming skills to guide military operations all over the world. Only she was probably happy staying in an office with a computer as her partner, while Jack flew over her now and then and thought about what might have been.

When Jack was assigned at JBAB in Washington, Emily or Zoe hinted that the two of them were in the same town and should get together for a drink sometime. He always promised he would, but he never tried.

He'd bet a hundred bucks that Shannon had told them the same thing. Neither one wanted to go into details about their breakup. It was simply that they never started.

Funny how life works. Or doesn't.

He picked up his cell. "Hello, Captain Morell. How are you tonight?"

She didn't waste time with small talk. "I wanted to call and tell you that my father and Zoe's mom are going to be parents."

"No news flash there. They have been for thirty years."

"No, you idiot. Alex is having a baby, a new one."

He laughed. "It's hard to have an old baby."

"Shut up, Jack, and listen to me. My father is going to be somebody else's father too. Isn't he too old for that? The whole thing is impossible. I'll be carrying around a baby and everyone will think it's mine and I'll have to stop and explain that we're sisters."

He laughed. No matter how old she got, Shannon always thought he was dumber than rocks and she needed to explain things to him. "We could go back to biology, Shan. I could explain how it happened between your dad and Alexandra. Even show you if you like." When he heard her mumbling, he changed the questioning. "Have you talked to Zoe? I saw her a few weeks ago when I went home for my dad's funeral."

"No. She's not answering her phone and she never remembers to charge her cell. Dad buys her one for Christmas every year and she loses them as fast as she loses boyfriends."

"I'll call her, but the last time we talked, she said she wasn't feeling well and might stay home for some R and R. Zoe's always running and running until she breaks and falls over. If she's back in New York, I'll find her."

"How can you find her when I can't?"

"Several months ago, I flew in and had dinner with her and her newest boyfriend. A nice guy, as actors go. I'm guessing he lasted a month with Zoe. He gave me his number and said if I was ever back in town he could get me tickets to the play he's starring in."

"You might try her at the bakery. If she's not there I'll call him."

Jack sat down on the leather couch in his hotel room. Since most of his flights were overseas, it didn't make sense to rent an apartment, and staying at the base was boring. Most times he simply rented a room and made use of the room service and gym on the handful of days he was in DC. "When's the last time you saw Zoe, Shan?"

"Almost a year. We'd planned to have tea, but Emily couldn't get away anywhere, and Zoe couldn't come all the way home. I didn't push it. I've been busy at work."

Jack knew how important their teas were. Maybe they were finally growing up, or worse, growing apart. He hated that, but he hadn't been much better at keeping up.

He went back to Laurel Springs three or four times a year, but he never stayed more than a day or two. Half the time he didn't call Emily and Fuller when he was in town. They were busy with their lives. Emily was a stay-at-home mom who wrote for the paper and published a few children's books a year. She was homeschooling their sons, and with more kids planned, she'd have her own one-room schoolhouse in no time.

"Jack, are you still there?"

"I'm here, Shan."

"I'm sorry I called, but I have to talk to someone and you seem to be the only person alive to answer the phone. I can't talk to Dad or Alex. I don't want them to think I'm upset about this. They called me all excited, like this was their first child."

"And, of course, you're obviously not upset."

Jack swore he could hear her teeth clinching. She didn't want to talk to him, but he was her last choice. He decided to put away all the battles between them and all the reasons why they'd never work. She needed a friend. Someone who knew her and her family and the whole town she grew up in.

"Talk to me, Shan. I'm listening."

Within an hour they'd gone through all the reasons why a sibling was going to affect her life, and had moved on to laughing about other news from home.

Jack finished his third beer and said, "I asked Fuller how many kids they planned to have. He said kids made Emily happy. They'd have as many as she wants."

"It's not like they don't have help," Shannon added. "Emily's mother babysits a couple of mornings a week. Fuller comes home for lunch, and from what I hear, he does most of the cooking. His dad keeps the lawn mowed around that beautiful house, even eats dinner with them a few times a week. Word is he's sober most weekdays. My dad says he sits in the front yard like a lawn ornament and the boys run wild around him."

"Emily's all right now, Shan. We don't have to worry about her. Turned out all she needed in life was a mechanic."

"He's a lot more than that, Jack. He's redone the old garage and has four employees now. Some say he'll be rich one day. He cleaned up that junkyard called Wilder's Fort and hired Tanner Whitaker to run a used-car lot."

"Isn't Tanner that shy kid who never talked in school?"

"Yes, but he's related to half the town. They all buy their cars and trucks from him off the lot and Fuller guarantees them to run for a year. Emily said Fuller's thinking of going in with Tanner and buying a car dealership."

"Smart."

Shannon agreed. "You getting another beer?"

"I'll have one if you do." Jack put down the phone and walked the three feet to his hotel fridge. Then he plopped back down and waited for her.

By the time they'd run through most of the kids in their high school, both were a long way from sober.

"You have to get up in the morning?" Jack asked.

"Nope. I'm off Sundays. Usually work from home after an early run."

"Me too. Only I'm stuck in DC for another week."

"What hotel?"

"The Hilton downtown. They call it the Capital Hilton."

"I'm close to there. We could burn off some of the calories from all the beer we've been drinking tonight with a morning run."

"Sure." He tried to sound sober. "Six o'clock?"

"I'll be in the lobby of the Hilton at seven. Last one there buys breakfast."

He hung up and poured the rest of the beer in the sink. Jack never drank alone unless he ordered pizza. Then it was usually only one beer. Tonight had been fun. Just friends talking about all the people they knew and loved.

Somewhere on his way to his bedroom, it occurred to him that he'd just made a date with Shannon.

Zoe was right. He was a masochist.

Good news: it was hard to argue and run. He'd be safe till breakfast.

thirty-eight

Mack

MACK HELD ALEXANDRA in his arms all night. He wasn't sure he even closed his eyes. There was something exciting about her being pregnant. He'd love watching her grow with their baby inside of her. He couldn't wait to watch her cuddle a newborn to her breast. Even in her late forties, her beauty took his breath away.

He spread his hand over her tummy. A child. He'd be a new father at fifty-two. Mack couldn't help feeling like he was touching a miracle with his hand.

But he could remember all the nights of walking the floor with a baby crying. And the panic when your tiny child has a fever. Alex wasn't young. There could be all kinds of complications.

She could die. The baby could die. He could die of

worry any moment. Nothing in his career had ever scared him as much as this. Mack swore he felt a heart attack coming on. By the time the kid started puberty, Mack would be bald and have knee problems.

They had nothing they'd need to bring a baby home. No crib. No clothes. No diapers. No security system.

He'd install that tomorrow.

Alex wiggled and rolled to face him. She patted his face as if she knew he was awake. "It's going to be all right, Mack. You are a great dad, and you'll be just as good the second time. Gray, maybe a little wrinkled, but just as good."

She settled against him and went back to sleep.

Alex was right, he decided. He'd done it once. He could do it again. If he could remember all the rules. Toddlers swallow everything. They'd need to carpet the stairs. Buy baby locks for all the cabinets and drawers. Nowadays even peanuts could kill kids.

Mack carefully slipped from the bed and decided he'd better start a list. He'd need to call his mother and tell her. She'd been hoping for her first great-grandchild. Maybe she could tell the folks at the retirement home where she and her sisters lived that the kid was a great-grand. After all, no one would believe at eighty she was having only her second grandchild.

The phone rang. 2:37 a.m.

Mack figured it was a wrong number, but he picked up anyway. Why not? He was awake.

"Mack," a panicked voice whispered.

He checked the ID. "What's wrong, Emily?"

"I'm going into labor. She's not due for a month and

my parents left to visit my brothers and their families in Norman. Kind of a family reunion without me. I was happy not to have to go this year and we were sure the birth wouldn't be for a month."

"Emily." Mack was fully awake. "What can I do? Take you to the hospital? Find Fuller?"

"No, Fuller's here. He's loading the car now. I was wondering if you and Alex could come over and baby-sit the boys. I asked Zoe first, but she begged to be at the birth. Her exact words were 'I'll just die if I don't see what having a baby is like. You've got to let me watch.' Fuller wasn't too into the idea, but how could I say no?"

Mack fought to get a word in, even if she was the center of the crisis. Shy Emily had suddenly turned into a chatterbox. "We're on our way. Be there in five."

"Thanks."

He hung up and turned toward the bedroom. Alex, pulling on her sweater, was smiling at him. "I had time to dress while you and Emily talked."

"How'd you know what she wanted?"

"When you yelled her name, I knew we'd be driving Mother or watching the kids. Why else would she call at this time of night?"

Mack nodded. "Right. What should we take? They probably won't be back home before breakfast. Food? Games to play? Handcuffs? Those boys are wild."

"Just get dressed, Mack. I'll back the car out."

"Right." Three minutes later when he dropped into the passenger side, he said, "Promise me you'll deliver on time. None of this early stuff."

"I promise our child will come on time. Only problem is, he's got the calendar with him. All other dates are just guesses."

"Him—you think it's going to be a him? Definitely, I think so too. We've both had a girl. Now it's time for a boy. I'll get to do things Shannon never liked doing. I won't have to buy a princess dress every Halloween. I'll teach him to work on cars. I forgot to do that with her. We'll go fishing and actually eat the fish we catch."

Twelve hours later Mack walked through the Wilders' living room and playroom. It looked like a war zone. Toys, empty juice bottles, several pairs of socks and Cheetos must have snowed the one minute he wasn't looking.

Charles, the oldest at seven, had thrown up twice because he kept yelling that he didn't want another brother and complaining that no one asked him. Edward, the five-year-old, thought Mack and Alexandra had come to play with him and cried whenever he wasn't the center of attention. Ernest, the baby, just broke things. Mack had given up on trying to stop him from eating the marshmallows under the table. He'd broken two of his brothers' toys, tipped over any glass within reach and found Alex's purse when no one was looking.

Add two dogs to the mix, a cat that sneezed and a hamster that was MIA. Mack felt like he was an inmate at the worst insane asylum in the world.

His wife, on the other hand, seemed to be enjoying

the show. She cooked, gave Ernest a bath in the sink and read stories even when no one listened.

When Zoe dropped by in midafternoon to tell them Emily had had a five-pound baby girl, Mack talked Zoe into entertaining the boys, which wouldn't be too hard since Ernest was asleep in the laundry basket.

Then he walked Alex down the hallway to a bedroom that looked like clothes had exploded from the closet. He didn't bother to hang anything up; he simply spread a quilt over the mess and said, "Right now I have to put my baby down for a nap. You've been up since two this morning."

Alex didn't argue. They cuddled atop the quilt and both fell asleep immediately.

Two hours later they awoke to a quiet house. Both panicked.

When they rushed down the hallway, somehow everything was clean and in the right place. Even the Cheetos were gone.

Take-out pizza was on the table and all three boys, along with Zoe, were eating.

Alex hugged her daughter and told her she was wonderful.

Mack glanced out the window and saw half a dozen high school kids climbing into a car. Drama students, he guessed, since Zoe had spoken to their club last Friday about being an actor in New York City.

From the looks of it, she'd paid them for cleaning the house, helping with the boys and bringing in pizza.

He turned back to Zoe without saying a word to Alex. "You'll babysit for us, too, I hope."

"Of course I'll keep my baby sister. I plan to teach her to dance."

"It's going to be a…" Mack stopped, remembering the day he'd just had with the Wilder boys. The screaming. The crying. The chaos. "Maybe it'll be a girl. They're easier, I've heard."

Alex laughed. "Either is fine."

Mack nodded as he looked past his wife and noticed Ernest putting a slice of pizza on his head. His older brothers did the same thing, then started slapping their slices at each other as if they were in a sword fight.

"I'm voting for a girl." Mack caught a flying pepperoni and ate it.

thirty-nine

Fuller

FULLER ROCKED HIS fourth child in his arms as Emily ate Jell-O. "What are we going to name this one, Em? I would say Emily after Emily Dickinson, but I've already got my Emily."

"Harper, of course. I sent Mom a picture. It's being passed around the family reunion now. She has already told me that she's the most beautiful baby ever born. Black curls at birth." Emily smiled. "Just like her handsome papa."

He brushed the baby's hair, thinking she had her mother's eyes.

"For once I agree with your mother. Where is she, anyway? I figured the minute you went into labor, she'd be driving ninety to get here. She hasn't missed a birth before. All nine of the grandchildren, until now."

"She's with the other grandkids tonight. I told her not to miss the time with them, even if my baby comes early." Em laughed. "She told me not to dare have my baby early."

Wilder winked at her. "And we both know you always listen to your mother. She'll probably think you planned it."

"I swear, it's like my brothers and I got together and plotted so many grandkids that she'd have to be constantly on the move trying to run all their lives. Best thing we ever did."

"Sounds like a good plan. Her one son-in-law is so far down the list she hasn't picked on me for two years. Last week I heard her refer to me as 'that man who lives here' like she'd forgotten my name."

"You'll never be that lucky. Now hand me Harper. It's time for her to eat."

Wilder handed over his daughter, then stepped out of the room as a nurse rushed in to help Emily.

To his surprise, his dad was sitting in a chair at the end of the hall. Not in a waiting room. Not too close to the birthing room.

Moving closer, Fuller said in a low voice, "You sober, Pop?"

"Yeah, but I won't be for long."

Fuller squatted down and patted his father's knee. "Tough day." The old guy had been in the waiting room at dawn when Fuller rushed out to tell him he had a granddaughter. For once, Fuller hugged his dad. "What's wrong? I promise the baby is fine."

"I got some bad news, son, and I don't want to tell you because this is a happy day for you. Lord knows you haven't always had your share of them and I don't want to take this one away."

"Dad, what's happened?" Fuller's chest tightened. He had so many he loved now. So much to lose. He knew Em and the baby were fine, but what about the boys? The house? The garage?

Bill cleared his throat. "You'll find out soon enough, so I might as well say it. Son, your mother's done come home to nest and she swears she's not leaving. Alice Ray is bossy as ever and must have grown into being a good cook because she's as round as she is tall."

Fuller burst out laughing so hard he was sure Em probably heard him. When he finally calmed down enough to speak, he put his hand on his father's shoulder and said, "She's your problem, Dad. Not mine. I barely remember her."

Bill looked so sad Fuller almost felt sorry for him. He hadn't been much of a dad, but he'd stayed. Alice, on the other hand, hadn't wanted the party to end, according to his grandpa. He'd told Fuller that Alice was a good girl, but she loved the glow of neon. By the time she could pass for eighteen, she was belly up to the bar.

"She ain't my wife," Bill grumbled. "I never married her. She said I wasn't fun enough. I was older than her, and that matters when you're young. You think we should tell her to keep on moving down the road?"

Fuller shook his head. "I promised Grandpa if she

ever came back she'd have the house to live in. Since you're already in it, I suggest you either bunk at the garage or propose. It won't look right if my daughter's grandparents aren't married."

Bill scratched his dirty hair. "You mean I got to get married because you had a baby?"

"Afraid so."

His dad stood and handed over a stuffed bear. "I brought the baby a toy. I wouldn't have if I'd known she's going to make me get married."

Fuller smiled as his father walked away. Fuller turned back to Em's room. He'd wait until she finished with Harper before he told her the news. His family tree was a twisted mess, but he planned to make sure that the branches budding now would grow straight and tall.

Loving Emily had given him direction. Since the night she'd first kissed him, he'd been building, changing to be the kind of man she needed him to be. He'd even taken Connor's tassel back the first time Larady invited them to dinner. Turned out Connor hadn't even missed it.

forty

Jack

JACK TOOK THE stairs down from his third-floor room.
When he walked into the lobby of the Capital Hilton, Shannon was there, staring at the elevator doors.
The huge clock above the doors marked the time as
exactly seven o'clock. He couldn't help but take one
more second to let his gaze drift over her. Running
shorts, a light windbreaker and an old academy T-shirt.
Except for her blond hair being a few inches shorter
than he remembered, nothing had changed. She still
stopped his heart.

He walked up behind her. "Waiting for someone?"

Shannon jumped in surprise, then swung around
and hit him on the shoulder.

Welcome home, he thought. Nothing new.

"I'm not late, Shan. You can stop staring at the elevators. I'm right here." For a moment she looked like she might move in for a hug, but she stopped herself.

The ever-proper Shannon Morell. Never do anything on impulse.

"Ready to run?" He moved his open palm toward the door.

She hesitated. "I plan to go to the Air and Space Museum as soon as I leave here. Mind if I drop my bag at the desk? I can change in the restroom."

"Fine. You can change in my room if you like." He felt the oddest need to introduce himself. She'd probably call him some names for acting so formal, but he gave it a shot. "Shan, it's me, Jack Hutchinson. You've known me forever. I'm not some stranger. You don't have to worry about me stealing your bag."

"I know. It's just been a long time."

She dropped her bag off and they walked out. "You want to run to Ford's Theatre and back?"

He nodded, not even sure of the direction.

They jogged, warming up in the cool air. Then she turned off on a running trail near the park and it was a full-out run. Jack knew exactly what she was doing, pushing it, fighting to prove she was as good as any man.

Deep down he wondered if she didn't think her dad had wanted a son, not a daughter. Mack tried with the girl stuff, but he was an airman at heart. And so was his daughter.

When she finally slowed, it took a few minutes to catch her breath while Jack did the same.

"You're in great shape."

"You too." She didn't look at him, but she slowed to a stroll. "You happy, Jack? When I think of you, I always think of you being happy. You so wanted to fly."

He thought of saying *since when have you cared?* Old wounds heal slowly. But the past was the past. "I am happy. Love the work I'm doing. Flying the best planes in the world. I've done exactly what I planned to do. I've seen the world. You?"

She hesitated too long. "I love my work too. Very interesting. And who wouldn't love living in DC?"

Even though he told himself he didn't care about her anymore, it bothered him to realize that she wasn't happy. And that she felt the need to lie to him about it. He could always tell when she was lying or bluffing.

When they walked through the lobby, he picked up her bag, and without a word between them, they rode the elevator up to his room.

He motioned for her to use the bathroom first. While she showered, he stared out the window, wondering what had happened to them. It seemed, for thirty years, he'd loved three women. Part of him still did. Zoe and Emily had loved him back in their own ways, but not Shannon. Except for that one snow globe moment she probably didn't remember, it had never been right between them.

Jack grinned, remembering the night Emily told her husband she'd always loved Jack.

Fuller didn't even blink when he turned and stared at Jack. His voice was low and deadly serious. "I figure I've got a choice. I can either beat the hell out of you or take you on as a friend. Neither'll be easy. Em will be mad at me if I hurt you in a fight and I've never had a college boy for a friend. Not sure I'd want one. Kind of an albatross, if you ask me."

"Do I get a vote?" Em asked.

"No," Fuller answered.

"What about me?" Jack didn't much like the idea of a fight. The only fight he'd ever been in happened in second grade. Zoe had ended his beating by slugging the guy. "I should have some say in this, Wilder."

"No. I've made up my mind." He offered his hand. "We'll be friends. But don't ask to borrow money and I'll never lie to Emily for you, so don't even bother asking. Anyone else in this town is fair game, though. If you exaggerate a story, I'll back you up."

Funny, Jack thought as he looked out at DC. All those years ago. Half a continent away, and somehow, he considered Fuller Wilder probably his best friend.

The bathroom doorknob rattled. "I'm out." Shannon broke into his thoughts and his room. "Shower is all yours."

He turned. She was wearing a towel. The dead crush seemed to have found a defibrillator. He couldn't stop staring.

Without a word, he walked into the bathroom and stepped into the still-warm shower. The smell of Shannon was all around him.

Jack took his time, letting hot water pour over his muscles. How could it be possible that he could still be attracted to her? It made no sense. It wasn't love, that was for sure. If it was love, he would be attracted to Emily or Zoe. He cared for them. But there were no sparks. They were just his friends.

Shannon, on the other hand, haunted his dreams. Seeing her standing there in that towel that came up high and hung down low was writing new chapters in his imagination.

He thought maybe he'd have breakfast with her, maybe go to the museum for the day. It was Sunday. Neither had plans that she'd mentioned. If they spent the day together, they could begin to build on something. Friendship, a closeness, lovers? Probably just companions.

That was, if he could get his mind away from one towel long enough to put a sentence together.

Jack closed his eyes and pushed his face into the stream of hot water. Hell, he was stepping into the same trap again. Liking her. Planning a future. Being knocked down. He knew the flight plan of their relationship. How many times did he have to crash and burn?

A tap on the door pulled him back to reality. "You decent? I left my bag in there."

He didn't answer.

She pushed the door open and felt her way along the counter in the fog.

Jack just stared at her. In the cloudy air he swore he could see all the Shannons he'd known. The little girl who was a year younger than him, but challenged him at every turn. The teenager who stood eye to eye with him and argued about everything. The woman who wanted to plan his life with no mention of love.

She was right one time when she said he'd followed her to the academy. He might have gone a year earlier, but she'd said she was applying first. She'd pulled him into the dream of flight.

All through school she'd been there. Track meets, spelling bees, debate team, everything he tried, he'd always been competing with Shannon.

Funny thing, he was a year older, but now and then, when she won, he was so proud of her.

Every memory from childhood and college had her in the background. Even now, when they were both successful, they were still competing.

He pushed his head under the shower again, thankful that hotels never ran out of hot water. When he pulled out and looked over to see if she was gone, he found her standing there in that same too-little towel, staring at him.

Maybe she was remembering too. Or maybe she was thinking he'd cracked up and decided to take the world's longest shower. He didn't care.

"I don't want to fight anymore, Shan. I don't want to compete or debate or argue. You win."

She tilted her head as if she'd lost him in the fog. Perhaps she saw the little boy in him, the high school kid, the cadet. All of them had loved her and all had been turned away.

He didn't move as she dropped her towel and stepped into the shower. Slowly, her stare never leaving his eyes, she put her hands on his face and kissed him. Then she moved skin to skin with nothing between them. Nothing. No words. No arguments. No lies.

He finally pulled her to him with a need that shook them both. In the fog and the waterfall, they discovered what the other wanted, needed, without saying a word.

When both were out of breath, Jack picked her up and carried her to bed. Neither one had had enough in the shower. He combed his fingers through her wet hair as he kissed her deeper and longer than he'd ever kissed a woman.

When he finally pulled away, he saw her smile.

For a long while they didn't talk. They just made love; they held each other; they drifted in and out of sleep.

And, for once, they got it right.

forty-one

Zoe

ZOE WALTZED AROUND the bakery, slowly, as if time itself moved to the silent melody. The tables and chairs had been shoved back against the walls. The counter moved over to allow more room. The bay windows had been opened to accommodate tiny tables that could be set for only two.

Zoe wanted to surprise her mother and Mack. She'd show them what the bakery could become. Now that Alex was expecting, she'd probably love the idea of Zoe sharing the bakery space.

Zoe could see every detail in her mind. Everything would be painted light pink, with yellow curtains framing the doors. The sign outside, written in two-feet-high cursive, would read The Little Teashop on Main. In the spring, she'd plant pots full of flowers, and in the fall, she'd decorate in wreaths made of real fruit like they did in Williamsburg.

Her mother might even be excited about passing the place on. She'd loved the bakery, but it was time to move on, and now Alex could know someone would love it as much as she had. Zoe would take on more and more of the load.

Of all Zoe's wild dreams, this one filled her heart. Since she was eighteen, Zoe had felt like she'd been a vagabond looking for just the right place. Searching for where she belonged, where she could shine. She'd used up all her energy looking, it seemed, and now she wanted to be close to her mother. In the little rooms upstairs, she'd have her own space, her own world, and she'd have her dream. Planning the teashop was far more exciting than rehearsing for a play, and once it opened, there would be no critics to rain on her parade.

All those years in New York, she'd been acting happy. But here, she'd found peace. Her body often felt tired. She blamed it on being run-down. Poor eating habits. Too much drinking. Not enough sunshine. But this dream was too important for her to slow down.

Until now, her dreams had never worked out. But this one just might. When she'd first come home in her early twenties, she'd felt trapped in a world of sameness. Yet when she'd left for the city, she was lost, like adventure, success, excitement were made of smoke and floated just out of reach. All the parties were simply distractions. The men just bit players in her life.

All the plays and wild parties were camouflage for not knowing where she belonged.

Who knew that the place she'd finally fit was here? Laurel Springs, the town she'd grown up in, could also be where she grew. She could shine here. Belong here. Here she didn't need to prove anything. Here she was already a star.

The drama teacher wanted her to help with the one-act play competition. The dance studio, open only on Saturdays, had a sign in the window wanting a ballet teacher. She could do that. She'd had lessons since she was six. And, best of all, Emily wanted her to turn one of her children's stories into a play for the elementary schools. A tale of a rabbit who had to learn to share.

Zoe could do that. She'd even direct it. Every child would have a part and they'd all be stars.

This place wasn't Broadway, it wasn't New York, but there was magic here, and that was all Zoe ever wanted to do: create magic.

She lit a dozen candles on the tiny tables in the bakery. She even put them on windowsills around the room so the space looked like a twinkling wonderland.

Maybe, once the teashop was up and running, she'd be open for lovers to share a pot of tea on rainy days. Every season, the tea would change, filling the shop with a new aroma, and her mom would think of just the right scones or cookies to go with them.

They'd keep her future little sister in a crib in the warm kitchen and take turns spoiling her. Zoe would sing her to sleep. The bakery would be a grand place for her to grow up, just as it had been for Zoe.

Some people see what is, but Zoe had always seen what could be. She saw the best in others. The beauty in clutter and the colors of the night. When she was a child, she'd believed that when she was dancing, nothing could ever hurt her.

Now, as she turned thirty, she realized the real world didn't work that way. She'd loved New York, but it hadn't loved her back. Dreams had faded. At first, the bit parts were great, but now she wanted more. The lifestyle she'd been living was obviously making her sick, a little broken and wanting to come home.

Her mother always said she could start over, and that was exactly what she planned to do.

She'd see the doctor and get vitamins. She'd get enough sleep. Give up everything that was bad for her. Maybe even start running like Shannon did.

Zoe whirled faster and faster as she danced around the tables, making all negative thoughts fly away. The pain in her head tapped in rhythm, but she didn't stop. She didn't even slow. She'd take pills later to sleep, but right now she wanted to dance.

The idea for a teashop on Main Street had been in her mind for years. A place the three little princesses could go, even if they were thirty now. A place where couples could talk in a relaxing atmosphere. A shop where strangers could fall in love. And, best of all, sidewalk tables where people could relax and simply watch the world go by.

She'd never asked her mother to share the space until now. This was Alex's bakery, her mom's dream, or at least it had been, years ago. Now, every time

Zoe came home, she saw how Mack was pulling Alex away from working. First, with travel, and later, with the idea of retiring early and finding something they could do together.

Today, he'd pulled Alex away from baking one more time as they talked about the baby. Soon any dream Zoe had of running the teashop with her mother might be gone. Now, somehow, she had to make it happen on her own.

She twirled and twirled like a ballerina performing her last dance. She didn't want to start the teashop on her own. Nothing had ever worked on her own. The child in Zoe wanted her mother back, even as the adult realized her mother deserved a different happiness.

She'd make it. Her mother had always been there for her, and that wouldn't end. There would simply be one more in their family to love.

Zoe took a bow as if crowds had been watching her dance. The room silently cheered back. She darted up the stairs as if she were running off stage, leaving her dream of a teashop behind for the night.

The apartment seemed too big now that she'd stayed here alone. It looked hollow, kind of like her life had in New York. Each semester in school, her friends seemed to change. Once she was out, friends shifted in and out, never staying around long enough to talk of "remember when" days.

One more reason to plant herself here where she'd been born.

She switched off the lights quickly and went to bed without bothering to watch the news. Since she'd been home, she couldn't get enough rest and the headaches had followed her home from the city.

As she slept, the sweet smell of gingerbread and lemon cake was replaced with the heavy odor of something burning.

"Candles!" Zoe shouted as she came wide awake. "I forgot to put out the candles!"

She ran down the stairs and straight into smoke. The bay window with its lace curtains at the front, where she'd shoved the tiny table with three candles burning, was now on fire. The flaming tablecloth draped to the floor making the fire cascade. The breeze from the long, tall windows fanned the destruction.

Reaching for the phone, she dialed 911. Yelled "Help!" then dropped the phone. For a few seconds she didn't move. The fire fascinated her as it slowly worked its way toward her. It crawled along the baseboards and reached the door. The glass in the top part of the door reflected the flames. Beautiful and frightening at the same time.

Zoe had no shoes. She couldn't run to the door. Any way she looked promised burns on her feet and legs at least. She ducked behind the counter, hiding. She'd wait for the firemen. They only had to come a few blocks. They'd be here soon.

Fire reached the stairs to the apartment. That way was cut off now. The heat made her bare arms and legs feel sunburned. She couldn't move. Couldn't think.

A huge roar of splintering wood around the door and shattering glass sounded from the other side of the counter. Smoke rushed to escape first, and flames seemed to run to catch it.

Zoe peeked over the counter to see a dark form barreling through the hole that had once been the front door.

"Zoe!" Mack's booming voice echoed off walls.

He stormed straight toward the steps. "Zoe!"

"I'm here." She heard her voice squeak and she jumped up from her hiding place.

Mack jerked his coat off and tossed it over her head. A moment later he picked her up and ran.

In what seemed only a few steps he sat her down atop his car. "Stay here. Don't move. There is glass all over the street."

Then he left her and ran to direct the fire truck in. Suddenly, twirling lights turned Main into a stage. Four firemen jumped off the truck. Cars stopped in the middle of the street to shine their lights toward the site.

Zoe slipped her arms into Mack's coat and crossed her legs beneath the tent she'd made. She had a front-row seat. The flames seemed to fight back against the firemen. Dying in one spot and rekindling in another. Dry wood popped, sending tiny stars into the night. Glass shattered, then clanked against the sidewalk. The air warmed, but the horror of what she saw chilled Zoe to the bone.

Finally, the last spark fired toward the sky and blinked out as water washed over it.

The beast took a smoky breath and died, but the front of the store was a mess. The "Sweetie" sign was still hanging just below the balcony, but "Pie's" and "Bakery" had tumbled in the flames.

Zoe guessed that if she had any burns she'd be feeling them, but the third fireman was so cute she let him take a look to make sure. With her thin T-shirt she wore as pj's, he was able to make a complete search of her exposed limbs.

When everything settled down, Mack opened his car door and carried her to her seat.

"It's all my fault. I lit candles. I was dancing," Zoe finally cried.

"Nope," he said over her confession. "It was an accident."

"But I…"

"Did you mean to burn the bakery down?"

"No. I didn't. I just wasn't…"

He stopped her again. "If you didn't mean to, Zoe, then it was an accident. I'll tell your mother all the details in the morning and she'll feel the same way I do. She'll just be happy you weren't hurt."

Ten minutes later when she was settled on Mack's couch with her mother on one side and Mack on the other she told them what had happened, even how she shoved the chairs and tables to the corners so she could see just how much room she'd have for a tearoom.

To her surprise, her mother asked no questions about the damage. She simply said once more how much she loved Zoe's idea of a teashop. She even suggested they use the insurance money to not rebuild the bakery as it had been, but to transform the space into a teashop.

"I could still be a baker, but I no longer want to run a business. You take over, Zoe. Do it how you like. I'll come in a few mornings a week to bake. Mack said the kitchen behind that counter that saved you only looks like it has smoke damage."

"Two days, Mom?"

"Two days. You'll have to get someone else to do the decorating. I'll do the cookies and breads. Maybe pound cakes for the holidays."

"You'll bring my baby sister?"

"Of course. You loved being in the bakery and so will she, or he."

They talked for an hour. Then, as her mother went to bed and Mack locked the front door, Zoe whispered, "Mack, how come you were driving by the bakery tonight?"

He barked a laugh. "Your mother wanted peach lowfat yogurt. You have any idea how hard it is to find at midnight in a small town? I was on my way home to tell her the bad news when I drove by and saw the flames. When I brought you home, I guess we both forgot about the yogurt. I don't even want to think about what might have happened…" He didn't finish. Mack simply straightened to attention and pulled all emotion inside.

"Thanks for being there, Mack. You know you're still my knight in shining armor."

He smiled. "I hope I always will be, kid."

Zoe giggled at the idea that he thought of her as a kid. "Good night, Pop."

She'd never called any man her pop, but it seemed right now.

"Get some sleep," he said as he moved down the hallway. "We'll start on the teashop in the morning."

forty-two

Shannon

JACK COVERED HIS eyes with his arm as Shannon clicked on the light. "What time is it?" he asked.

"Eleven. If we hadn't ordered room service, we'd both be dead by now." She puffed up her pillow and folded her arms over bare breasts. "Jack, I've never done anything like that. I feel like a marathon runner. It was far more…"

"Eleven at night?" He obviously wasn't paying attention to her rambling.

Standing, she pulled a change of clothes from her bag. "Do me a favor, Jack. Don't say anything. Nothing. You'll just ruin it."

"You're leaving?" He still sounded half-asleep.

"Of course I'm leaving. I have to report at seven tomorrow and probably so do you."

"Six." He rolled off the other side of the bed. "I'll take you home. If you'll tell me where you live." He laughed. "I just slept with a woman and I don't even know where she lives."

She didn't laugh. "I'll catch a cab. Go back to sleep."

"We need to talk about this, Shan."

"No, we don't."

"But…"

She opened the door and was gone before she could bear to say more. She'd spent the day in bed with Jack and didn't want to hear reruns of the play-by-play. They hadn't just had sex—they'd made love, and she didn't want to talk about it.

After putting her shoes on in the elevator, Shannon ran out as soon as the doors were opened. Logic told her there was no way Jack could have followed her down, but she didn't want to face him.

She was trying to tell him how great it had been and all he seemed to want to know was the time. Well, time was important. If she was lucky she'd get four hours of sleep before she had to start getting ready to make the commute. Maybe he was right. They probably should give it some time, think about what happened.

Shannon couldn't believe she'd just stepped into the shower with him. What if he'd turned her down? It wasn't like she just stepped into the wrong room. What if he'd yelled "Get out"? Shannon shook her head so hard the cabdriver stared at her in his rearview mirror.

She was overthinking it, she decided. Maybe if she

put some space between them, they'd both figure out what had happened. *Wait*, she almost said aloud. She knew what had happened, and if she dared go down that road, she'd probably have the driver turn the cab around.

She needed a shower and sleep. No. Wrong. She didn't need a shower. Shannon took a deep breath and tried to think logically. Sleep. Work. Don't talk to Jack. She could follow that.

Only when she got home, she was wide awake and spent the rest of the night remembering. By morning she wondered if there was a twelve-step program for getting over the best night of her life.

Jack called twice the next morning, but she didn't pick up. The next day, he called at noon, leaving a message that they should meet for drinks after work.

She didn't answer.

At six he called and said, "We can't end this without talking. Damn it, Shan, pick up the phone."

She never called him back.

As she did whenever she was sad, Shannon threw herself into her work. Ten hours a day, twelve, fourteen. By the end of the week, she was too tired to think or run or eat.

She finally made it to her apartment about eight Friday night. Knowing there was no food at her place, she raided the vending machines in the laundry room in her building and headed up.

The elevator was too slow, so she walked up the two flights. As she turned the corner, she saw a man in uniform sitting on the floor, his back against her door. As she slowly crept toward him, she realized Jack was sound asleep. He'd probably had as bad a week as she'd had.

When she tapped his head with a bag of chips, he blinked awake and looked up at her. "Evening, Shan."

"What are you doing here? And how did you find my place, anyway?"

"I called Zoe."

"Figures."

"I thought we could go to dinner. Have a date. You know, do something ordinary people do. It's Friday night, and I'll have to work Saturday, so we can't do much else."

"I know what day it is, Jack. No thanks to the dinner date. Maybe some other time. I've had a long day, and if you're flying tomorrow, you should just go home and get some sleep."

"It's been a long week." He slowly stood as if his body was waking up one joint at a time. "Let me get this straight. You step in uninvited to my shower. You have wild, wonderful sex with me all day and now you won't eat dinner with me."

A neighbor two doors down opened his door and had the nerve to stand there like they were a street show.

"Go away," Shannon snapped at the neighbor she'd never even smiled at.

"Not a chance. It's my hallway, too, lady, and there's nothing interesting on TV. If you want my opinion, I think you should give the captain a chance."

"I don't want your opinion." Shannon unlocked her door and Jack followed her in.

Jack closed the door behind him without saying a word.

Shannon fired up without looking at him. "I don't want to have dinner. I don't want to talk. I know all about your family, your life. You probably can't tell me about your job. So what's left?"

She tossed the chips on the couch and turned to face him. "It was fun, Jack. We'll have to do it again sometime."

To her surprise, he didn't say a word. He simply stepped closer and kissed her. Not a hello kiss, but the kiss of a man who knew her well.

She felt like she was made of memory foam, because she melted perfectly to him. His warmth relaxed her tired muscles and his gentle touch calmed her all the way to her soul.

The long week, her fatigue, any sense of reason seemed to fade.

Without a word they made love on the couch, then in her bed. After they slept an hour, Jack woke up and stumbled to the refrigerator. When he couldn't find food, he found a number to an all-night delivery service. He ordered groceries and stumbled back to bed.

When a knock sounded at the door, Jack put on his pants and ran to pay the guy. Then he brought in two bags and dumped them out on top of her. Cereal, milk, cookies and bananas.

Shannon searched through the bags. "Where is the real food?"

"I don't want to waste time making anything. I'm starving." He opened the cereal box and poured the milk in. Then, sharing a tablespoon, they ate dinner.

As he fed her the last bit, she said, "I still don't want to talk about this."

"Fine with me. As long as we keep communicating as we have been, I might go mute." He set the box down and pulled the cover over them. "We'll eat the other box for breakfast."

"I'm still hungry."

"Oh, I almost forgot dessert." He jumped out of bed in a run and was back with a mixing bowl before she had a chance to ask questions.

"We could have used that earlier." Shannon looked at the bowl like it was a new invention.

"Stop talking," he ordered as he crumbled a dozen chocolate chip cookies in the bowl, then added pieces of bananas, then topped the bowl off with milk. "I discovered this dessert one summer when Mom thought I was old enough to be left alone. I've never shared the recipe with anyone, not even Sweetie Pie's Bakery."

She laughed. "Something tells me Alex doesn't want it."

But when he fed her the first bit, Shannon changed her mind.

She laughed. Everything in her life made sense. Everything but Jack. Nothing he did seemed to belong in her organized world.

Odd how right he felt, though. Their bodies seemed to have cell memory for each other. Even when they were sleeping, they found the other.

When she woke the next morning, he was gone. A note on the half-empty milk jug said he had to fly out early. He'd be back in a week, hopefully. Would call when he had time. He'd signed the note "Love, Jack."

Shannon sat down on the couch, dug out the smashed potato chip bag, held it to her chest and cried harder than she'd ever cried.

How many times in her life had her dad left a note like this? He'd be called into service. She'd wake up and her grandmother would be in the house. Ready to step in and be the parent for a while.

Only she hadn't had a chance to say goodbye. Not to Jack now or her father. Maybe they both felt like they were being easy on her.

Every time Dad left, every time he was late returning, every time Dad didn't call when he said he would, Shannon thought the worst. He wasn't coming back. He'd left, just like her mother had. No matter what her grandmother said, she always feared her dad wasn't coming back.

The sun was just coming up on Shannon's Saturday, and she wished she could go back to work, where she didn't have to think of anything but programming.

She'd always known that if she let Jack in, he'd break her heart. Maybe he did love her. Maybe they were right for each other. But she felt like she'd already lived one lifetime waiting, and she didn't want to live another.

She *wouldn't* live another.

Standing, she tossed the note in the trash, picked up the rest of the chocolate chip cookies and curled in front of the tiny TV. She watched every old movie she could find until Sunday morning, when she finally fell asleep.

When she woke, she showered, dressed and went to work. The fact that she was four hours early didn't seem to register in her mind.

forty-three

Jack

JACK FOUGHT THE urge to call Shannon every night, but he knew how it would go. She'd be mad, accuse him of being like her father. Swear she never wanted to see him again.

That was the problem with falling in love with the woman you'd been in love with all your life—you knew her too well. You could argue both sides of every argument.

He'd always compared her to every woman he'd ever kissed or slept with or even talked to.

Like it or not, Shannon was the benchmark by which he measured every woman.

Finally, on Thursday night, he called Zoe just to

check in. Thought he might mention that he'd seen Shannon. That was all. Keep it light.

Zoe answered after the first ring. "Jack! You slept with Shan."

It wasn't a question. "She's called you." Not a question, a statement of fact.

"Of course she called me, and Emily, too, but Em couldn't talk. She's busy. Can you believe our shy little Em has four kids? She's building her own tribe."

"Wilder probably had something to do with that." Jack had to give the man some credit.

"I heard his mom moved back." Jack commented to keep the subject off him. "How's that working out?"

"I don't know. Em says no one has seen either of them for three days."

"Maybe we should…"

"Oh no you don't, Jack. First we talk about what happened between you and Shannon. Details. I want details."

Jack thought about hanging up. He wasn't sure he knew what happened, other than the great sex. Finally, he gave up a little. "It was bound to happen sometime, Zoe. We bumped into each other, and for once, we forgot to fight. In fact, we gave up talking. Seemed to work well."

"I swear, you give fewer details than Shan." Zoe giggled, suddenly making Jack smile. "Of course, I've slept with you, Jack, and don't remember much happening then either."

"That's because we slept, Zoe. Nothing else happened."

"I know. Do you realize you were the only one that got away? If I felt better, I'd fly up to wherever you are and show you what you missed."

"You're sick? Shannon said her father told her you came home to rest but I didn't know you were sick."

"That's the least of my worries. I burned down half of the bakery last weekend. I have no boyfriend, no job, no apartment in any city big enough to have a Walmart, and I'm thirty and still living with my mother. Oh, and by the way, Mom is pregnant."

"I know. Shan called and told me. I guess you could say that's what brought Shannon and me together."

"I don't want to hear it. I have a feeling for the rest of my life people will be asking me about my sibling. Shannon and I will fade into the woodwork as the two older sisters."

"You like being an only child, Zoe. I've always known that. Now tell me about the fire. Anyone hurt? How bad is the damage?"

Jack leaned back in his chair and listened to every detail. Even the part about two of the firemen still monitoring her recovery, though there were no apparent wounds.

They talked into the night. Late enough that he wouldn't be tempted to call Shannon. Two more days, maybe three, and he'd be back in DC.

He ended the call by lecturing her to go to the doctor.

"I promise. I'm tired all the time and can't seem to shake this headache. The doctor here is sending me to a specialist in Dallas."

"You'll go."

"I'll go as soon as I have time. Oh, and, Jack, I love you."

"I know. I love you, too, slugger. I'll try to get leave to come home and help you remodel."

"Bring Shannon."

He hung up, thinking *Fat chance of that happening.*

forty-four

Zoe

A MONTH AFTER she'd promised Jack she'd see a doctor, Zoe walked out of the doctor's office, telling herself she wouldn't cry. *Cancer* wasn't a word she thought she could say out loud.

She'd always rattled on, telling all her friends about every detail of her life, but not this time. Now she couldn't even put her problem into words.

Brain cancer. And the good news was, she wouldn't have to suffer long. The party called her life was about to end. The doc said she could do several things, maybe stretch a few months to a year. No promises, though. And they might always find a cure before her time was up.

She spotted her mother waiting in the car. There

was no use dragging out the results of her tests. Zoe needed to tell her mother now. Only Zoe wasn't sure she could be that brave. She could run the streets of New York. She could have more lovers than she could count. But she couldn't bear to see her mother cry.

"How did it go?" Alex asked as soon as Zoe crawled in the car.

Zoe took her mother's hand and said, "The doctor said I need to slow down. You were right. I'm exhausted." She couldn't say the word. She just couldn't. "I need to eat better. I need to rest." She took a slow breath and added calmly, "He wants me to come back in a month."

A single tear ran down her mother's cheek. "We'll do whatever we need to do to get you better, honey."

Zoe nodded, burying the word, the diagnosis, deep inside her. "I agree, but I want to keep working on the teashop. The Hutchinson brothers got the frame up, and Jack and Shannon said they'd be home next week to help with the inside work." If she didn't think about what was growing in her brain, it wouldn't be real.

Alex smiled. "Sounds like a plan, honey. But to tell you the truth, I can't see those two working together on anything. Not Shannon and Jack."

"Me either, but it'll be fun to watch."

Alex pulled out onto the street. "And you'll take a nap every day, and no more late nights."

"Yes, Mom, I'll be careful. I'll get strong again. I have to. Who else is going to teach my new sister to dance? Don't worry about me, Mom."

Silently, they both agreed to keep the conversation light. Alex had taught her daughter well. No matter what happened in life, keep going, keep dancing.

forty-five

Shannon

SHANNON SAT IN her car, waiting at the airport. Jack said he'd be back in a week and it had been a month. A month and six days.

He'd sent flowers twice and a note once saying there had been delays. Then, yesterday, he'd left a message on her machine that told her simply to pick him up. He gave the time and place. Nothing else. He'd left no way to contact him.

She couldn't say no. No matter how mad she was at him, she couldn't leave him stranded at an airport.

She watched him walk out to her car. She'd always thought, even when he was in his teens, that he was a man built in balance. Only tonight, he looked tired, and she wondered how many hours it had been since he'd slept.

As he neared, she stepped from the car.

He tossed his coat and suitcase in the back, then came around to her. She'd spent an hour waiting and thinking of what she'd say to him, but before she could start, he wrapped his arms around her and lifted her off the ground. His hug was strong and solid as he buried his head into the hollow of her neck.

They just stood there like that for a long time. Holding on. People passed and smiled, then hurried on as if they thought they were intruding.

"I had to hold you," he finally said. "I had to smell you."

His need was too raw. She didn't know what to say.

Without a word they climbed in the car and she drove out of the airport. "Where to?"

"Your place." He leaned back and closed his eyes.

She had to wake him when she pulled in the underground garage at her apartment building.

They climbed out and he followed her in. She wanted to set some ground rules, maybe tell him they could be friends. She was willing to go as far as friends with benefits. But there had to be set times. No showing up at her door. He had to agree to organization that fit nicely into both of their schedules.

But she couldn't say anything. It was like she could feel his mood and knew all he wanted was her.

That night they made love slowly, gently. Then they slept, wrapped up in each other. All night, over and over, even in his sleep, he touched her. Moving his hands over her body as if memorizing every line.

He loved her. She'd always known it, but tonight she glimpsed just how much. No matter how often they fought or turned away from each other, he still loved her. She was a part of him.

Tears dripped on her pillow when she realized she felt the same. She hated that he left her to fly. She hated how he pushed her buttons, always making her angry. But deep down, in a place where there was no conversation, no pretend, she also knew one fact: she loved Jack. No matter how hard she fought it, she loved him, and she would until the day she died.

A little before dawn, Jack woke her up, kissing her throat.

"Stop that." She tried to push him away.

He moved to her shoulder. "Wanna go back to Texas with me today? It's about time we helped Zoe out."

"I have to work Monday."

"Can you get off work? A week. Maybe two. I have a feeling we need to be home."

If he hadn't been kissing very private parts of her, they could have been having this conversation in the hallway.

"I can." She usually ran two weeks ahead.

"Good." He slipped off the bed. "I'll shower while you pack."

She followed him into the bathroom. "I'll shower with you. It'll save time."

He grinned, obviously knowing that she was wrong, but not wanting to mention it. Two hours later they took a cab to a private airport. He borrowed a friend's plane and they were in Laurel Springs before dark.

All at once they were surrounded. Zoe had to show them all the work that had been done, and explain the plans for the last stage of the teashop. Emily invited them to dinner at what felt like an indoor playground.

They all were excited and happy to see each other. The girls were together again. Shannon didn't think any of them finished a conversation the entire meal.

Zoe looked tired when they dropped her back at the bakery. She moved up the steps like an old woman, barely saying good-night.

"I'm sleeping here," Shannon whispered.

"So am I," he added.

"No, you are not. We're home now. Your mother's expecting you."

Jack frowned. "You're kidding. We're not sleeping together?"

"Right."

"Shan, marry me, tomorrow. I can't stay here all week and not sleep with you. Every night while I was gone, all I thought about was sleeping beside you, holding you. You've got to marry me or I'll go mad."

"Yes," she said calmly as she took one step toward the stairs.

"Yes, what? I can come up? Zoe won't mind."

Shannon turned on the second step and faced him. "Yes, I will marry you, Jack. No, you are not coming up. Go home."

He moved to the bottom of the stairs. "You're serious. You'll really marry me?" One look at his face made it obvious that he was surprised by her answer.

"I love you, Jack. I've fought it forever, but I can't seem to shake it. Maybe it's going to be pure hell with you, but last month it was hell without you. I've decided no matter how bad it'll be, I'd rather be with you."

Jack frowned at her. "That didn't really sound like much of a yes. But I did like the 'I love you' part."

She thought about hitting him, but for once she simply answered "Yes."

He didn't have to say he loved her. She could see it in his eyes. Maybe he decided he'd stop while he was ahead, but Jack turned and walked away without another word.

He must have told his mother that night. Shannon told Zoe and Zoe told Alex and Emily. By noon, the whole town knew. The people who kept up with how the next generation was turning out all said they saw it coming all along.

As they worked together neither talked of the wedding, but it seemed both were constantly being pulled away from the group to discuss plans.

Three days later, when they finally found a few hours to be alone, Shannon cuddled close.

"You sure about this, Jack?"

"I'm sure. I think I have been all my life. You're the only one for me. Forever. We'll fight and make love until we're both gray." He lifted her hand and kissed the engagement ring that had been his great-grandmother's. "We'll have a ball running the globe. Just me and you. There's a good chance we'll be stationed together. If not, we'll have some wild weekends flying around. Seeing the world."

"And the baby?"

He rose on his elbow. "Now, Shan, much as you're going to love your new baby sister or brother, we're not taking a baby with us."

"Oh, yes, we are."

"No, we're not."

She faced him nose to nose. "Yes, we are."

"This is the dumbest fight we've ever had, and we've had some dumb ones. What makes you think Alex and your dad are going to let us take off with their kid?"

"Not their kid. Our kid. He should be arriving in less than seven months."

"What? Impossible. We used protection."

She patted his cheek.

"Don't give me that look, Shan. You're not pregnant. You can't be."

"What look?" Her anger had turned to curiosity.

"That look that says I'm dumber than rocks. You've perfected it over the years, but this time I know you're lying. There's no baby on the way. Both of us are smart enough to avoid that."

"Except for the first time. Neither one of us took protection into the shower."

Jack fell back. "You're right. I am dumber than rocks."

"And you're going to be a father. Is that so terrible?"

"No," he finally said. "Come to think of it, it might

just be the greatest thing in the world. It was always in my plan, just not seven months from now. Are you sure?"

She grinned. "I'm sure, Papa."

forty-six

Zoe

ZOE SLIPPED DOWN to her shop. She was too excited to sleep. The Little Teashop on Main would open tomorrow. Everything was ready, and the place had turned out just like she'd planned. Her dream had come true. Boxes of teas from around the world were on the far wall mixed in with teapots and cups of all sizes. Tiny tables where close friends could put their heads together to talk and lovers could whisper across a candlelit table were scattered about the shop.

But tonight would be special. Shannon and Emily would come, and Zoe would set out their tea. They'd relive the ritual. Strengthen the bond of friendship.

Zoe was so proud of herself. For once, her world had turned out just as she dreamed it would.

The headaches were there, but happiness and pills pushed them to the side. Once the shop opened, she'd drive back to Dallas and tell the doctor that she might not be gaining weight or sleeping better, but she'd decided not to die. She had too much to do.

Slowly, she began to dance around the teashop. Her thin body waving like a willow through the shadows. She was a princess again, dancing in a little palace of her own making. She was on stage. A star. The candlelight streaked her vision into long colors of light as she whirled.

When the girls tapped on the door, Zoe let them in and they took their seats. Everything was perfect. Beautiful teapots from England. The aroma of spices drifting in the air. Scones and tea sandwiches and chocolate kisses scattered on the table.

Emily raised her glass. "To unicorns and fairy dust."

Zoe giggled. "To princesses who never grew up."

Shannon clicked her cup. "To friends forever."

"And to Forever Tea," Emily added.

As darkness fell outside, they drank their tea and talked of all that had been and all that would be.

Fuller picked Emily up first, apologizing for interrupting, but he couldn't get his daughter to stop crying and his dad was threatening to give the boys whiskey to settle them down.

Shannon asked him about his mother, and Fuller said that it turned out it wasn't just him that caused her to leave. Alice Ray didn't like kids, period. She claimed she'd get to know all her grandchildren when they were twenty. Until then, she thought she'd stay with Bill. He liked her cooking and they both liked watching crime shows. At her age, that was enough, she claimed.

When Emily passed through the door, Fuller kissed her on the cheek as he always did. The love in his dark eyes always amazed Zoe.

Jack came next, saying his mother wanted to talk to Shannon about the wedding details. She had an idea about how to incorporate the grandkids into the wedding. Jack made a face. "The last thing I want in my wedding is my brothers' kids, but Mom thinks she can talk Shannon into it. Good luck with that."

Shannon passed him, promising she might just agree with his mother just to irritate him.

Before they left, Jack took the time to hug Zoe goodbye. "I'm heading out tomorrow. Shannon will stay for the shop's opening, but I want pictures, slugger. What you've done here is grand."

Then everyone was gone, and the shop was quiet.

Zoe climbed the stairs smiling. Each day she seemed to grow a bit more frail. Just climbing the stairs took her breath away but her heart seemed to swell.

Lifelong friends. The best kind, and she hadn't lost them when she'd gone away.

At the top of the stairs she turned and looked down at the shop. This would be her place. Folks would come in here to make their memories, and she'd be a part of it all.

As she lay down, she laughed, knowing that tonight, in her sleep, she'd dance. Around and around and around. She'd waltz across a marble stage wearing a fairy dress that touched the floor. She'd be so nimble her feet would barely touch the ground as she twirled as a packed house cheered.

Only the strangest thing happened: as she danced she seemed to grow lighter and lighter.

Then, sometime in the stillness on Main, Zoe flew away.

Fall 2018

forty-seven

Jack

JACK PARKED HIS old Ford, now considered a classic, a half mile down from Cemetery Road. He wanted to walk. To think. After five years of traveling, he and Shannon were finally moving back home. Like birds coming to nest.

Both their careers had taken a few turns. Jack had walked away from flying to teach at the academy he loved, and Shannon had gone freelance so she could stay home with the kids.

They had a place in Colorado Springs during the school year, and his brothers were building him a house on the edge of town where the creek bends. They'd stay in Laurel Springs on holidays and all summer.

Best of all, Jack decided, he and Shannon had finally run out of anything to fight about. Though he often teased her that he missed the wild makeup sex. Every year, between Christmas and New Year's, Alex and Mack would keep their kids and he and Shan would fly away somewhere to just be alone.

They'd make love without fear of being interrupted and spend hours talking about how much they missed their children.

They had their vacation all planned, but first Shannon had something she had to do today.

Jack would wait and watch as he did every year.

He stepped over a place where the cemetery's fence was down, and walked near the trees that were bowing low with the dawn's chilly rain. The earth crackled with fallen branches beneath his feet, but he kept moving.

Silently, he scanned the grounds until he saw them.

He watched as two women moved between the graves. One spread a blanket; the other set out cups. They were little more than shadows against the gray sky.

Jack paused. A crunching sound in the leaves to his left drew his attention.

"I figured you'd be here." A voice echoed from the other side of a hundred-year-old cottonwood.

"I just got in town. Shan's not expecting me until later today. I kind of feel like a spy, but I had to get here in time to watch. How about you, Fuller?"

"Yep. We're not invited but I come to watch every year on this date."

"We love them. How could we stay away?" Jack whispered as he moved closer to the tree. "There's such a grace about this tea. Shan calls it their Forever Tea."

"Right. It's almost like they're dancing."

A light rain made the whole world cry as the two men watched. Shannon and Emily drank their tea. Toasted Zoe's grave, which had a butterfly carved on the stone.

"Watching them like this, I can almost telescope their whole life." Jack's words caught in the wind and drifted around the men. "The little girls, the young women, the mothers."

As they folded the blanket and moved away, Jack and Fuller walked back through the trees. Jack knew Fuller hadn't told Emily he'd silently join the tea, just as Jack never told Shan he watched.

"You got a minute, Jack?"

"Sure. What's up?"

"I want to show you something."

They climbed into Fuller's new pickup and drove toward Main. By the time they parked in the alley and jumped out, the rain had turned into a steady drizzle.

Jack followed Fuller to the side of The Little Teashop on Main that Alex still managed with the help of three employees. Like two spies, they leaned around the corner.

Fuller pointed and Jack looked over his friend's shoulder.

Three little girls, all dressed up as princesses, were sitting at the table in the bay window. Mack and Alex's daughter in a fluffy green dress, her red hair curling past her shoulders like a cap. Emily and Fuller's daughter in white with yellow bows even on her tennis shoes. And his own daughter in pink. Three princesses with wobbly crowns and chocolate icing on their cheeks.

"Alex set it up while Em and Shannon had their tea with Zoe. It's the girls' first real tea, but I have a feeling it won't be their last."

Jack watched, feeling like he was drifting back in time. He remembered watching from the sidewalk the day another tea party had started. The girls hadn't noticed him, but he'd seen them all dressed up. Laughing. Dreaming. Dancing.

That was the day it had happened, he decided. The day he'd fallen in love with all three. One became a dreamer. One became a fighter. And one danced away to become a memory.

* * * * *

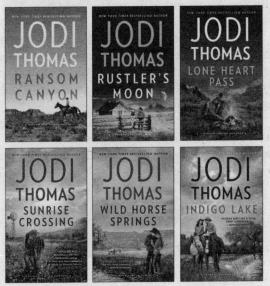

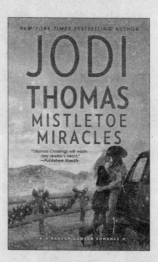

From the beloved and *New York Times* bestselling author of the Ransom Canyon and Harmony, Texas series,

JODI THOMAS,

comes a powerful, heartwarming story about generations of family and the ironclad bonds they forge

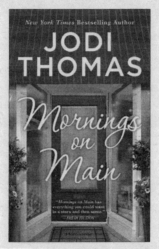

"Compelling and beautifully written, it is exactly the kind of heart-wrenching, emotional story one has come to expect from Jodi Thomas." —Debbie Macomber, #1 *New York Times* bestselling author, on *Ransom Canyon*

Order your copy today!

HQNBooks.com

PHJDMOM1019

Get 4 FREE REWARDS!

We'll send you 2 FREE Books <u>plus</u> 2 FREE Mystery Gifts.

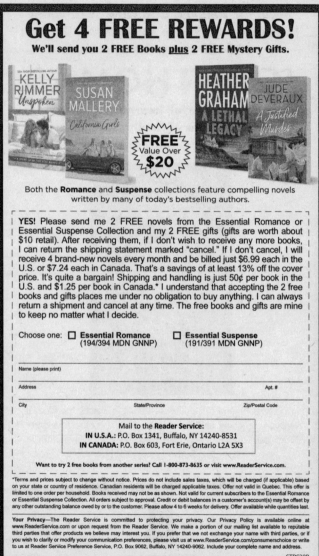

FREE Value Over **$20**

Both the **Romance** and **Suspense** collections feature compelling novels written by many of today's bestselling authors.

YES! Please send me 2 FREE novels from the Essential Romance or Essential Suspense Collection and my 2 FREE gifts (gifts are worth about $10 retail). After receiving them, if I don't wish to receive any more books, I can return the shipping statement marked "cancel." If I don't cancel, I will receive 4 brand-new novels every month and be billed just $6.99 each in the U.S. or $7.24 each in Canada. That's a savings of at least 13% off the cover price. It's quite a bargain! Shipping and handling is just 50¢ per book in the U.S. and $1.25 per book in Canada.* I understand that accepting the 2 free books and gifts places me under no obligation to buy anything. I can always return a shipment and cancel at any time. The free books and gifts are mine to keep no matter what I decide.

Choose one: ☐ **Essential Romance**   ☐ **Essential Suspense**
                      (194/394 MDN GNNP)   (191/391 MDN GNNP)

Name (please print)

Address   Apt. #

City   State/Province   Zip/Postal Code

Mail to the **Reader Service:**
IN U.S.A.: P.O. Box 1341, Buffalo, NY 14240-8531
IN CANADA: P.O. Box 603, Fort Erie, Ontario L2A 5X3

Want to try 2 free books from another series! Call 1-800-873-8635 or visit www.ReaderService.com.